Here I Am!

Here

I Am!

Pauline Holdstock

A JOHN METCALF BOOK

BIBLIOASIS
WINDSOR, ONTARIO

FIRST EDITION

Library and Archives Canada Cataloguing in Publication

Title: Here I am! / Pauline Holdstock.
Names: Holdstock, Pauline, author.
Identifiers: Canadiana (print) 20190116684 | Canadiana (ebook) 20190116730 |
    ISBN 9781771963091 (softcover) | ISBN 9781771963107 (ebook)
Classification: LCC PS8565.O622 H47 2019 | DDC C813/.54,Äîdc23

Edited by John Metcalf
Copy-edited by Emily Donaldson
Text and cover designed by Ingrid Paulson

 Canada Council for the Arts / Conseil des Arts du Canada

 ONTARIO ARTS COUNCIL / CONSEIL DES ARTS DE L'ONTARIO / an Ontario government agency / un organisme du gouvernement de l'Ontario

Canada

ONTARIO CREATES | ONTARIO CRÉATIF

Published with the generous assistance of the Canada Council for the Arts, which last year invested $153 million to bring the arts to Canadians throughout the country, and the financial support of the Government of Canada. Biblioasis also acknowledges the support of the Ontario Arts Council (OAC), an agency of the Government of Ontario, which last year funded 1,709 individual artists and 1,078 organizations in 204 communities across Ontario, for a total of $52.1 million, and the contribution of the Government of Ontario through the Ontario Book Publishing Tax Credit and Ontario Creates.

PRINTED AND BOUND IN CANADA

Here I Am!

Chapter 1

THURSDAY

I will tell you first how I got on board without a ticket. If I don't you will think I am making it up.

It was easy. First I walked through the big gates with a big crowd of people—but that's no good. You will just wonder how I got to the gates and how did I know where the boat was. I will answer the first question but not the second one because everybody knows where the boats are. Well. I ran away from my school when I couldn't stand it anymore and I ran all the way down Princes Street. You can't get lost because there are great big fat arrows and they have DOCKS written right on them in capital letters. And anyway I knew the way because I have a good memory. MyDad took me there right after when MyMum came home from the hospital so he could show me where we were all going to go when she was herself again and he could take us on holiday to France.

I had to keep running all the way so if I saw anyone they wouldn't say Oh hallo! Are you lost? When I came near the big sheds where passengers wait for their boats I slowed down because I was exhausted. I was on my last legs! (That's what you say. As if you have extra sets.) There were a lot of people in the doorway all talking to each other and undoing their cases and doing them up again and looking in their pockets and hugging and being all sloppy. I said Excuse me excuse me excuse me and everyone I said it to sort of moved out of the way just a tiny bit so I could get by and they were so busy doing what they were doing that they did not even look at me.

Inside it was even bigger than I thought and I could only see legs. It was a good job I looked up high because over on the other side there were two giant notices hanging in the air. One said PASSENGERS with the arrow pointing left and one said VISITORS with the arrow pointing right. (Actually, if you were the arrow it was pointing to its left but don't worry about that. It might confuse you.) I followed the sign that said PASSENGERS because I was going somewhere. And because there was not a sign for PEOPLE WITH NO TICKETS. (That is only a little joke to cheer you up in case you were confused. By the arrows.)

The crowd of people trying to get out of the door for PAS-SENGERS was even bigger than the crowd of people who had been trying to get inside the shed. I was amazed at how many people were going to France all at exactly the same time as me! I got in really close behind a Mum and a Dad and their kids and sort of squeezed through the door at the same time as them. On the other side you could see the boat only it was a ship. It was gigantic and it was covered all over with strings of coloured triangle flags. They are called buntings. I know that because MyMum told me when we went to the fête up the road for some jam. She said to MyDad I don't care if it's church. I've run out. They had triangle flags everywhere and that is when she told me what they are called. I asked her if it was the same as Cry Baby Bunting and she said Oh don't remind me. Then she played Lucky Straws until she won a bottle of sherry and then we went home. Well we started to go home but we had to go back because she had forgotten to buy the jam. And then we went home.

Anyway. I could see the ship and I could see tiny people up at the top of the gangplank trying to get inside. The top of the gangplank was higher than a house. (That's just a nestimate. You can't tell exactly because it depends how big the house is.) I could see it even with all the people in front of me. Everyone had to walk all squished together in between big wire fences like the cows in front of us when MyDad had to stop the car only they were hedges then not wire fences. And there wasn't any music then either. Did I tell you I could hear music? It wasn't in my head like it is sometimes. You will see in a minute why not. There was not a lot of room between the fences. Someone said Where's your Mum? And I started to run. I said Excuse me excuse me excuse me because it worked before and sometimes I said Mum! Mum! as well. I pretended I could see her up ahead and she was calling me to hurry up.

And now I will have to stop telling you this because I have thought of something bad. It is very difficult to think about and I can't do rocking and writing at the same time. You know what they call rocking. Unhelpful behaviour. I'll just stop for a minute and do counting.

All right. Now I'm better. So. We started going up the gang-plank. There was a big clump of people stuck at the top and now my heart was really loud. It was unbelievable. I thought this is what Panic means. It is not at all like Picnic like I used to think it was when I was little. A man said Let him through please and I said Thank you. And then I remembered and this time I said Mum! Dad! A lady said they're just inside there. It's OK. I squeezed by and I had done it! I was actually inside the boat. I ran where she pointed and joined up with a Mum and a Dad and a little boy and girl and they didn't even notice. They were talking to some other people and arguing about which way to go. I gave the girl a hug and she looked really frightened. It made me feel funny too because I don't like touching strangers but I did it because that is what you're supposed to do if you're normal. The adults were still arguing so I said This way and the boy followed me then so did everybody else. They were all still talking and they talked all the way up the stairs. At the top I dashed away really fast and went through a door to the deck outside. I was a board! I told you it was easy.

It was noisy and windy outside. Some rusty music was coming out of a loudspeaker. I thought people were clapping too but it was all the coloured flags flapping. Nearly the same thing. It was really confusing. The people were all talking at the same time only they were practically shouting because of the wind and the flags and the music. I went to stand between two big clumps of passengers. They were looking over the rail and waving. I have told you how high the rail is so I looked under instead. It made me dizzy. All the people who were walking about on the ground outside were really tiny. They were like toy soldiers only people. There were hundreds. Some of them were waving back up at the people who were waving down. There were still more coming out of the big shed and going towards the gangplank where I came up or to the other one where I didn't. When I dug two water channels in the wet sand at Seagrove it was just like that.

A man said they're going to play and he pointed to some people down below They were getting musical instruments out. They made a lot of bad noises and then when they had all had a little practice they started to play. I could hear something like Christmas but the sound kept blowing away and you could only hear the loudspeaker. It was playing a different tune. The people next to me waved down to the people on the ground and some of the people on the ground waved up. I started to feel dizzy like when I have to lie down and do screaming. I rested my forehead on the rail like I rest it on the tree in the playground but it didn't help so I squeezed back out and went to look for somewhere away from everybody. I thought if everyone is up here all around the edge I will find somewhere inside and I went in and down the stairs again. There were still tons of people coming up. When I got down I turned right and went along by some places that looked like shops but they were closed. Then there were more stairs. They had a thick blue rope across. I ducked under and ran down. At the bottom there was another big rope across with a picture of a red hand hanging from it. I thought Good. No one will come here and I ducked under again. I started walking along the corridor. There were so many doors! It was unbelievable. If you looked in the open ones you could see a little room with a bed. They were all the same. Cabins! Silly me! And just when I thought Cabins a door of one opened and two people came out talking to each other. They went along the passageway up in front of me and they didn't look at me at all. But then they stopped and the lady said Oh no! She started looking in her handbag and the man said I'll go back for you and I thought Oh no just like the lady. She said No. I'll go back. I went into one of the open cabins and closed the door. If she had been looking she would have thought I just disappeared. That's how quick I was.

There was nobody inside. Thank goodness. But just standing in the room did not feel safe. I wanted to do real hiding like tight because the panic was getting worse so I went underneath the bed. It was not very high. I wriggled right under until I felt safe and curled up. It was nice and quiet. I thought I could stay there until we got to France. It was better hearing things all tiny and far away and there was a big soft sound like humming. I was exhausted. I had been awake a long time because I had got up really early to see if MyMum was awake remember? Oh no. I have not told you yet. I will tell you about it later. But only if I feel like it.

Anyway I was exhausted. I was exhausted for what had happened to MyMum and exhausted for trying to make people understand and exhausted of being mad with them and their stupid faces and all of the stupid lies you can hear in their stupid voices when they say things they don't really mean and you know they don't understand and they think you are lying anyway when you are not. I tried not to think about screaming because if I think about it I remember how nice it is and then my mouth opens and my throat just does it all by itself and I can't stop it. So I listened to the humming instead. It was nice and soft and plain and far away and not all jumbled up and batting on my head with all different noises like outside with all the loud people and the rusty music and the wind and the clapping flags and everything at the same time. There was another kind of loudness too. It was everywhere and it was huge only it wasn't up close and banging in my ears. I liked it. It was sort of far away and inside me at the same time. And then I was sitting in MyDad's car and we were at the traffic lights and waiting and waiting and waiting and MyMum was outside and waving at us through the window and smiling but MyDad didn't see her. He said These lights are a bloody long time. Then something banged on the roof of the car and when I opened my eyes there were two suitcases in the room and I could see people's legs walking about on the carpet. One set of legs for a man and two for grannies! I could tell by their shoes and by their podgy granny feet. One of the suitcases disappeared and landed on top of my bed. I could hear my heart ticking and my teeth were all nervous and ticking back. The man said When you've unpacked your cases will fit nicely under your birtls. I thought What? It sounded a bit rude so I closed my eyes. One of the grannies said Thank you and the man said Thank you thank you very much and went away. I could hear the door closing. And I could still hear my heart juddering. The grannies laughed. One of them said This is it Clare. We're sailing the ocean blue. Me and you. And they both laughed again. The other one said Never mind the suitcases. Let's go back on top again and wave goodbye. I could hear the first one saying I expect it's gone by now and then the door closed.

I opened my eyes. No legs. All quiet. Only silly me stuck under the bed. I am not really a stupid person but it was a really stupid idea to hide under a bed. I must have been mad.

Like a lunatic I mean. I needed to wee straight away so I crawled out and went into their bathroom. Everything felt a bit dangerous especially the grannies. I did not want them to know I was all by myself so when I had finished and washed my hands a hundred times (eight really because I had to be quick) and had a big drink of water I peeped out into the corridor. If I could find a different place to hide and stay there all the way to France even though I was starving I could get off with the rest of the people and go straight to the police station to ring MyDad. The policemen would give me something to eat. I could see some people nearby and lots of people up at the end. I waited until the nearby people were farby and then I slipped out of the room. That is what thieves do only they usually slip inside places and when they leave they run off with jewels and money. I ran off empty-handed haha. I could not steal a whole suitcase or a sink or a toilet. I did not go back under the big blue rope because it wasn't there. I went the other way instead to see where the farby people were going. All the doors looked the same. One of them opened when I went past so I walked a bit faster. A man's voice said Well he knows where he's going. We'll just follow him and a lady's voice laughed even though it wasn't a joke. There were two other people coming the other way. They both said Hallo! And my heart did a little jump but they were talking to the people behind me. Thank goodness! They went by me and stopped to do chatting with the people behind. I heard the second people say Yes up on the sun deck. It's really nice and a man said It won't be in the rain. They were all still laughing when I went round the corner at the end of the passageway. I followed some people through a door and then it closed behind me. We were in a lift! But how was I to know? A lift on a boat! I did not expect that. Someone said Sun deck anyone? And everyone said Yes Please! When the doors opened I could see we had come to exactly where I had started. Everyone got out and went outside to do looking over the rail. It was a bit surprising. We were still in the same place but the band on the ground had packed up and gone home for tea. After a minute the loudspeaker stopped playing music and made a nannouncement. It said, *Ladies and Gentlemen it is now time for all visitors to leave the fare well lounge and disimbark the vessel. Please make your way to the exit door at the port side—the left hand side—of the lounge. Thank you.* And then it said it again. (You probably think I am making up the words but I am remembering them. I remember all the separate words people say. Miss Kenney even made me say what was on the wireless.) I could see people walking down the gangplank a little way away. It made me feel funny. I started counting. I thought If I get to three hundred and thirty-three I will change my mind and be a visitor and go down the gangplank. I did not know whether to count slow or fast. I wanted to see MyMum again but it was nearly time for MyDad to come home and probably he would start to cry when he saw her. I decided to count just normal but go to my second favourite (five hundred and fifty-five) instead. I had got to four hundred and twelve when the loudspeaker came on again and guess what? It was the Captain. He said *Ladies and gentlemen good afternoon. This is a message from Captain Pondringum. Welcome aboard. In fifteen minutes we shall be conducting a lifeboat drill. Please listen attentively to all further announcements and follow the instructions carefully. Thank you.*

Everyone started looking around and moving about and some of them were saying What are we doing? Where are we going? They had not been listening very attentively. Someone said boat drill. You know—like fire drill. The loudspeaker came back on and it was someone else. He told all the passengers to go to their cabins if they had not done so already to get their life jackets and to assemble with their life jackets in the Queen's Room on the quarter deck. I did not have a cabin so I did not know where to find a life jacket. I wanted to do the boat drill then I would know what to do if we started sinking. It made me very nervous. Some people already knew what to do because they were walking about with their life jackets on and their chests puffed out. Some people think they know everything. Show-offs. They were going over to the stairs so I followed them. A man in a white uniform was standing by the stairs. He had a whole bunch of life jackets and he said You need your life jacket. Where's Your Mum and Dad? I said I think MyMum is asleep and it was kind of true and not true. He looked at me a bit funny. I said I'll go and get her. He said No you won't. You might miss her (and that was a bit true too). You stay here. There were people all coming now with their life jackets and it was getting confusing. He said Here take this one in case she forgets yours and he pulled out a really tiny one from the bunch. I was a bit insulted but I said Thank you because you have to. Then I said I can see her! and I went up the stairs. It was really loud in the Queen's room. I was glad because the noise kind of covered up the lie I said about MyMum which was still playing in my head. Everyone was talking at once and making jokes. Most of the jokes were about the Titanic. I started counting. I heard the same joke eight times—*Women and children first*. It made everyone laugh (except me). It means women and children get saved first when the ship is sinking. I don't know why it made all the men laugh. I expect they were just nervous. Sometimes I laugh when I am nervous. Actually lots of times. It is one of the things MyDad always says we have to talk about because it makes life difficult. The other joke was Man overboard and that was a little bit funny because it's what MyMum used to say when she chopped carrots and they fell on the floor. It was a tie between Abandon ship! And Man overboard! Three each.

The room got more and more crowded and some of the people had to stand on the stairs. I could not see very much. Twice I had to move my place because I could feel the person beside me looking at me. Then the announcement began again only this time it was a man with a microphone. He was standing on a little stage. He explained what the ship's whistle would do if we were in danger. He asked everyone to be quiet and we had to wait quite a long time because people were still making jokes. When he started speaking again nobody heard because his microphone was switched off. Then we heard the ship's whistle blowing and his microphone came on again but not so loud. Someone shouted Turn your microphone up and the whistle stopped and he said *Followed by one long blast*. Everyone was saying What? and not really listening while he said it all again. Some people were saying How many? So I said Seven (because I had been counting). Eight if you count the long one. And he was saying—*The signal to go your lifeboat station*. And then the ship's whistle sounded again and we couldn't really hear him.

When it had stopped he said *Please attend carefully to the following instructions. At the sound of seven short blasts followed by one long blast* (eight see!) *of the ship's whistle all passengers must go to their cabins and put on their life jackets. You must then make your way to your assined emergency station where you will await orders from the officer in charge of your station.* Two people started whispering the same joke again. Perhaps they hadn't heard it before. The man with the microphone said *You will find the number of your emergency station on the instructions posted in your cabin. The instructions also show how to put on your life jacket. We will review these instructions with you now. Please follow along. Place the life jacket over your head and grasp the tapes in front with opposite hands. Pass the tapes behind you and cross them at the back then bring them to the front and tie them securely with a double bow.* Everyone looked like people in a book. The man beside me could not make a double bow. He looked as if he was playing with his willy so I started laughing. It was very hard to stop. It was my nerves. The lady on the other side next to me said Where's Your Mum and Dad? so I went away to stand where she couldn't see me. I could hear that kind of ringing starting. Not in the ship (that would have been a fire). In my head. When I started listening again the man was saying *Thank you Ladies and Gentlemen.* He said *That is the end of the lifeboat drill. Cocktails will be served here in the Queen's Lounge at five thirty—but not to anyone still wearing a life jacket.* Everyone laughed at the same time so I put my hands over my ears.

When I took them off again someone else was telling all the passengers to put their life jackets back in their cabins. I did not have a cabin (you know that) but I am good at solving problems so I thought I would find a place to hide my life jacket. I took it off and started walking with everyone else but the man at the bottom of the stairs was still there. He was saying Borrowed life jackets only. Please take the life jacket you brought from your cabin back to your cabin. Borrowed life jackets only. So I gave it to him. That is because I usually do what I'm told even if it makes me feel a bit sick. He didn't even bother to say thank you. He just kept saying the same announcement because lots of people wanted to leave their life jackets there. They were probably not very smart. Like Miss Kenney.

I was worried not to have my own life jacket but you could still see England through the window so I went exploring. I was amazed! There was a great big round room like in a palace and guess what? The floor in the middle was missing! There was only floor all the way round the edge—with shops!—and you could see down past the other floors to the bottom. But the most amazing thing was coming down from the ceiling. Hundreds of electric lights hanging down in a bunch! They went right down through where the floor ought to be. You couldn't fall through because there was glass on the sides. When I looked across to the other side of the hole I could see stairs going down there. All right I thought. This is even more complicated than the hospital where I went to be tested.

I heard the ship's whistle and thought about my life jacket again but it was only three blasts so it was OK. Lots of people started going all in the same direction to go outside. I wanted to see why they were doing that in case it was a nemergency. It wasn't. They just went and leaned on the railing again. When I found a place to stand I could see what they were all looking at. We were moving away from the dock. Sideways! You could hear the band playing again but you couldn't see it. Then we started going frontways and everyone went crowding up there in a blob to see where we were going. Someone said Get in here son. You'll get a good view. There was a boat way in front spouting water. It was shooting up as high as where we were standing and we were getting wet.

After the spouting nearly everyone went inside. I carried on walking to the other end of the boat so I could find a really quiet place. That was when I saw the swimming pool. I could not believe my eyes. It had about a million sunloungers round it. Exaggeration! (Of *course!*) There were a hundred and sixty.

There were some more people looking out over the railing at the back of the boat. They were probably looking at England because you could still see it kind of floating away. I think one lady was crying. Her Dad had his arm round her. When I turned round to find somewhere else to be I saw a sort of serving place like a café. It had a clock and I remembered—six o'clock! I decided to go and find the cocktails instead in case they were something everybody has to have. Like a life jacket.

The cocktails were easy to find. It was a sound like a whole load of bees and some giant pigeons. You could hear them before you even got there. I didn't want to go in there at all but if everyone was going to be having them it might be food and I was hungry. I was just going in when a lady in a uniform said Are you looking for the playroom? so I said Yes. And it was a big relief even though it was only just true.

She said Your Mum and Dad should have taken you there. I suppose they were thirsty…And she did a funny little huff out of her nostrils. She said Come with me. I'll show you and she started walking. Then she said What's your name? I was alarmed. (*Abandon ship! Emergency!*) I said Franny because that is what MyDad calls me when my hair is getting too long. She sucked in her cheeks a bit and then she said We mustn't try to be clever, must we. I said I don't have to try and she stopped walking. She did some breathing without saying anything. When she thought of something to say she made her lips all pointy and then she pointed with her finger and said It's just through those doors there. Have a nice time. Bye-bye.

The playroom was nearly as noisy as the cocktails and all bright colours. I could feel the itchy bad school feelings coming back but there were some biscuits on a table like at a party so that was a good thing. I put two in my pocket because you mustn't eat without washing your hands then I looked for a place by myself. There was a jigsaw puzzle on a little table behind a fat plastic climbing thing. Only two puzzle pieces were joined up so there were forty-eight left to do. The picture on the lid was of a parrot eating a nut. For a little while the itchy feeling went away. I joined up twenty-seven pieces even though someone was crying and interrupting me. I could have finished it but someone else went up on the climbing thing and dribbled on me so I left. The lady in charge of everyone was busy with a toddler that had been sick over her shoes so that was all right.

When I was going up the stairs again I met two men coming down. One of them said Hullo-hullo! I didn't answer because when someone says it twice you don't have to. I did not know where to go next. There were people everywhere. I went to stand at the rail again. The sea was all smooth. I liked doing looking under the rail. It was very soothing. That was how I discovered this other thing to help me be normal. To hang on to. (MyDad's joke.)

After I had been doing it for a long time a boy came and said Shove over will you. I looked at him out of the side of my eye. He had a big bulge in his nose. It was disgusting but he probably couldn't help it. He had probably put something up there like a nut or a button and it got stuck. Poor him! (I didn't laugh out loud. It might have been dangerous.) He saw me looking at him and said Staring! And then he stood on my foot and said Are you a crybaby? I said No I never cry. He said Liar liar! Pants on fire! and then pressed down hard. I wanted to get away but I didn't want him to follow me so I didn't move. I just stood still like the cow when it got stuck in the hedge by Gran's. I didn't even blink. He took his foot off and kicked me on my shin bone and said Bye-bye twerp. I had water in my eyes. There were wavy lines everywhere I looked. But I didn't do crying.

When I was sure he had really gone I walked away. That was when I saw the door with the red hand on it. I didn't know what was inside (because I hadn't opened it yet!) but I needed somewhere no one would follow me especially him so I opened it and went in and closed it behind me. It was half dark with only a little long window high up near the ceiling. It was lovely and quiet. There were four towers made of dark blue cushions and two towers of yellow ones. That's what I thought but they were really mattresses. (You will see.) They were blue like MyMum's best dancing dress only she never puts it on because MyDad doesn't do dancing. He says it's cissy. Especially the Loco-motion. There were one hundred and fifty-six. I did quick counting. I can do that. You just have to do a little bit and then you do times tables. It was easy because they were all the same size. If they were different it wouldn't—oh never mind. You would probably not be interested anyway. Sometimes people yawn when I talk about sums. They don't even cover their mouths. I think it is because they don't understand. (My cousin has a puppy that yawns when it doesn't understand why it can't take a biscuit off the table.) Anyway I was lucky to find the mattresses because I could squeeze behind the ones at the back. It was lovely. They sort of pressed on me after I got behind them and I felt safe like when I make a barricade. I did not even need to scream anymore. I just closed my eyes. I thought about being lucky and I thought about MyMum and how she looked lonely when she was dead.

🦢

You probably want to know what happened. I will tell you.

It goes like this.

It was Wednesday. It was just MyMum and me and not MyDad because he had gone to Ipswich. I was singing. I was getting ready for school like I always do and I was singing Be My Be My Baby because it's MyMum's favourite. I thought she was still in bed so I shouted Mum! Get up! when I went past her door. I didn't shout Dad! because I have already told you he had gone to Ipswich. That's quite far.

I went into the kitchen and climbed on the stool and got my cereal down. My Snap Crackle and Pop had all gone so there was only boring Weetabix. I got a bowl and put it on the table and put one in and then got the milk. If you pour it round the edge it makes a nisland and it doesn't go all soggy on the top. I got a spoon and started eating. (I sat down on the stool first. Of course.)

I didn't hear MyMum yet so I called out again and some milk ran down my chin. It was embarrassing. I thought I heard her in the sitting room and that made me remember I hadn't fed Jackie yet so I got the tin of birdseed. It says Cadbury's but it's where we keep his food in case there's a mouse. Not a pet mouse like the ones I killed but a sort of wild mouse. Except it lives in the house. I am telling you things right now because I am not sure I want to remember the next bit. I could tell you everything like the colours on the carpet and the patterns on the curtains and how I killed my mice and what Jackie says when you talk to him and what it says on the side of the Weetabix box and the label in my shorts and what seven nines are and the front page of the Radio Times. I could tell you everything I know but then I would be an old man and I would die too so you would never know about MyMum. But you'd already be dead anyway. Haha. I'd better just tell you.

So when I went in the sitting room I saw MyMum in the big armchair. She didn't turn round and say Good morning Sunshine! She didn't even move. I said Mum! I'm up! And she still didn't turn round. I said Can I sit on your lap and eat my cereal? She was wearing her fluffy dressing gown. It's made of the same stuff as my blanket. She didn't say No so I went to get my cereal. When I came back she was still sleeping. (Well you know she wasn't because I've told you what she was but I didn't know yet.) So I whispered Mum! I'm getting up. I put my cereal down. When I looked up I saw her eyes were open. I laughed because she was just staring like the time she got the telegram. I said, Mum! Stop it! but she didn't. I watched her really hard. I thought she was tricking me. Then I looked at her dressing gown. When I sit on her lap and she does breathing the fuzzy stuff moves just a little tiny bit. It tickles. I left my cereal on the little table and I climbed up. I put my cheek on the collar. It didn't tickle. I said You're dead aren't you. That's when I knew. She didn't burst out laughing like she would if it was a trick. But I still had to ask her something because her eyes were open. I said What are you looking at? And she didn't answer. I said Mum! What are you looking at? And she still didn't so I said Mum can you see me? and I put my face in front of hers—like right in front—and I looked right in her eyes—like right in—and then I was a bit scared because I couldn't see her and I couldn't see me either in the black bit. I said You will get tired like that Mum. Go to sleep. But she didn't so I reached up very carefully so I wouldn't hurt her eyes and put their lids down. It was better then. She looked like someone having a really nice sleep. She looked cozy. I wanted to have a little cuddle but it was time to eat my cereal so I got down and ate it. I sat beside her on the floor with my shoulder next to her leg. When I had finished it was time to go to the toilet and brush my teeth and comb my hair and then I would have some time left over to call 999 (that's Emergency). I had just finished combing my hair—it took a long time because of the sticking up bit—when I had a new thought. It was What?! like that with a rounders bat. What?! It meant what do you need an ambulance for if you're already dead? I felt really silly because I was already nearly phoning it. It made me go a bit red so I stopped looking in the mirror and went to look at MyMum instead. She hadn't moved. Of *course*. I felt a bit strange then. It was like everything underneath me the carpet the floor the dirt everything had fallen down a big hole and I was still standing there. I was standing on the air. Thin air! Not even that! There was nothing underneath me at all. I thought I would fall down the hole too if I didn't think of something quickly. And then I heard MyMum's voice only it was inside my head. It said *What's next Frankie? What's next on the list?* It's what she always says to me when I get lost in the day and begin to feel a panic. So I thought Go to the toilet and brush my teeth and comb my hair and…GO TO SCHOOL! Then I knew what to do. It was easy. I would go to school and I would tell them about MyMum and they would know what to do when the person is already dead.

First I went to MyMum and told her. I got on tiptoe and whispered it into her ear because I was a bit embarrassed. It was like when you talk to Jackie and then you remember he doesn't speak English.

I got the funny feeling again (only it's not funny) so I got down and put on my coat and my shoes. MyMum looked lonely all by herself. I went back and said Don't worry Mum. I'll tell them. They'll know what to do. And then I gave her a kiss and then another one because she didn't notice. And then I went to school.

On the way I saw the milkman. He was just going home. I knew that because the bottles in the back of his float were empty. He waved. I wanted to call out but my throat wouldn't work. It was like what happens when you have a dream. After he'd gone past I turned round to try again but he was already driving round the corner.

I was thinking about it a lot when I fell asleep behind the mattresses but I don't remember anything else until I felt them moving and then it was the next morning.

Gran

Dear Lord. I still don't believe it, seeing her like that.
I knew at once she weren't alive, even with the curtains
closed. I said, Patti? I don't know why I was whispering.
Patti? She could have been a waxwork. If you didn't
know. If you forgot to breathe. It wasn't her. It was what
they call her remains. Patti was long gone. The room
was full of it. I wanted to get out quick but my God,
poor Patti. I put the end of my sleeve over my nose and
went over to her. I didn't like to look at her face, it
seemed indecent with her mouth open. But I wanted
her to know it was me and I'd come and I'd help her,
so I touched the back of her hand. Cold as a statue in
a church.
I found her doctor's telephone number in her address
book on the hall table. I could hardly dial, my hands
were shaking that much. I waited in the garden for him
to come. That bloody dog barked at me the whole time,
as if I didn't have enough to wreck my nerves.
When the doctor come he took a look at her and then we

went into the kitchen. He said, Where is Mr Walters, Mrs Walters?

I said, Ipswich, I think.

The doctor said, Hmmm. It's going to be rather a shock.

I said, We can't leave her here like this and he said, No of course not. He said he'd be calling the police. A sudden demise like this, Mrs Walters, he said. It's a matter for the coroner.

After that it weren't long before they took her away, poor love. I couldn't watch. I cried my eyes out soon as they'd gone.

When I pulled myself together I made another telephone call. The telephone makes me all jittery. I got the number of Len's company through Directory Enquiries and rung them up. It took all my patience and in the end it didn't do no good. They rung Ipswich and Ipswich rung back and then the first lot rung me and said Sorry, he's already left. Useless. I'm glad I don't have one.

I went down the school next. I said, I've come to collect Francis Walters. He needs to come home with me. The secretary said, I'll have to check with the Head. You're his gran aren't you?

When she come back she said, Yes, that's all right. I'll just go and fetch him. But then she come back without him. She said, I'm sorry. Miss Kenney says he's absent today. And just then her telephone rung so she said, Excuse me, and I was left standing there. But there was no point in staying. There wasn't any way I could bring myself to talk about any of it to a complete stranger. I went back to the house. I thought, Right. If he's not at school he's got to be

hiding. But I don't know if I believed it. Not really.
I went all over looking for him when I got back. Every
room. Then I went outside and looked. In the coal cellar,
in the shed, down the end of the garden. That's when I got
really worried. I didn't bother going next door, not with
the dog there like that. No point. He's terrified of it. No,
I thought. The police station is where I go next.

They asked a load of questions. But I wasn't much help. I
hadn't seen Patti or Frankie since Tuesday so I couldn't tell
them much. I was only going there this morning with the
fish I always fetch her. They took a load of notes all the
same. They've been very kind. They said I could wait here
if I wanted and they made me a cup of tea.

That was hours ago. They've been back since. Asking a
load more questions, this time about poor Patti. One of
them started talking overdose. I'm not joking. Not in so
many words, mind you. Things like "access to sleeping
pills," "tranquilizers, painkillers." I know exactly what he
was getting at but no. She'd been through all that *and*
come out the other side, poor love—and no thanks to
Len. No. That wasn't it. It was her diabetes. I know it like I
know my own self. She'd never have done it on purpose.
Never would have. I don't care what they find. I won't
ever believe that. Even if things were rocky with Len she
still loved him—I'm not blind—and she loved Frankie to
bits. Tantrums, panics, silly behaviour, screaming—none
of it mattered when push come to shove. She put up with
it all. And more. Seven days a week. Unlike Len. And if
anyone ever said a word against him, against Frankie—

well, look out! Too right, she could have been my own daughter! She gave them a bollocking down at the school when they kept him in for not eating his Brussels. And good for her. But I don't think it helped in the long run. Know what I think? I think that's when they come up with the word "difficult." It was when she went down the school and made all that fuss that time she said they treated him like a trained monkey. But I would have done the same in her shoes. I know I would. You stick up for your own, don't you.

She had her faults—who doesn't—but I never minded helping her out. She was more like my own daughter, was Patti, and I never blamed her for the drinking. Probably would have done the same in her shoes. Bloody Len. He was never there, for God's sake! Always some excuse why he had to add another day. Come back a day later. Some load of codswallop about a new account, top priority order, breakdown on the A23, whatever popped into his head. I saw through Len years ago. Still using the same smile to get his own way, wriggle out of trouble. Well it works when you're a lad in short trousers but it don't get by me coming from a grown man with that silly pencil moustache. Never mind he's my own flesh and blood, I couldn't have put up with him, not in her shoes. But this now. Oh God, poor Patti. I can't believe she's gone. It don't seem possible.

Ah, dear Lord, no good going over and over it again. Letting myself in the front door. That feeling that come over me. Nothing can't help her now. Not all the love in the world. Nor all the questions neither. And no use getting angry. Too late. It's all too late.

Question is—the real question—where's Frankie? First thing I thought after I come to my senses. Where's Frankie? What kind of state is he in by now? Poor little bleeder. With no Len around. No sodding Len. Poor little bleeder.

Let's say he run off. Been running ever since, on and off. He could be anywhere. But there's a limit. You only have to draw a circle, don't you. With his house in the middle. So where's the search party? I tell you what. These police are too busy asking bleeding questions. That's what. Not to mention the tea. They'd be better off down the pub getting the lads out. Those lads wouldn't be hanging about. When Margie's chimney caught fire they was all there before the fire brigade. Anyway I wouldn't mind betting he's not running at all. He's hiding. That's what it is. He does that when he can't cope. Same as me with a migraine. I put a pillow over me head. Makes everything go away. That's all you want to do, isn't it. And imagine… Well I can't imagine…Poor Patti. He must have seen her. Must have. And then he run away. Oh poor little monkey. The poor things the both of them. And she'd been trying so hard. I know she had. She come round the week before and she told me while Frankie was on the swing. She said, I've done it, Mum—that's what she always called me—I'm off the pills. She said, And I'm not going back on. They don't do me any good. She said, Len is really pleased. He agrees.

I said, A bit late in the day.

She said, No, you can't blame him. He was only ever trying to help. Only ever.

She told me about some fight they'd had before. Said he'd been trying to help. She said it turned ugly.

I said, You tell me. Cat and dog, you two.

She said, I know but he was trying. He only wants to do the best, Len does.

I said, Wants a quiet life more like.

She laughed then. No hope of that with me and Frankie, she said.

Well if they don't find that boy soon, he might just get his wish. Please, God. Don't let it be both of them.

Chapter 2

FRIDAY

I don't remember what happened while I was asleep. No one does! Night time is like a big tunnel. Like if you are walking along all awake and then suddenly you are in it and when you wake up you you are out again only on the other side. It's like you start all over again until you come to the next one. (Like 'Go Back to Go' on my game.) When I opened my eyes the mattresses were budging. Like an earthquake. Or a niceberg. I stopped breathing. Completely. I could hear someone else. Then he started grumbling. I couldn't understand the words he was saying—he was probably French—but I knew he was fed up. I could hear dragging and sliding noises and then huffing and puffing and then the door closed and it was all quiet. I stuck my head out a little bit. The foreigner had gone but so had the first tower of mattresses. Time to get up I thought. So I did. I opened the door just a crack and looked out. It was daytime but it was still really early you could tell. Everything was pink. I could not see any other people. If the foreigner came back to the red hand room he would certainly notice me so I walked away fast.

The sea was pink. Yes really. It looked like glass all smooth. Pink glass! And the sky was pink too. There was no one else out on the deck. I didn't know if people were allowed outside yet so I went along to where one of the metal doors was open. They have a little foot sticking down for souls who are not strong enough to open them by themselves. Lucky me! I passed a man on the stairs but he was the only person. I went you know where and there was nobody in there either. I waited for a long time with the door shut sort of like hiding but not. When I could hear other people walking about and talking it was all right to go outside again. It was bright blue then like it is supposed to be and the sun was shining. I wanted to see how far away England was. It had completely disappeared! Yesterday you could still see a lumpy grey line at the back where it was. Today it was only sea. I looked for France at the front but it was not there yet so I went to the rail on the side to do looking at the sky and making the edge go away. It was a good job they had a rail for that. MyDad would have said it was something to hang on to.

Three ladies came and stood a little way away. They were gossiping. You could tell. They were wearing P.E. shorts and plimsolls even though it was not school and white towels round their necks like boxers (but they weren't!). I sat down on a round iron thing to wait for them to go away. You call it a capstan because MyDad said. One of the ladies tapped her friend on the arm and pointed at me. It was very rude. You could tell she didn't know how to behave because when her friends looked everybody laughed. I didn't know what to do so I just did a sort of smile and looked up at the sky. I pretended I was bird watching. The sea is not really a very good place for that. It felt a bit lonely. Some doorbell music came on the loudspeaker and they all started walking again. One of them called out Come on! You'll be late.

I didn't know what she meant because I wasn't going anywhere (except France) so I put my head down to pretend I was shy. Actually I am shy so that was easy haha.

When they had gone I stood up and carried on looking. The sea was so shiny and smooth you felt like swimming in it but there was nowhere to climb down even if you were brave. I looked. Anyway I can only do twelve strokes. So maybe not swim. Maybe walk. Like Jesus. Holding my arms out sideways. Look. Jesus walking. That would be good I thought if we started sinking. Especially if you didn't have a life jacket—like me.

—What are you doing?

(That was a boy. He was a noying you could tell.)

—Nothing.

—Can I play?

—No.

—Why not?

—You're a noying.

—A what?

(See what I mean?)

When he had gone I carried on looking through the gap between the wire and the top rail. If you do that you can't see where the sea stops and the sky starts. If you stood on tiptoe you could make the top rail come down just enough so you couldn't see the line where they joined up. If you did it right the sea and sky looked like all the same thing. The only trouble was if people saw you doing it they asked you questions. The first man who came by did it.

—See any fish?

I shook my head but I felt silly. We were way too high up even downstairs to see a fish. You could see a whale but that wouldn't count. It's a mammal.

We had a fish in a goldfish bowl at home when I was little. It jumped out and flopped down the back of the sideboard. I waited for it to come out until Blue Peter came on then I gave up. I ate my cheese on toast and put my jarmies on and went to bed. In that order. In the morning I told MyMum—that's what I call her when she isn't here—and she got it out with the egg flipper. It had fluff all over it like the stuff at the bottom of your coat pocket. And it wasn't bendy any more. That was the funny thing. The not funny thing was when I said you could fry it. MyMum laughed and laughed. But I meant it. It wasn't a joke.

(By the way that's what I will have to call her all the time now. All the time. Forever and ever. By the way.)

When the man left I carried on looking but not for fish. I liked making the line disappear. I could have done it forever (and ever). To make it come back you had to breathe out just a little tiny bit of air so you were a bit shorter. Just a bit. Not even a quarter of a ninch probably and then it came back. When you breathe in it disappears again because the rail comes down. It wasn't magic. It was because you're taller when you breathe in so you can't see the join. It looks like all the same thing. You can't tell if it's air or water.

I did a nexperiment to see if it was better with my mouth open. It was like the sea and the sky were filling me up both at the same time. I was breathing blue in my mouth. Blue in. Blue out. Blue in. Blue out. Blue in. Blue in. Blue in. Blue in.

—The man came back. I could see him out of the side of my eye.

—Still no fish?

Some questions are just stupid. You don't even have to answer them. Probably. I blew out after he had gone.

I don't like being with people when I am trying to enjoy something. It's too hard when they are talking to you all the time. And they always ask you things you don't want to talk about.

I went exploring instead. I wanted to see everything before we got to France. They let you go wherever you liked. Nearly. They had that special sign when you couldn't go. It was a hand like a traffic policeman in a book but red. It's the sign for stop like on the door of the room where I went to bed. It is also the sign for Hallo but that's in other countries. We did countries with Miss Kenney. If I went through a red hand door by accident I decided to just say Hallo. That would surprise them.

It was a lot of walking. I stopped once to watch two boys and a girl playing a game with slidey things on the floor outside. Its real name is the deck and that's why they have deck chairs. Someone had painted white circles where the slidey things were supposed to go. The boys weren't very good and nor was the girl or perhaps they weren't trying. Their two Mums were just doing sitting. After a minute and eighteen seconds they stopped playing and started eating Smarties instead. One of the Mums said Well? Give him some of your sweets then. That's what he's after. (She wasn't very observant.) The tall boy said As long as he doesn't want to play too and the Mum said Ronald! He held out a brown one. He had a wart on his thumb so I didn't eat it. I just said thank you. The Mum was still telling him off when I left.

I went upstairs to another deck and threw the Smartie over the side before a wart could grow on me. I could not see where it went. It just disappeared. I thought that will happen to me if I fall over the side.

I made two important discoveries. Number one was that there were twelve decks. Yes really! I saw a picture that was like the side of the boat fell off so you could see inside. Twelve! They don't all have numbers—some of them have names instead—but I counted them anyway. Then I decided to check and go and count the real decks. On the way to the real stairs I went past the big dining room I was too scared to go in last night. They were having breakfast! And it wasn't waiters like last night. The food was waiting for the people! It was all on big long tables and the people were getting up and walking about and taking whatever they wanted. It was a big muddle. Some people were being greedy and not sharing. I saw a lady pick up a whole big jug of orange juice and carry it away just for her and one man had so many fried potatoes on his plate they were falling off all the way back. So then I was even more hungry. I wanted to go in and take some too but I didn't know where to take it because I am shy (you know that) and I didn't want to sit next to someone else's MumandDad and anyway I didn't have any money.

Number two was how you spell Ocean. I always thought it was Otion. It was on a kind of map on the wall next to where it said PURSER. It was covered in glass like a picture but with a frame sticking out like a box. At the top it said Atlantic Ocean. (I always thought it was Atlantick too.) There was a cutout boat on it to show it was the sea. Halfway down there was a red line going all the way from one side to the other. It looked like the equator. It goes all the way round the world because I have a globe pencil sharpener. The equator is where you twist it apart so you can empty the bits. The map said English Channel as well. They made the letters small so they could fit in the channel. It's not very big.

After that I double checked the decks in the right order starting at the top. I had to go outside to start. There was only one man up there. He was all by himself. He had a little tin and a rag and he was polishing the gold bit that holds the rail up. It was already shiny but he was polishing it anyway. I only counted ten decks. It was still a lot of stairs. Two hundred and eighty-four. When I had finished everything properly I went back to the dining room to have a nother look because I could not stop thinking about food. Nearly all the people had gone and I could see to the other side. And guess what! They had a table like in Infants. It was in the corner with some play blocks and a wooden fire engine. I expect it was for little kids to be messy there so their parents could be greedy in peace. Some waiters were doing clearing up and some people were standing and doing jokes and laughing at each other. There was a lot of food left and some of it was on the floor. I wished I had been there. I could see a whole piece of toast that had fallen down. It had the jam on top. I was just going to dash in when one of the waiters saw me and waved. I pretended not to see him and went away—without running. And without any toast.

Outside I did reading on a notice board. It said

Breakfast 7 a.m. — 10:30 a.m.

And then it said

1,316 souls on board

I read it three times. I was just going to read it again when
a big girl beside me said What does that mean? Souls on board.
And her Dad—he was behind her—said People On The Boat.
That's what sailors say. I went outside to sit in a deckchair and
think about it.

I know about souls because we have them at school. There is
a chart on the wall in our classroom with a ladder going up to
heaven and we have to bring our pocket money in to save the
little Piccaninny souls and the China Boy and Girl souls. There
are Red Indian Brave ones too. If you bring sixpence you get a
cut-out soul wearing the right costume and the right headdress
and you colour it and stick it on the ladder. If you bring another
sixpence you can move your soul up to the next rung on the
ladder. When they get to the top rung they are in Heaven. But I
had not seen any on this boat. Not one. Well maybe the man
with the tin but he was a grown-up. Certainly not one thousand
three hundred and sixteen. (You probably want to know what
happens when your soul gets to heaven. Answer—You start again
with another one. If you bring another sixpence.) But Sister Vin-
cent said we all have one of our own and we have to look after
it. I don't think she meant a cut-out. It was a bit confusing.

When I had finished doing thinking I was still starving (that's
what you say) so I went to look for France again in case it was
nearly time to get off. It was too windy to stand at the front for
very long so I went all the way round instead. Twice! Then I
went all the way round the deck with the lifeboats on. Three

times! (No wonder I was exhausted.) I said when you have gone round three times France will be getting near and you will see it. I only said it in my head. No one could hear me and that was a good job because anyway I was wrong. I couldn't see it anywhere. I didn't know what to do next so I did looking because I could feel a panic coming. I stood at the rail for twenty-eight minutes. I know because I did counting and I'm very accurate. That means I get it right. (Miss Kenney always asks me questions just to make me show off when we have visitors. Sometimes I stop doing things on purpose because you're not supposed to show off. But they always write down what I do anyway even if it's nothing.) To get it right you have to use alligators. Like one alligator two alligators three alligators four alligators and then to know the minutes you have to divide by sixty but you probably can't do that in your head like me. You'd probably have to have a piece of paper. I was counting how many alligators until a nidea came then I had to go because a lady having a walk came along and said You don't give up, do you? I walked away really fast and I looked back at her to make her feel bad, and then I went downstairs to where the playroom is so she wouldn't come by me again. That's when I decided to have a little rest in the yellow tent. I was exhausted.

It was refreshing inside the tent. If you blinked really fast you could make it go turquoise. Then you could pretend you were not worried. If someone came in and said What are you playing? You could say Going to sleep. I am playing going to sleep. They would not stay for very long.

While I was there I remembered a whole dream. All at once. It was about the time MyMum fell down and went unconscious (that's like dead but not). I could hear MyDad's voice. He was so tired it sounded like letters on a page all in a straight line all the same size. He was saying Yes. Seven Worcester Terrace. (That's where I live but I expect you guessed that.) Yes. Come at once. Only he didn't sound at all like he wanted anyone to come. He sounded like he wanted to go to bed. I didn't want to dream who was going to come. Instead I dreamed MyDad going out into the garden and meeting a chicken. The chicken became a big white duck the same size as me—forty-five inches—so I woke up.

That's three foot nine. By the way. Two of my favourite numbers—together!

When I had finished blinking I went out to have another look for France because it was Number One on My Plan. I made it number one because it was the furthest place away from my house and especially my school and I didn't want to go to Gran's. And anyway MyDad promised we would go to France when MyMum was better. MyMum wasn't better but she wasn't sick anymore either. (That's true. By the way.) So this was my plan.

My Plan
1. Go to France.
2. Find a police station.
3. Ring MyDad.

I was a bit worried about my plan. Even when I blinked.

While I was outside I had a stroke of luck! (That is much better than only a stroke like Grandad haha.) It was after I went out of the playroom. I found a piece of cheese. A big piece. Just what I needed. I found it by the swimming pool. (Yes I know! A swimming pool on a boat! I was amazed too when I got on. I had not been on a big boat before.) You had to be careful at the pool. A big notice said *Children must be accompanied by an adult* except they got the spelling wrong when they painted it. People always put their ens in the wrong place. You could find biscuits there if you were quick. There was a sort of little hut where they served the souls Bovril and Cocoa in mugs with biscuits on a plate. People threw their biscuits at the seagulls but they were not very good shots. I found some under the chairs. That's when I spotted the brown paper on the ground right near door of the hut and in it was the cheese. It was much too big for a sandwich so it probably fell off the ledge where the waiters put the mugs of Cocoa to take them to the souls in the deckchairs. I stuffed some of it in my mouth. I had it in both my cheeks and I put some in my pocket. I could not fit any more in. But then I had a nidea. I needed a cache. It's spelled like that. It sounds like stash but it's spelled c-a-c-h-e. I saw it in True Tales of The Great White North and I asked Miss Kenney how to say it and then I asked if it was spelled right and she said You really are a remarkable little boy. So I still don't know. Sometimes she is not very helpful. Maybe lots of times. A cache is where hunters (in the Great White North where I told you) put their leftovers when they catch too much food. A kind of outdoor cupboard without any doors. Or a fridge only not electric and they don't tell anyone where it is.

I looked everywhere until I found the best place. It was behind the red box on the wall that has a little window and a naxe inside. It would have been better if the cheese could be inside too but not really because then everyone would have been able to see it. So actually it would be worse. There was a gap behind the box. I reached up and pushed the cheese into the gap. It just fitted. I told you I was lucky.

I went inside next to get a drink of water because cheese makes you thirsty. There was a water fountain right outside the toilets. When you pressed the tap the water came out in a shape like a bridge. Or maybe a rainbow. It was quite hard to do because the edge of the dish was about forty-two inches high and you know how tall I am. Anyway it was hard to lean over and I got water in my ear. It made me miss MyDad. I could hear him laughing in my head like a nimaginary Dad. But I wanted my real one.

I heard a girl say Do you want me to press it for you?

I said No thank you.

I carried on drinking.

When I had finished she was still there. I think she wanted to be my friend. Or perhaps she was thirsty. She had brown curly hair like knitting and brown skin and white eyes with brown in the middle. I think she was a coloured person. That is what you say. Not piccaninnies like on Miss Kenney's ladder. MyMum said Miss Kenney is wrong. Actually she said Miss Kenney is a nobstacle to human progress but I think it's the same thing.

The girl said You're always by yourself. Is there something wrong with you? She had glasses and she looked at me hard right through them. Perhaps she had bad eyes. I hope so because my chin was dripping and I didn't want her to notice.

I said I don't think so.

She said You should make a suggestion.

I said What do you mean?

She said A suggestion. You can ask for anything you want and put it in the Suggestion Box.

I said Where?

She said At the Purser's Office. Kay? You should ask them to make a shorter drinking fountain.

(She had noticed!)

Then she said You don't have anyone to play with do you. Do you want a friend?

I said No thank you.

She said Why not?

I said Sometimes friends make me mad.

She said Would I make you mad?

I said Only a little bit.

She said Well then. That's all right then. We're friends then. Kay?

I said Kay.

She said What sitting are you?

I said Pardon?

She said You know. Dinner. Half the people are in first sitting and half the people are in second. I'm in first. You could ask to be in the first.

I said You mean tea. And souls.

She said Put it in the Suggestion Box.

I said What?

She said Oh never mind and then she went so I carried on exploring. It was much better if I kept on walking around because then people didn't talk to me. I still had to be careful where I went though or they might say You again! I did so much exploring I was tired to death. (That's not a nice thing to say. By the way.)

I found the Purser's Office. It was true what she said about the box.

After that I found two places to sit but each time a nadult came and said All by yourself? so I stopped doing that. I didn't even have a ticket.

I went up to the next deck where there are not so many people and I saw…Guess! A dog! I did not know they let dogs on a boat. It belonged to a man who was sitting on one of the deck chairs with his face looking up. He was not seeing anything because he was blind (*and* there is nothing to see. At sea.). You could tell he was blind because his dog had a handle on its back and a little cloth under it with the same stamp as the ones on the collection box outside Tesco's. I saw him sitting there on Thursday but I hurried past because he looked a bit suspicious. I didn't see his dog then even though I'm observant. It must have been lying down really flat. There was a nempty deckchair next to his. A dog would be a good friend to have so I decided to go over. Blind men are definitely not suspicious.

I was still nervous climbing up. He knew I was there even though I was very quiet because his head made a little move like when a fly lands on you. He didn't look at me because he couldn't. He just turned his head a tiny bit and then turned it back again.

—Hallo! (It was him!)

—Aak…! (That was me. It wasn't a word it was only the sound I did when he made me jump.)

—Hallo. (That was me again. I was trying to be normal.)

He didn't saying anything. I was still a bit scared and I didn't know what to say because it was not my turn. But I couldn't wait forever.

—You're a blind man aren't you? (That was three turns for me. Now it was definitely his.)

—Yes I am.

—Is it terrible?

He was doing smiling and not answering at the same time.

—Can you hear me? (That was me.)

—Yes. I can hear you. No. It isn't as terrible as you think.

—You know I think it's terrible?

—I'm just guessing.

I told him I liked guessing too. I said I'm guessing the name of your dog right now.

— Shall I guess your name?

— No. It's Frankie.

—Pleased to meet you Frankie. How old are you?

—Seven. (That was probably the biggest whopper I'd ever told. I'm only just six. But everyone always thinks I'm seven.)

—I expect you want to say hallo to Alec.

—You said it!

—What?

—His name.

—I'm sorry.

—I don't care. There are lots of things for guessing all the time.

Alec was standing up wagging his tail like mad and doing smiling too.

—Do you want to pat him?

I was nodding. I was so stupid. Nodding!

—Yes. (It sounded really loud.) I started getting off the deckchair but he said Hold on. I have to tell him first that it's all right.

—OK Alec. Playtime!

I said Hallo Alec. You're a nice dog Alec. Good boy Alec good boy. His fur was all soft and he really loved me you could tell. He was pushing his nose all over me.

The blind man said Tell him to sit so I did and he did it.

I said Look! (Silly me.) But he got up again.

—No sit Alec. Good boy. No sit. He's doing it but he keeps getting up again.

—Alec sit. (That was the blind man.)

—Are you cross?

—No not at all. That was just my voice for a command.

—Like a norder?

—Exactly.

—Like *I command you to lie down*. I did the voice and Alec really did lie down. But only for one second.

I said Look! (Again! Double stupid.) He's standing up again. He's smelling me.

—Perhaps you've got something in your pocket.

—Can you see? (That was me.)

—No. But Alec can always smell food.

The cheese! I had forgotten about the cheese.

I said I have to go now. Bye-bye.

—See you again. (That was him.)

—Hahahahahaha. (Me.) (You probably knew that.)

I had forgotten all about the cheese. Of *course* Alec would smell it. He's a dog. Dogs have really amazing noses. They can smell where the FA cup is if it's stolen. They can even smell if you have been touching it. Even if you wash your hands. Even seven times. And they can find people. They just have to smell where you started out and they can follow your smell all the way to where you are. Only no one could find me now even with a dog. Unless they were a really good swimmer.

I looked for somewhere to go and eat the cheese. After a little while (that's what books say and this a book. Right?) I found the perfect place where no one takes any notice of you. It was like The Regal in Yardley Street where you go to the pictures (but I've finished being surprised). Inside it was all seats and all dark and some boys and girls were watching with the sound up too loud. They were gawping at a stupid film where the people weren't even real. Well actually they weren't even people either. They were a mouse dressed up and a broom (see what I mean?) and not even a real mouse and a real broom but flat like drawings. I sat in one of the itchy seats that tips up. The music was too loud. It made me think about the bad things that had happened to me so I couldn't eat anything. I tried to make a list of good things. I couldn't think of any. The noises on the film made me want to scream a bit and then I had to rock so I wouldn't. The music got louder and louder and there was crashing and clattering and a whole lot of banging and all right it scared me a lot so I closed my eyes. I got down low and put my arm over my head until it stopped. I forgot all about thinking. I could only do wishing. Like I wish MyMum was still alive. And I wish MyDad was here. And I wish I could go to a police station in France. It was a good job the loud noises stopped. The terribleness sort of flaked away and every-thing started to get all joined together (like the blue). Blurry and fuzzy. Like my blanket when I was little.

I had a bit of cheese and I tried to stay awake to enjoy all the blurry furriness but I went to sleep anyway. When I woke up the lights were on and the film had finished. The dream I had been having vanished but I definitely had it and it was definitely about MyMum. I could sort of hear her voice in my head but I didn't know what she had been saying. It was like when I'm watching telly and she says Frankie! I've been talking to you for five minutes! Said.

There was no one else in the pictures. The itchy seats were all tipped up and they were a horrible colour like you-know-what. If you step in it. I thought Time to find somewhere else. Really fast. But not running. That only makes people stare.

Outside the sea was all pink again like when I got up only dark pink. It helped me to calm down. It was smooth like counting.

There weren't many souls on the deck. The clock by the swimming pool said a quarter to seven so half of them were probably finishing their tea (except they call it dinner). That meant six hundred and fifty-eight were not having their tea. Dinner. Six hundred and fifty-nine if you count me. They could have all been looking at the sea if they wanted to but they weren't. There was only an old lady an old man and a nordinary man still sitting in their deckchairs and a nother man having a cigarette with his friend and a lady pushing her baby round in a pushchair. So six hundred and fifty-three were somewhere else. In their cabins washing their hands I expect ready for their turn or having a little sleep. I'm good at arithmetic. (I wasn't counting the baby you know. It's probably not a soul. Even though it's a board. A board is what sailors have to say. Like All a board!)

I decided to see if there was any more food I could get with no money (that's not the same as steal. By the way.) in between when the first people came out and the new people went in. I sneaked behind a great big china vase right next to the door. It was shiny yellow and green and it was bigger than a barrel. The edge of it would have come up to my chin but I was on my hands and knees so I could pretend to be looking for something if anyone noticed me. The plant in it was gigantic. It looked like a palm tree indoors. Actually I think it was a palm tree indoors. It had leaves like in the Bible hanging down all the way round. It probably needed watering like MyMum's. The droopy leaves were good for hiding. There were lots of people waiting to go in. No one noticed anything unusual especially not me. Joke. They were all talking at once and not listening to each other. I think they were over-excited.

I had to do breathing carefully with no noise really really small. (That's what I thought MyMum was doing by the way when she wasn't. Breathing I mean.) The people who had been having dinner started coming out. I waited until the doorway was sort of crowded so I could sneak out and dash round the edge of the door.

I darted in—that's what you say like for a narrow—and dodged between the people who were still inside and did really fast looking. It's what hawks do. They have to. They look down while they're flying along so they can spot things on the ground and then swoop down and catch them. They have to be ready. So that's what I did and straight away I spotted a chip on the edge of a table. I snatched it and flew off (but I put the chip in my pocket not in my beak ha ha.) I was just rushing out again when I spotted a whole basket of rolls on a trolley so I snatched one of those too before I went out and no one noticed. That's what I thought but I was wrong. It made my heart stop and start again. A lady was talking right to me. She was wearing a dress that had no shoulders and no sleeves and a diamond necklace. She said *Wasn't* that a dreamy dinner! (So *she* wasn't very observant!) And then her dad talked to me as well. (*And he was!*) He said It's all right kiddo. We won't tell. I didn't answer. I just kept saying in my head Don't answer Don't answer Don't answer. Just fast walk away. As fast as you can.

All the way back to the pictures my heart was even going faster than my feet.

There was someone hoovering up at the front but no one else was in there. I ducked in behind the seats at the back where they make a kind of triangle with the wall and sat down on the floor. I had to wait for my heart to sit to down too. I did breathing. Slow breathing. Trying not to make a noise.

I was not even hungry any more.

I ate the chip but it was sort of burnt and I couldn't make the roll go down quickly. I had some of the cheese that was in my pocket too. On the last swallow I thought of a joke. Only it wasn't very funny. My neck went all hard and the bread kept getting stuck. That's why I couldn't swallow. It was nearly making me panic so I got out before the hooverer could notice me. That was a relief. A relief is what MyMum always says. *Well that's a relief then Chuck.* Said. (Except it's like I can still hear her talking.)

I couldn't stop thinking about my joke. Do you want to know what it was? *I'm a soul who stole a roll.* It made me feel a bit sick even when I thought about it. And then it got even worse because…the cheese! I had stolen two things! It did not seem like stealing when I picked it up because it was on the floor but it was. So stealing plus dirty. Plus still not seeing

France. It made my legs wobble. I didn't know what to do next. I hate that. That's when other things can get inside your head like Lie down and do screaming. I did not want those things to get in so I decided to go to bed until I heard the boat stop. I have never had wobbly legs in bed.

I went along all the way past the place where everyone had been standing on Thursday when they were waving to England and I found the door with the red hand where the blue and yellow mattresses were. There was nobody to see me. (*That's a relief then Chuck!*) BUT THEN. I could not open it. Someone had locked it. They didn't have to lock it if it had a red hand! My heart was beating so fast it was making me rock. I don't like it if I have to do rocking. I did not want a strange man to say Hallo hallo. I'm a doctor can I help you? It would be even worse if I cried like I sort of wanted to. Then it would be a kind granny and you can never get away from them. Or a mum and mums always guess the truth straight away. (Nobody knows how they do that by the way.) I thought I might have to Just lie down and do screaming. Or maybe I would have to run away again except I would have to jump off the stupid boat first. I even went to the railing to see how far down you would have to jump. (Hint—not a short way.) Then I remembered the helpful thing and did that instead. It was much better than screaming and it was extra good making the line disappear because it was nearly dark. The sea and the sky were all pinky purple and the sky over the top of the boat was blue (navy blue!) and they had put the lights on while I was looking at the red hand so everywhere was pretty. I felt a lot better. You can only think of good ideas when you are feeling better. If you are not feeling smooth you can only think rubbish like

Help me help me help me. And there will probably be nobody there anyway.

While I was there the penny dropped *Ding!* That is what MyDad says when it drops. Or perhaps you don't know what *When the penny drops* means. You might be too young like me and need your Dad to tell you about the penny in the slot. Anyway *Ding!* Of *course*. The blue and yellow mattresses would not be in the room with the red hand anyway. They would all be at the swimming pool! Silly me! I felt really stupid. So I went along to see. And you know what? Someone had taken all the mattresses off the folding beds and piled them all up against the side of the little hut and put a kind of fishing net over them. A fort! Perfect! I squeezed in behind them and nobody saw.

It felt a bit lonely. Nobody knew where I was. Especially MyMum. She probably couldn't know anything anymore. She certainly couldn't see anything because I closed her eyes. I pretended she did know. I pretended she could see me. I didn't have to pretend she could talk to me because I could kind of hear her—*Forts again you!* I thought if she could see me I would be all right. And so would my cheese. I needed my cheese to be all right because if my cheese was all right I would be all right. But I don't expect you will understand that. MyMum would say it's silly superstition.

The mattresses made me feel sort of safe. You could climb on if you were sinking. Even without a life jacket. I thought MyDad will be worried mad. He is probably looking every-where to see where I am. He has probably called the police and probably all the policemen in Southampton and in England too have been looking. And their dogs have been sniffing. Perhaps everyone has been. My Gran and her friend and Aunty Julie. Perhaps they still are. They would have to have really good binoculars to find me. Or a telescope like the one that lets you look on the moon.

Sometimes jokes only make you feel worse.

Miss Kenney

Miss Kenney is sitting in a deckchair in the shade at the back of her house with a glass of lemonade. A beaker, because glass could break. Glass always does. She has removed her nylons and left them, neatly folded, just inside the kitchen door. It's Friday afternoon. She has been to confession the same as every Friday, obtained absolution and picked up a piece of plaice from the fishmonger's on the way back. She saved the penance Father Morecambe gave her—five Hail Marys, three Our Fathers, and an I Believe—for the bus, something she's been doing lately. It makes the journey go more quickly. The concrete pad beside the yellow lawn is giving back the heat of the day. She won't last long out here even in the shade.

Friday. The start of her ordered, her orderly weekend. That she's *earned*. Saturdays are for shopping and sometimes the pictures if there's a good one on like *Lawrence of Arabia*. And she must remember to take her sandals in to get that strap mended tomorrow. She can't bear a sloppy appearance. Sunday is for Mass—but perhaps she'll have a headache and won't be able to go—and then the afternoon and the whole blessed evening to herself. She doesn't go to see her dad anymore. Pointless isn't it, really, when they don't know who you are?

Inside, her treats are all lined up on the coffee table. Tea cake, butter, jam, a pot of Tetley's, milk already in the cup, sponge fingers she'll eat right out of the packet, the *Evening Standard* and the *Radio Times*. And her weekly box of chocolates. The curtains are partly drawn against the sun. And the neighbours. You wouldn't want to be on display when you sit down to your treats, especially with a whole box of Milk Tray. You can't forget food rationing that easily, even if it's been nearly ten years. But never mind. She might have cheated a bit, even pinched a tiny little bit now and then in the war—who didn't?— but her conscience today is all bright and shiny and she can enjoy whatever she likes. Thank you. She's worked hard for it. The bottle of sherry for later is still in the sideboard. She can still say she doesn't drink because, well, she made a vow that VE Day, didn't she? Actually it was the morning after, when she was sicker than she'd ever been in her life and hopes never to be again and it was more of a promise to her poor Eddie, who wasn't there because he never came back and who she hoped wasn't watching from up there but she doesn't like to dwell on that and anyway sherry doesn't count does it? It's medicinal. That's what she'll have when she settles in later after her fish. The television's already on with the sound down low. Warming up.

So, yes. An ordered, orderly weekend. Out of reach of the disobedient, unmanageable lot of them. Thank God. Thirty-two she had this year. Thirty-two six-year-olds! No one has any idea. It's impossible. No wonder she needs a pick-me-up. She'd go mad otherwise. To be honest, sometimes she wonders why she didn't stay in factory work. At least your mind was your own around the machines. And they didn't talk back. But she was only twenty when it came up and the opportunity was too good to pass over. Trained, certified, and posted to a primary school in less than fourteen months. Almost too good to be true when she'd never been that good herself at maths. Or spelling. Actually she didn't think about the teaching part much at the time. Only the pay and the holidays. And being able to say she was a professional person. Her first day in her own classroom was a bit of a shock, though, she has to admit. Fourteen of the children in tears by playtime. She couldn't help taking it personally at the time (she knows better now), despite what the head said to her. Try not to take it too personally, he said. Oh, and here's a tip: Don't forget to smile. It's a great help. She's never forgotten that. But it hasn't helped. Not one bit. You have to be strict with them. She's found that out. It's the only way. They run rings round you otherwise. It wears you out. With any luck she'll get that summer cold that's been going around. Three days at home right now would be just the ticket. No, the twenty-seventh of July can't come quickly enough in her opinion. The last day of school before the holidays. She won't have to force a smile then. Bye-bye. Dear.

Miss Kenney doesn't know what to think when she hears someone at the front door. It's a bit of a surprise.

I had a mouthful of teacake. I'd have swallowed it first if I'd known who it was going to be. I was thinking it was boy scouts again like last week or someone else collecting. But the Head! He said, So sorry to disturb you in the middle of your tea. Polite or sarcastic. I can never tell with Mr B.

I asked him in of course. You have to. I was so mad with myself. My nylons were still in the kitchen. The television was on, my magazines were all over the settee. I made him a space and asked him to sit down. Crumbs everywhere. He said, Would you mind if we—? and pointed to the television. I said, No. Not at all, and sat down. Sat down beside him! What was I thinking? (Well I know what. I was thinking about my nylons and how on earth I could I pop out and slip them back on again without him noticing.) He said,—Um turn it off?

I am so slow!

I got up and switched it off and asked him if he'd like some tea. I said, I can fetch another cup. It's no trouble. He said, No, thank you. No. He said he had just come from the school. The police had asked him to meet with them there to check the registers. I nearly choked. Wondered what on earth I'd done wrong. Well you do, don't you, when you hear the word police? It's the first thing comes into your head. But I always do the register right off the bat. *Always*. Well, I've only forgotten once or twice—or three times perhaps—this whole year. And it's usually on Sports Day, or trips, or special assemblies, the days when everything's out of order. So no one can really blame you.

He said they were trying to ascertain the whereabouts of Francis Walters. It seemed there was some family difficulty and he'd gone missing, apparently. He asked me how long Francis had been away. Of course, I knew exactly. A day and a half. It's bliss when he's not there. Pure bliss.

He was away Thursday afternoon, I said, and he was away all day today. Mr B. said, Right. So no note, then? I said, No. He'll bring one on Monday I expect.

He said, It might be a bit more complicated than that. There's been some troubling news. That's when I felt a sort of cold hand on the back of my neck. I said, Oh, yes? He said, I probably shouldn't say too much just now. At the moment all they want is to find out if Francis seemed all right the last time you saw him.

I laughed out loud. All right as Francis Walters ever can be, I said. You know what he's like.

He didn't answer that. He said, But he wasn't poorly?

Not that I know, I said, and then I remembered. I said, But now you come to mention it, he wasn't well on Wednesday. Apparently he'd had a—you know—bilious attack in the dinner hall. I let him spend the afternoon in the infirmary until home time. You have to, don't you, the dears? Do your best for them, I mean when they're poorly.

He ignored me again, which was a bit rude, I thought. He said, So that was Wednesday? But on Thursday morning he seemed all right, did he? Some of the children were extremely upset by what happened to Mrs Mahoney, you know.

I'd forgotten all about that. I said, Oh yes, terrible. Terrible shock. Terrible. I had my hands full I can tell you.

He said, But not Francis?

I said, No. Same old Francis. He makes a nuisance of himself all day long. *As* you know, I said. I can hardly finish a sentence without him interrupting. And the things he says! The questions he asks! I think sometimes...

Well! Mr B. wasn't even listening. He just cut right in exactly like Francis, now I come to think of it. He said, You almost sound as if you'd be happy to see the last of him. That made me so mad I didn't hold back. I said, Mr B., I have put it to you on more than one occasion that my classroom would run more smoothly—But then I stopped. Mr B. was looking at me with a sort of sad smile. The way you look at the ones you've just used the ruler on. It was verging on insulting, so I didn't say anything else.

He said, Well, all right, thank you, Miss Kenney. I'll let them know what you've told me. They'll probably want to come and have a word themselves too. Just to be sure. My hands were shaking when he'd gone. I sat down and I couldn't even pour the tea. The truth was, I couldn't even remember seeing Frankie after Mrs Mahoney. And not only that, I hadn't even taken the register, Thursday afternoon. I filled it in this morning.

I had my supper and felt a bit better afterwards. Two glasses of sherry helped. To be honest I thought that was the last of the business about Frankie. I certainly wasn't expecting to hear the doorbell again at half-past eight. I switched the television off this time. Mr Bladgeworth was right. It was the police. Actually only a police-woman, and she was probably younger than me. She said she just wanted a quick word and no she wouldn't have a cup of tea, thanks. She sat down and said, You must be worried sick. I'm sorry.

I didn't really know what she was on about. I said Well, yes, I am a bit.

She said, Have you any idea where Francis might have gone when he left school on Thursday? His whereabouts are still unknown as of this moment. I said, Well I suppose he went home for his dinner. He didn't come back in the afternoon. She said, Miss Kenney, it's very important that we gather all the information we can, in light of Mrs Walters' demise.

I think I went red. I know I did. I started tidying up the newspapers so she wouldn't see. She said, Someone *has* informed you, haven't they? I was on fire. I said, What do you mean? She said, Miss Kenney, hasn't anyone told you? Mrs Walters was found dead at her home in Worcester Terrace this morning.

I said, Oh, no! I had no idea! My face wouldn't calm down. She said, And Francis wasn't at school today? We really need to be sure of our facts here. I said, Oh I'm quite sure. Absolutely certain. Of course I was sure. I'd had the best day all year without little Mr Bossy Boots Frankie Fartface getting up my nose. But of course I didn't *say* that. Even if it was true. Little wretch.

I don't know why I felt so guilty after she left. As if I'd done something wrong. As if it was my fault his mum died. I poured myself another sherry. You can blame the teacher for a lot these days but not that one. No thank you. I'm not taking that one on.

Miss Kenney tidies up. She's missed *Take Your Pick* and by the time she's done the washing up it will be *Friday Night Playhouse* and she's not in the mood. She could do with some company. Her bright, shiny weekend is tarnished. She wishes her friend Hilda were around, but Hilda is in Switzerland. Switzerland! On a coach trip! The prospect of Friday, Saturday, Sunday all to herself is suddenly as inviting as Shingle Spit in January.

Len

Len Walters sees the police car in the street as soon as he drives round the corner. He pulls up at the curb thinking they've finally come about the damn dog next door, thinking, Good. He is still inventing Patti's rant, smiling, as he gets out and slams the door. When he looks up he sees for the first time a young constable stationed at his own front door.

Good God, how life can pull a fast one! Leading you on one minute then grabbing you by the throat the next. What in God's name has he done?

In seconds the two officers from the car are standing in his path, blocking his way to the house.

Hello, hello, he says brightly. What's all this then?

One of them says, Good evening Mr Walters, and announces himself as Detective Sergeant Mickleson. Len is too busy ransacking his memory of the last three days to reply.

Sergeant Mickleson says they've been trying to reach him concerning the whereabouts of his son, Francis. He says, Can you tell us where your son might be at this moment, Mr Walters?

Len says, Well if you just let me get in the house, you lot, I'll take a look.

Sergeant Mickleson says, Uh no, sir.

He says there is no need to go in. There is no one in the house. They will go down to the station together. If he wouldn't mind.

—My wife—

The detective interrupts. He says, That's what we'd like to discuss, sir. At the station.

—Is that where my wife is? Are you detaining my wife? What's she been up to now? But no one is smiling. He tries again.

—Arrests a bit thin on the ground tonight, are they?

Sergeant Mickleson, holding open the door of the police car, says, Let's just get out of the street shall we, Mr Walters?

Obediently, Len climbs into the back seat and waits while the officer closes the door and gets into the front. The uniformed officer has already turned the key.

The two policemen sit in silence as they pull away. It seems like a good idea to place himself on their team. Len asks if they've had a busy day, suggests they must get used to all types sitting in the seat behind them. The policemen stare obdurately ahead.

—At least tell me if my family's all right, says Len. He says he is sure they would like to know the whereabouts of their families, if they were in the same boat.

—Car, he adds weakly.

The officer in the passenger seat says he will be fully informed down at the station. Of what? he wants to know. Of what? Though somehow he doesn't want to ask.

She's gone beserk, he concludes. It is all he can think of. She's been into something that's made her crazy. She made herself a cocktail, mixed things you never want to mix. That's it. She's gone out of her head. Some kind of damage. Some kind of harm. God. If she's hurt Frankie. If she's so much as.

—Where's my son? His own voice interrupts his thought, blurting now, urgent.

—Almost there, Mr Walters, says the officer.

At the station a policeman behind the desk takes his name and makes a note of the time. He says the detective sergeant has some telephone calls to make. He says he is to wait in the interview room. The officer who had been driving takes him there and he sits down at a table.

—Won't be long, the officer says, while they're making the calls. He goes out and shuts the door. A young policeman, a boy really, is standing in the corner. A young woman comes in with tea. The smell of it makes him nauseous.

Len Walters leans forward in the chair, propping his elbows on the interview table, his thumbs behind his jaw, his fingers pressing his temples, his forehead, as if by physical pressure he can knead a single cogent thought from the throng of images now at riot in his brain. He's begun to imagine the worst. They've found Francis. Dead of course, his eyes wide open, at the bottom of the coal hole where he fell while Patti was in a stupor. Or, worse, he'd had a tantrum and Patti put him down there. As a punishment. Stuffed him down there and closed the lid. Or she smothered him first because he wouldn't stop his tantrum and she couldn't cope. Then she realized what she'd done and swallowed the first fistful of pills she could lay her hands on.

His mind is racing, switching gears, switching track. It was a traffic accident. A bus overturned. They're in the hospital. He can't think fast enough to trap the narrative he needs, the story of what happened while he was driving the A3 down from Ipswich. Why didn't he leave earlier? He could have been home sooner. Perhaps even in time to stop whatever it was. But he knows why. He likes the drive. He makes it last. It gives him time to catch his breath between the pleasurable creaking of the bed in the room over the pub and the emotional onslaught that will greet him at the door. He likes the stops along the way, the Nag's Head at lunchtime. The peaceful drive through Epsom. No demands. No questions. No suspicions or recriminations.

And no Frankie.

Oh Frankie. They're not telling me where you are. They said no one was home but they're not telling me where you are. I hope to God you're at Mum's and not in a ditch somewhere. Or worse. Did you set this up, Patti? Oh God, is it something I've done? I haven't done anything that could hurt you, Patti. I would never do anything, you know that. Is it the pills again? But you were off them. You were OK. We were OK. Oh God, Patti. If you could walk through that door right now. Get me out of here.

At last the detective sergeant returns. He has another man with him. Detective Inspector Isherwood, he says. They take their seats on the other side of the table. Len waits again while the detective sergeant rummages for a handkerchief and blows his nose.

—Right, Mr Walters. I'm afraid we have some—

Len Walters' blood roars in his ears. He completes the sentence in his head even as the detective is speaking.

—very bad news for you.

But the man's next words: Your wife—seems to jolt the chair from under him. So that he is suddenly standing, repeating My wife? My *wife?* Drowning out what the inspector has to say and suddenly shouting, My son. What about my son? Where's my son? Pressing with his hands, leaning into the table and aiming the words directly across at the stony face of the inspector, who waits patiently for him to finish before he resumes.

—Your wife, Mr Walters, was found dead at your home this morning. Her body is being held at the Coroner's office in Chapel Street.

It is not what he expected. He has no idea what to do with the information. He is not equipped. He says, Then what are we doing here? He wants to say, She needs me, but he says again, Where's my son?

The inspector does not answer either of his questions. He says, Let's start at the beginning. Tell me where you were on the night of Tuesday, July the eighteenth, Mr Walters.

Chapter 3
SATURDAY AM
(That's the morning)

I was starving when I woke up (not really so don't worry)
but I had to stay where I was because it wasn't light yet only
electric light. Yes really! They kept the lights on all night so
you didn't have to be afraid of the dark (and do screaming).
Getting up was as tricky as going to bed. I had to be careful
people didn't see me. I was sure they wouldn't let you sleep
all by yourself on the deck. At least I didn't think they would.
If a sailor saw me walking about at night he would say What
are you doing sunny (only it wouldn't be!) out here all by
yourself at night? And then I would be scared even with the
lights on.

So. I needed to wait for it to start lightening—but not thun-
dering (haha)—and then do spying until it was safe to get up.

You know why I had to do hiding at night don't you? It's
because I didn't have a cabin. And I didn't have a cabin because
I didn't have a ticket and I didn't have a ticket because I didn't

have any money (you know that). But I got on board anyway. (You know that too. I'm just reminding you.)

I was all achey and cold. My bedroom was not very comfortable. The floor was too hard. I had tried pulling on the bottom mattress so I could lie on it but there wasn't room to pull properly and it was too heavy anyway. I was afraid they would wobble. Then people would think it was a rat. A giant one! (That's another joke.)

When it was proper light I got up. I had to walk fast I had been waiting so long. It was a good job they had the little feet to keep the doors open. The only person I saw was somebody cleaning. He was polishing the clips on the stair carpet. He was a foreigner too but he could speak the right language. He said God bless my soul. (So *he* had one.) I didn't know what to say back. I said Excuse me. And he said Sir. So I said Excuse me sir. And he said No. Pardon me. You're the sir. Then when I went by him he said Thank you sir. Mind yourself sir. I was very confused. In fact I was completely puzzled. I expect it was because he was foreign.

I had a nasty shock when I looked in the mirror in the toilets. I was all dirty! I washed my hands fourteen times and washed my face and dried it on the roller towel. I did not know you could get so dirty. It is because I am always hiding behind stuff or crawling on the floor looking for food and useful things. I didn't have a comb so I used my fingers. My hair was sticking up a bit at the back but I have seen lots of boys like that. And some of them even make it stick up at the front. On purpose.

When I was all clean I went out again to find my cheese. My cache is not very handy. I was even more starving thinking about it. I pretended I was a refugee. .They come from Hungary so that's really funny. But not for them haha. MyMum said sometimes refugees don't eat anything for days and days. Sometimes weeks and months so I am really lucky. I think she exaggerates. But I think she is right about the lucky bit.

Or maybe not. Sometimes I forget that MyMum is dead. But that is probably better than remembering.

Stolen Goods. That's what they call it. I had to stretch up high. A good job no one could see. I broke off a big piece and put the rest back for later. (That's like remainders when you do dividing. MyMum taught me dividing. She said Sometimes I think school is holding you back.) It tasted disgusting. I put the remainder in my pocket because I still had another important thing to do. Go up to the front. I wanted MyDad to be with me. It would have been better. I knew I was not going to like it. I was right.

Sea. All the way round.

Just like yesterday.

I could not see France anywhere.

Not anywhere at all.

I had never felt such a big panic coming. I expect you know what I wanted to do. But then I thought Perhaps it isn't true. I thought Check. You have to check. You have to go inside again and look at the map. Then you will know if the thing that is giving you a bad feeling is true.

When I got there the glass was open like a door. Someone in a white uniform was just moving the boat. Some souls with white towels round their necks had stopped to look so I did too. The sailor had moved the boat right out along the red line. He was just locking it up again when another sailor in a black uniform came along and said something I didn't understand. It sounded like Complexmanoover Philips!

It might have been French for Good morning Philips because Philips said Good morning Captain back.

Captain! I tried to get behind one of the soul's legs but I couldn't. The Captain said I don't know where we'd be without you to keep us on course hahaha. One of the souls said Probably still in the English Channel hahaha. The Captain said That wouldn't do at all would it son? And he looked right at me! I said I wouldn't mind. And everyone laughed their heads off. (That's only what you say.) I had not been so scared since I got on board but it was all right because they all ignored me after that so they could carry on laughing so I just disappeared myself.

It took a long time to calm down. I had made a very Important Discovery but there was nowhere for it to go inside my head. It was worse than that. It was a Terrible Discovery. I can't even say it out loud, it made me feel so funny. I felt like Jackie my budgie when he was trying to get back in his cage because the door was shut. He went bananas. (Bananas was just to cheer you up.)

I went to where the sailors had put deckchairs all along the side and I sat in one to think about the Terrible Discovery. As soon as I sat down I knew it was true.

We were not going to France. *Ever*. And the red line was not the equator. It was to show where we were going. We were going to America. We came out of the end of English Channel just like the cut-out boat. And now we were out in the Ocean where the sailor in the white uniform put it. Pointing the wrong way. We were in the Atlantic Ocean and we were going on it right over to the other side. The other side was definitely not France. I am not daft. It said New York and New York is in America. Everyone knows that. And even if they don't they know it's not France because it's two English words. The red line on the picture was joining up Southampton to New York. There was nowhere to get off in between because you can't get off in the Ocean it doesn't matter how you spell it. And there wouldn't be any police stations anyway. That was kind of a joke. And kind of not. I couldn't think of a joke. I was too worried. I wished the cut-out boat didn't have glass over it so I could turn it round and point it back the right way.

I needed to make a new plan. Here is my first one in case you've forgotten:

Old Plan
1. Go to France.
2. Find a police station.
3. Ring MyDad to come and get me.

It was a good one. Better than just staying at home. You don't want to see your Mum get buried. That would be horrible. And I didn't want to go to Gran's. Gran is all right but her house smells of cat pee. (She says it is certainly not Lady Beaverbrook. Lady Beaverbrook doesn't do that. It is the tom from next door. Or the ferret.) So France was a good idea. MyDad wouldn't mind coming to get me. He would like it. He says the vanblonk there is unbelievable. That is a word he says when he likes something. *Unbelievable!* (MyMum only used to say it when she got mad.) MyDad went to France with Uncle Norman. When he came back he had thirty-seven bottles of wine. That was one of the bad rows they had when he said MyMum had managed to drink a whole suitcaseful all by herself. He said *managed* to drink like she had been trying really hard and it was difficult. Actually it would be difficult. But maybe not for MyMum. She can do all sorts of things. She said I'm just saving you from the clink. Destroying the evidence. I didn't understand that bit until I found out after. The clink means prison. Where they put people who have stolen goods.

If you look carefully at my plan you will see how good it was. I do not speak French (it is a foreign language) but if I found a police station I would be all right. I could mime being on the telephone so they would know what I wanted and I could draw MyDad and write our telephone number down. They would be able to read the numbers. They are easy to learn because there are only nine. Ten if you count zero. Numbers are amazing. You only need two and you can write down one million. Even a billion. But that wouldn't help if there were no police stations or telephones. I didn't even want to say haha. The Atlantic was not very funny.

This was my new plan. It only had two things on it:

New Plan
1. Stay on the boat and don't get off until it goes back to England. (*If* it goes back.)
2. Go home.

I would have to have a wash every day so I didn't look like a nurchin. MyMum used to say that when it was time for my bath. That was before I grew up. She used to say Come here my dirty little urchin (she used to drop her ens like lots of people). I used to like being little. It was easy. You got wrapped up in a towel.

I would have to have breakfast too because the Atlantic could take a really long time and *You can't travel on a nempty stomach.* (That was MyGran.) And anyway I was starving.

Also I would have to be extra careful. It was probably like the trains if you didn't have a ticket. The fine for not having a ticket on a boat would be gigantic. If they found out about me and asked MyDad to pay he wouldn't have enough money and they would put him in prison.

I added another number. Just in case.

3. If MyDad is in the clink go to Gran's.

I would be brave and put up with the smell.

When I got to the dining room nobody cared about me having breakfast. They were all too busy gobbling food. It was unbelievable! This is what you had to do. First you didn't have to pay any money or have a ticket (or run in and take stuff!). Everything was free. You got your own plate from a huge pile and then you just went to the big tables and you could take whatever you wanted. I saw the same lady as before and this time she was carrying *two* jugs of orange juice. Two! Everybody got whatever they wanted and some of the people even helped you—like if you couldn't reach the baked beans.

This is what I had. A fried egg some fried potatoes a pancake (yes pancakes! For breakfast!) and some baked beans. Actually it was a whole big puddle. I had some bacon too but I didn't eat it. I will tell you about that in a minute. I took everything to the children's table where there were two twins eating some porridge. One of them licked her spoon while she was looking at me. I said Hahaha. Goldilocks and Goldilicks. The other one put her tongue out and a bit of porridge fell off so I didn't say anything else.

I went back a second time. I got some toast. Four pieces just in case. A lady said to me Here. Have a plate. And use the tongs next time.

Tongs! That is a funny word. I tried not to do rude laughing.

I had to go back again to get some jam.

So do you want to know why I didn't eat the bacon? Listen to this.

—There you go laddie. (The man helping me with the baked beans.)

—Thank you. (Me.)

—And you'll be wanting this. (The man putting a bit of bacon on my plate.)

—No I won't. (Me.)

—*No I won't?* (The man again. He was doing mimicking.)

—Yes. (Me.)

—Yes or no laddie? Make up your mind. (The man. But you know that.)

No. (That was me except I said it in my head in case he thought I was being rude and not making up my mind.) I really just stared at the bacon.

—Ah go on. Put hairs on your chest.

See what I mean?

The next thing after breakfast is brush your teeth and I didn't have a toothbrush so that was my next job. Look for one. It was good to have important things to think about and important problems like washing yourself and finding food and toothbrushes. It was better than remembering your Mum. In the Atlantic. If you didn't have important things I expect you would go mad like the man up the road.

I went to the shops first. There was one shop that had everything you needed. Nearly. They had clothes and books and shoes and cameras—but you didn't really *need* a camera—and cups and plates and ashtrays and sunglasses and hats and pipes and watches (but actually you could tell the time by the sun too if you had enough practice) and all the other stuff for ladies that MyMum calls rubbish—like perfume and gold necklaces and earrings. They had lots of other things as well that you don't need at all especially on a boat. Like golf clubs and tea towels. But no toothbrushes. So actually the first thing is not true. They did not have everything you need. Not nearly everything. They did not have a bed for instance. Or a potato.

It was tiring thinking about things you need and things you don't need. There were so many things it made you want to close your eyes. The list of things you don't need kept getting longer and longer like a huge snake that would not stop growing. It was filling up my head so I stopped. I had to stop anyway because an old lady came and talked to me. She had yellow hair like my first teddy and red lips and she was wearing gold sandals. At first I thought she was very rich but her sandals were just painted. You could see a bit of the gold sticking up like the paint on our windowsill at home. Her skin was nearly the same colour as her hair. But with brown splashes on.

She said All alone again today? You were all by yourself yesterday.

I didn't know what to say so I said a lie. I said No I am with my Aunty.

She looked round like you do when you go *Where?*

I said She's sleeping. She's always sleeping.

She said So you *are* all alone then. We shall have to find you someone to play with.

She was the second person who had observed me by myself. The first one was Kay. That's what I called her because she said it twice when she came to talk to me. Kay was all right but I think the old lady was suspicious. I mean I think she thought I was. Suspicious. I was. I was suspicious of her haha.

I said No thank you and went away fast. I could hear the lady in the shop saying He shouldn't even be in here by himself. Little *monkey.* I didn't like her saying that. It's a special name MyMum has for me. Had. My little monkey mine. It felt nice. She wouldn't let anyone else say it.

It was better outside. I did not look in many places for a toothbrush because ugh. Someone would have used it. Instead I did some looking at the water so I could stay calm. It was going up and down very slowly. It was like being on someone's tummy when they do breathing. It is better when they do breathing than when they don't. I did looking for a long time and no one bothered me (for a change).

I did counting then to calm down some more. It was no good counting souls because I already know the answer so I did counting seagulls—not alligators haha. Do you want to know how many I saw? 0. Nought. I waited seventeen minutes before I gave up. I don't like giving up. I like things to have a nend.

I changed from seagulls to boys and girls. I made two groups in my head to put them in. YES and NO. Yes was for if I liked playing with them. No was for if I didn't. Twenty-two went in NO. YES got a 0. Like the seagulls. MyMum used to say Don't you have any friends Frankie? I used to say No. Then she used to say Oh you are a funny one.

But I wasn't making a joke. Playtime is the worst thing about school. When the bell rings everyone goes *Sshh!* all at the same time because Miss Kenney won't let us out *until*. They say Shush. We can't go out *until*. I'm never talking but they say it to me anyway and dig me with their elbows. Sometimes when someone won't stop moving or talking Miss Kenney makes them stay in. (I used to do it on purpose so I could sit in my desk but then she stopped letting me and she just used to say Let's all ignore Frankie shall we?) Then we line up at the door and Miss Kenney says no running until you're outside and everybody runs. Sometimes boys step on the back of your shoe and it comes off. And sometimes someone throws it in a bin or in a toilet. Everyone is pushing and shoving at the same time and yelling so it's a big roar. The words all jam together and sort of disappear into a bang. That is when I decide I will go to my tree. It's behind one of the classrooms. It's never sunny there so no one really stays. It's too chilly. I stand up close to the tree and lean my forehead on it. Sort of joined up with it so I feel better. It's quiet. Sometimes they run round the back if they're playing It. Then they hit me on the arm and say You're It. But only sometimes. And I don't mind because they don't mean it.

Gran

They kept Len all night after he finally showed up Friday. Not quite all night. Let him go at midnight, apparently. Probably needed the cell. He says they never locked the door, just wanted him there in case. In case what? He said In case they needed me, I suppose. Anyway they let him go so he went back to the house. On the last bus! Apparently there was still a policeman there. Plain clothes, he thinks. Someone in a car anyway, keeping watch. He must have been beside himself. They still hadn't taken him to see Patti. He said he couldn't face the bed, so he slept all night on the settee. Right next to the armchair. I don't know whether they'd told him that's where I found her. Dear lord. I thought about him in that room. I said, Did you manage to sleep? He said, Like the dead. I wonder sometimes about Len.

I thought about that policeman outside. I know what they were thinking having him there because I got close to thinking the same thing lying awake Friday night. Thinking about how Frankie wasn't at school. Marked Absent.

Hadn't even been there. And then thinking about what they told me at the station. Marked Absent Thursday afternoon an all. My blood run cold. Stone cold. Len? I know I'm his mum and everything but still. You can't help it. Your mind just takes you the worst places. But I didn't say anything. I tell you when I finally got home Friday I was in a right state. I'd been down the station all day. Margie didn't know anything about it. She only come round because she wanted her fish. But she knew something was up right off. She said, Good God what's happened to you, Em? I said, Not me, Marge. It's Patti. And Frankie. I didn't mention Len. I was too ashamed. But she asked. And you know for the first time in my life I was at a loss for words. I couldn't speak. I couldn't tell her. Not anything. I was blubber. You know when people say She's lost her mind. Well, that's what I done. I was blubber. Not blubbering. Just a sack of wobbly blubber. Margie was ever so kind. She just waited. Well, she put the kettle on. You do, don't you. But other than that she just waited. When I come to (that's how I think of it), I told her Patti was dead, died in her armchair, and Frankie was missing. She said straightaway, Are they doing a search? And you know what? I didn't even know. I told you I lost my mind.

She said, I'm going down the pub. And—you won't believe this—I laughed. I did. I laughed out loud. That got me out of it. I looked at her dead straight and I said, Have one for me, will you? We nearly had hysterics. It was the shock.

She said, I'll bring you one back. What do you want? Bottle of stout? Get your strength up.

Anyway, she went. She got all the lads out—there wasn't too many because it was early still— and they went door to door all up and down Worcester terrace and then the Barnham road both sides. She come back about nine thirty and said the police told them to stop. But they never. They carried on until closing time then they went back to the pub. She was waiting there with Reg and he let them back in. They said there was a police watching the house and there was a bit of fence across the front path. And no Len.

After the pub she got the eleven o'clock over to mine. She said, I'm staying the night, Em. Ever so kind Margie is. I made up the bed in the box room.

About three in the morning I heard her crying. But I didn't get up. You have to give people their privacy.

We were down the police station again by half past seven this morning. They were all drinking tea and you could smell bacon. Not exactly pulling out all the stops. They told me Len had shown up finally. He'd come down from Ipswich late. Seems the lads from the pub missed him last night by about an hour.

The relief. But it didn't last. They said No. It didn't mean anything. They said Patti had been dead since Wednesday and they still had some enquiries to make. *Wednesday!* One shock after another. Worried stiff I was. My own son. No, they weren't the only ones doing the suspecting.

He come in this morning just after we did. I heard his voice at the desk in the front. I don't know what I expected. A raving maniac? A ghost? But it was just Len. That kind of guilty look he always used to get. He said, Mum. I said, Len. What else can you say?

Chapter 4
SATURDAY AN
(That's for After Noon)

In the afternoon I saw the girl I called Kay up on the top deck. She was with her Mum and her Dad and they were coming out from the gap between the two big pictures of the sea. I didn't even know what was on the other side because I didn't know you could go through the gap. It was like a fence that didn't join up.

Kay said Hallo. You know what I just had? A Wimpy.

(I have always wanted one of those. They smell delicious. There is a Wimpy Bar in King Street but MyMumandDad say it's full of ton-up boys and I'm not old enough yet.)

Her Dad said it's called a hamburger.

Kay said Kay. Then she said You should get your Mum and Dad to take you.

I tried not to look at the Mum and the Dad in case they said something to me too.

The Mum said He can go and get one himself if he likes can't he. I expect that's where he was going. I would have hated it if she was looking at me but she was busy folding down Kay's collar where it was sticking up.

I said It is. (That was nearly a lie to start with and then it came true. I just wanted to get away fast.)

The Dad said Attaboy.

Kay called out Do you want to come to the Sea Shanties with us next?

I called out No thank you. (That was true.)

She said Kay.

I went through the gap. It wasn't a Wimpy Bar. It was a big long table with tin trays of food like the dinner hall at school and two cooks and you could go and get whatever you wanted and take it to one of the tables. I really wanted to get a Wimpy but there wasn't a special children's table like at breakfast and I didn't want to sit with anyone who would say SO. *Where are your parents then? Don't they want one too? Haha.* BUT! The blind man came in and joined on to the queue. I was still a bit suspicious of him but I thought I could just go and sit wherever he sat and pretend I was with him. I didn't have to talk to him.

I went in and stood a bit behind him. Alec knew. He wagged his tail. Then the blind man said Hallo? Someone we know? And he turned round!

It was really confusing. He was looking over the top of my head. I stayed really quiet and didn't say anything. I don't think I was being rude because he wasn't really looking at me. He was looking sort of blank. (That is what Miss Kenney said when she talked about me to MyDad. By the way. She said I looked blank. They talked about me for seventeen minutes and forty-five seconds. Miss Kenney kept saying And another thing and MyDad kept saying I don't think it's a problem. From the time I started counting, Miss Kenney said her thing seven times and MyDad said his eleven. I don't think they were listening to each other.) Anyway the blind man looked like Miss Kenney said I look. I thought he might be pretending or he might be doing counting like me. Then I remembered it was probably because he couldn't see me. Why did I keep forgetting that?

I just kept behind him and stayed quiet. Perfect! I thought. When he goes to a table I can go too and sit on one of the other chairs if I'm really quiet. Then everyone will think he's my Uncle and no one will be bothered that I don't have a nadult. He can be one.

There was a cook cooking the hamburgers. When the blind man got there he sort of felt for the plates. The cook of the hamburgers said Here you are sir and gave him one that already had a roll on it with the top off. He put a hamburger on top and said What else will you have?

The blind man said Tomatoes and onions and lettuce please. And you can put a stick of celery on the plate too if you don't mind.

The cook said Not at all sir. Mustard or pickle? Tomato sauce?

And guess what the blind man said. Everything! But that was not all. He turned his head towards me and he said What do you want on yours?!

I nearly fell down!

I said Everything. I was so surprised. And then I remembered Please. And then I remembered I don't like onions but it was too late.

The cook said I'll bring them over sir and the blind man said That's very kind.

Now I had to stay beside him even though I thought he might be only pretending.

He followed Alec to a table and sort of touched everything and sat down. I sat on a chair on the other side.

When the cook brought our plates he said I bet you're a big help aren't you? I didn't know if he was being sarcastic so I didn't say anything. Not even thank you.

It smelled so good I couldn't wait.

It was the most delicious food I have ever tasted (even with the onions) and I couldn't stop. It only took about two and a half minutes to eat it. I wasn't even counting I was so happy. I tried to slide out of my chair but the blind man said Finished already?

I was shocked. I put the celery in my pocket quickly. I said Can you see me? I couldn't help it.

He said No I'm afraid not. It was a good hamburger wasn't it? I said Yes.

He said You're the first little boy I know who likes onions. But you didn't eat your celery.

I said You *can* see me! I knew you could. It was a bit rude but it was like before. I couldn't help it. I wanted to say How did you know I was even here and who am I anyway? that would have been really *really* rude.

He said No. He said it kind of sad but he was smiling (at nothing!) and then he shook his head and said it again. He said No. I can't.

I said Yes you can or how do you know there was celery? Ha!

He said I could smell it.

I said Then how do you know I didn't eat…I was going to say It but I already knew the answer. He didn't hear it! I just said Oh.

And this time he smiled a really big smile.

He said Your brain's very busy isn't it? And just seven? Well well well.

And then suddenly I got scared because I guessed what his next question was going be so I did a great big lie and said I have to go and find my MumandDad now.

He said I'd really like to meet them. Tell them I'll be on the Sports deck this afternoon. Tell them to come and say hallo.

I said All right. Bye. Bye Alec.

Alec made a little noise when I was going away and the blind man said Shh.

The notice board near the Purser's Office said

FUNDAYS!

SATURDAY

9:00 a.m.	Fit as a Fiddle!	Sundeck	Adults
10:00 a.m.	Sea All around!	Cinema	Adults + children
11:00 a.m.	Treasure Hunt!	Atrium	Adults + children
2:30 p.m.	Sea Shanties!	Midships Lounge	All Ages
	Goofy Golf!	Activity Centre	5+
3:30 p.m.	Bingo!	Midships Lounge	Adults + children
	Wits Pit!	Queen's Lounge	Adults
4:00pm	Look Like a Star!	Beauty Parlour	Over 16
6:00pm	Cocktails		

They put the thing like a rounders bat and ball eight times. That means something is a surprise. Cocktails was number nine. It didn't have a rounders bat.

5+ that's my age. I went to the playroom to be by myself and think about it.

I got Five Go to Pirates' Cove off the shelf. The lady said That's a bit old for you isn't it? You can't read that.

I said Yes I can and she said Oh it's you and stopped talking to me.

I took it into the yellow tent.

No one ever believes you when you tell them about reading. It makes them bad-tempered. They didn't believe MyMumand-Dad at nursery school when they told them I had been reading books since I was two and a half. The lady said *Oh, yes?* Like when someone says the opposite thing. MyMum said Yes. The lady said What does he read exactly? MyDad said Anything really and she reached behind her chair for a book off the shelf and gave me the Ladybird book of Hannibal. I opened it and started reading very fast. I watched her with one of my eyes to see if she was impressed.

She said But he's not reading it. He's only memorizing.

That's when MyMum's voice got all high and squeaky and she said THAT'S BECAUSE HE *REMEMBERS* IT. HE'S ALREADY READ IT.

I stopped then. I thought she was going to say Silly moo. She said that once when we were in Boots and I started laughing and I couldn't stop. I fell on the floor and a lady came and told her off.

The lady in the nursery school said Could I have the book back please?

I gave it to her and she opened it at another page and said Read this. So I did.

Then she said Could I have the book back please dear?

I gave it to her and she turned some pages. Next she reached onto her desk and picked up a piece of paper and put it over the picture all kind of secretly so I couldn't see. She put the book down in front of me with the piece of paper over the picture and said Try this page dear and you could tell the words she said out loud were not the same words she was saying in her head. Even a nidiot could tell she was saying *I bet you can't read this.*

MyMum stood up and said You know what? Never mind. Just never mind and she got hold of my hand and took me away. I could hear MyDad saying Goodbye and then I could hear him saying I'm sorry. No it's all right. We're all right thank you. And then he said Thank you again.

I read three chapters of Five Go to Pirates' Cove. I was just starting chapter four when I heard the lady talking outside. I knew she was talking about me. She said They should find him someone to play with I'm not a baby-sitter. And then I had a good idea. Goofy Golf! And then I can be playing and be by myself as well.

I left the book in the playroom. I wished I could steal it but that is probably worse than stealing a roll. Stealing a roll is a nemergency. You could die of starvation if you didn't.

Goofy Golf was not really golf at all. Only the goofy part was true. They only had stupid cut-out trees made of cardboard and pretend hills and bridges and a pretend well. You got a pretend golf ball and a pretend golf club from the man or the lady wearing the blue jackets. Some of the kids were whacking each other and laughing. (You would not do laughing if you got hit with a real one. Uncle Richard didn't when he went to hospital. MyMum said Aunty Julie knew he was standing behind her when she did it.)

I went inside and waited to get a golf club. The man and the lady in the blue jackets were getting all mad with the big kids but they were still smiling so they looked really funny with crazy eyes.

I laughed and laughed and the lady said Goofy Golf is jolly good fun isn't it?

I said No and it made me laugh even harder.

That's when Kay came in. She came over to me and said What are you laughing at?

I said Them and my tummy started to ache.

Kay said Kay. Want to play?

I said Yes. You be the man and I'll be the lady and I made mad eyes with a big smile.

Kay said No. Stupid. Play Goofy Golf.

I said No thank you.

Kay said You're peculiar I can't play with you and then she said But you can still be my friend.

I said We're friends?

She said You're not just peculiar. You're a bit dim. Of course we are. And then she went away. I pretended I didn't care.

After Kay left two of the trees fell over because the floor was tipping up. The man stood them up again but then they tipped over the other way. The lady fixed it. She turned them sideways and they stayed up but it was no good. I told the man he needed to tell everyone to hold onto their balls because they were rolling away. He went and whispered to the lady and she whispered back then they did giggling. The lady came over and said Have you lost your ball dear? I'll give you another one. She said it like I was only two so I said No thank you. I could see in past her eyes. She was not talking to me at all.

I hate that. It made me start feeling bad. It was as if someone had made all the lights go dizzy and someone else had turned up the sounds. Everything was booming even the lady's voice and two big girls who were laughing and even the stupid fake golf balls that only go *ddth*. But this is what the trouble was. The loudness was right inside my head and not in the Fundays room at all. The people playing golf were like people on the telly with the sound down. But really they had come inside my head and their voices were making the sound inside it. Having a party inside my head! I couldn't stand it. I went away. Just like Kay.

🦢

MyMum told me one day it's all right to be by yourself when you don't feel good. She said In *fact*—she stuck her eyebrows up and opened her eyes wide like she always does when she tells me something important—in *fact* sometimes it's a very good thing finding somewhere to be all on your own.

I told her Miss Kenney says playtime is for playing with kids and not for standing by the tree.

She said It doesn't matter what Miss Kenney says about playing with kids if they make you feel bad.

That's when we had a nargument.

I said But Miss Kenney said we always have to obey the teacher.

MyMum said Miss Kenney *is* a teacher.

I said I know.

MyMum said So *think* about it! And then she answered the telephone because it was getting on our nerves. That's when I got mad and chopped up all the spaghetti with the chopping knife. When you chop it and it's not cooked it shoots away off the counter. I was trying to see if I could get it all the way across the kitchen. One bit hit me in the eye. When MyMum came back in she said *Unbelievable!* I just don't believe you sometimes. I've just spent ten minutes on the phone with Miss Kenney telling her there is nothing wrong with you.

I said I didn't say anything.

She said *What?*

I said You can't not believe me because I didn't say anything.

She did a funny face like if you're in a comic and you hit your finger with a hammer and she said Well it's a bloody good job I said Yes that's all I can say.

I went out to the garden to think about that. It did not make any sense.

I do not always understand MyMum. Sometimes I think she will be pleased and she's not. When I told her how Miss Kenney makes all the kids say their favourite colours one by one and then I have to tell the visitors how many reds how many blues how many pinks and all the other colours (I like that) she went into the school and told her off. I did not know you could tell off a teacher. MyMum said You can tell off any *mm-mm* (that was a swear) person you like. (I don't like it when she does a swear. MyDad has rows with her when she does that.) I said I like playing that game. But MyMum said You are not a trained monkey. I didn't tell her that a monkey could not do that because it can't speak. I could hear in my head all the things MyDad would say back.

I stayed outside until MyDad came home. He came to find me in the shed and he had his special kind voice on that always means he has something bad to say. He said Frankie. Mum (that's what he calls her even though she's not his Mum) and I have agreed that it would be a good thing if you see another teacher at the school.

I said what do you mean See?

He said Talk to. (That is the trouble when you talk to adults. They get mixed up.)

He said I think it's a good idea.

I said Who then?

He said We don't know yet.

It didn't sound like a very good idea to me. It sounded like they had only just thought of it so I didn't say anything.

Then he said Come inside and have some tea and he put his face down and looked inside my eyeballs. He said Cheer up Chuck. It might never happen. But I knew it would and I was right.

One day at school Miss Kenney said There's someone to see you Frankie. I knew she didn't mean see. She meant talk to you. It made me feel nervous. It was a skinny man and he had a little pointy beard. It looked disgusting up close. He put out his hand and said Hallo Frankie. My name is Mr Mack. Let's go in the quiet room shall we. I thought Let's not but I had to because grown-ups always get their way. He asked me tons of questions and I got confused. When Miss Kenney asks questions I always know the answer. Like what is seven sevens? Or where is the River Thames? (When Robert asked that in class she said London but I told her actually London is not a very good answer because the River Thames is actually in lots of places. She said I hope you're not trying to be a smart Alec Frankie.) Mr Mack's questions were useless. He asked things like How do you feel when you hear the bell for playtime? And Do you like playing outside or inside? All of the answers were the same. I had to say It depends about fifty times. Mr Mack was bored too because he kept doing a big sigh. He didn't come back again. Maybe he got the sack haha. It always makes you feel better if you do a joke. MyMum thought it was funny too.

A dog would be good for a friend. No one ever has a nargument with their dog. I would really love one. I asked MyMum and MyDad once but they said no. That was right after I laughed at my dead fish. It was the day after. They said I was not old enough to take care of it. MyMum said any little boy who can slide his dead fish along the kitchen floor just because he thinks it's funny doesn't deserve a dog. Only I didn't think it was funny. I thought it was interesting. It was like he was all frozen so he was really slidey and you scored a goal if he went between the legs of the green stool.

I got in trouble when he was alive too. I dug up some worms and I chopped them up on the top step so I could feed them to him. I put some in his fishbowl. Everybody knows fish eat worms. They even sell worms specially for fish. But when MyMum saw them floating about in the bowl she screamed a tiny bit and she came to find me. I had gone back to the step to finish chopping up the others. Some of the bits were still wriggling. It was very interesting.

MyMum said Did you do this?

It was a stupid question because MyDad was at work so it could not have been him. She said Did you? Did you. Did you? about fifty times. That's a nexaggeration. It was three times. I nodded for yes.

She said What with?

That was a more interesting question because I could not guess why she wanted to know what I did it with. So I said Why do you want to know? and she smacked me on the back of the leg and then she said Go away. Just go away.

Now I feel bad I wrote about MyMum because you will think she is not a nice person. But she is. Was. I know she was. That's why I don't have to cry.

Len

I had to tell them about Val last night. I couldn't avoid it. If I
could have kept it secret I would have. For your sake, Patti.
Out of respect, I mean. But they asked me to account for
my whereabouts Tuesday night. I said the White Hart just
outside Ipswich and they checked, didn't they. I'm so stupid.
I never guessed I was under suspicion. For your murder.
Dear God, Patti. I've been a shit in the worst way, but good
God you know I'd never hurt you. I couldn't believe it. Of
course they said there was no record at the White Hart.
They said if I couldn't account for my whereabouts I could
be detained, and they advised me "in the strongest possible
terms" to comply. I had to give them the name of the hotel
we used, I had to, and they checked that too. That's when I
had to give them Val's name. It took me a while to remember her surname. And I didn't have a clue where she lived.
Not that any of that matters. I'd let them put me in the
dock—I would, I swear!—just to get you back.
But they let me come back home. I couldn't face the
bedroom, so I got the travel rug and slept on the settee.

Or didn't sleep. I was awake most of the night. At first I started to pray to you, you know that? Really prayed, as if you could somehow perform miracles. Asking you over and over to come back to me. I bargained with you, said I'd give you everything, give you anything you had to have— booze, blues even. I'd give my whole life, I wouldn't care. Just to have you back. And have Frankie.

The later it got the more I started to think it had all been a terrible mistake. They wouldn't take me to see you yesterday so anything was possible in the silence and the darkness. I could think it was someone else. Even after what they told me. Even after they said it was Mum who found you. I began to tell myself she was mistaken. She was in shock. She couldn't think straight. It was one of your friends she'd found. She hadn't looked long enough. It wasn't you at all. You'd run off somewhere with Frankie. That's what I really wanted. Then you'd both be alive somewhere. After that I went round and round in circles. Convinced myself it was you. Mum identified you but you weren't really dead. Only unconscious. You would defy the odds and wake up. Yes, why not? You were awake and—at the very same moment in the middle of the night that I was lying on the settee think-ing it—they were taking you across town to the hospital. You do hear about miracles, don't you? Why not for me? For us, I mean. And if you could be alive, why not Frankie too?

Today everything's changed. I've seen you now and I wish to God I hadn't.

There's no mistaking dead. Not when you see it with your own eyes.

When I got up this morning I knew that was all wishful thinking but it still hadn't sunk in, not really. It felt good just to have made it through the night. I went straight to the station. Mum was already there. She can make you feel bad for no reason. It's as if she knows everything you do. All she said was, Len. But she had tears in her eyes. We both did. We'll get to the bottom of this, she said, and gave my arm a squeeze. But I couldn't squeeze back.

There was a lot of waiting around next. Verification this, confirmation that. So many forms to get typed up, a lot of "Sign here, please," statements, affidavits, you name it. After that they said I should go and find something to eat. As if I could. Mum said, I'll wait here. I've had breakfast.

I went up the road and smoked a couple of cigarettes. Julie was there when I got back. You can't look each other in the eye too long, times like this. We hugged each other. It's all you can do. There isn't anything you can say really either.

They came and asked if I was ready and I nodded. The others said they'd wait. I couldn't believe where I was being taken. Chapel Street's always only ever been a joke to us. *You wouldn't want to end up in Chapel Street!* Right.

Oh, Patti. I can't ever not see what I saw. I only looked for seconds but you were so far gone. Sunk down into yourself. Except for your belly. I couldn't help noticing you looked pregnant and my mind began to race. Thinking that was part of it. Afterwards, I asked, and the attendant was embarrassed, you could see that. It's part of the process, he said, sir. Looking guilty, poor chap, as if "the process" were his fault. He looked so crestfallen. I had to fight the tears, then. Oh dear God I won't forget it ever. Your face. Your poor face. They'd glued your mouth shut. You could see some of it squeezed out between your lips. Oh Patti. Oh my poor Patti. You never left me the time to make it all up to you. We'd never have had all those rows if we'd known what was coming. I keep asking myself if Frankie saw you. Where is he, Patti? I don't want to see him there next. He's all that matters now. Tell me where he is. I need your help.

When I got back to the station it seemed as if we were finally doing something useful. They were working in an interview room drawing up a list of places to look: the library, the railway station, the bridge over Wallingdon Road, the clock tower, One Tree Hill, the pet shop; making a list of friends' names—well there was only one—to add to the list of his classmates off the register; listing all the parks, sweet shops, toy shops. Mum working on it, and Julie. It was all bright ideas and brain waves until suddenly I couldn't stand it anymore. I broke down. We needed you, Patti. We need you. I can't do this without you. I don't know how.

I said, I need some air.

Detective Sergeant Mickleson said, It would be more useful if you could stay, sir. Would you like a cigarette? I said, Thank you, and he lit it for me.

Then Mum said, Ahem, and he said, I beg your pardon, and offered her the open pack. She turned to Julie and said, You want one, too, Julie? And when Julie said, Please, she took two and handed one to her.

So there we all were, puffing like chimneys, and suddenly it all seemed pointless. You wouldn't have sat there that long, I know that. I put mine out. I said, Look, haven't you got enough now? Isn't it time you got some officers out there?

Sergeant Mickleson said Most of our officers are conducting enquiries, Mister Walters—concerning Francis, that is.

I said, Shouldn't we be out searching? I mean, actually searching.

He said, It takes time to organize.

Mum said, I'll organize you.

He ignored her and said, I've sent someone to all the clubs, and charities, the SSAFA, the Good Samaritans... We'll see if we can't get some more manpower on it. That should help.

I just nodded. I tell you I was that close to losing it.

Chapter 5

SATURDAY AN
(Still)

The sea and the sky were different colours when I went outside
the next time. You couldn't make the line disappear. You could
always tell which was which. Sort of purple grey and navy
black. The line went up really really far. And down far as well.
(Of *course*.) You didn't even have to do anything. You only had
to stand still (if you could) and it did it all by itself. It was
soothing and woozy at the same time.

Then a man came and stood right next to me and ruined
everything. His hand was on the rail in my way. It was podgy.
And he was singing.

—*A sailor went to sea sea sea to see what he could see see see.*

I didn't want to look at him because it's a rude song. They
sing it at school. But he was carrying on anyway.

—*But all that he could see see see.*

He stopped singing and he bended down towards me. He
was too close. He said Do you know the rest?

It was *the bottom of the deep blue sea sea sea* but I wasn't going to tell him because that's the rude part. When the girls in the playground get to it they stick their bottoms out and smack them. And sometimes other people do.

He was singing it to himself anyway. But purposely so I could hear.

I just carried on doing looking far away so I wouldn't have to see if he stuck his bottom out.

I looked the other way and waited for him to go. Then I heard him say Cheer up it might never happen and I was scared he was going to put his arm round me. I could smell him doing breathing right by my ear. Eck! He smelled like a pub. Then he did a horrible thing. He whispered Boo like he was right inside it. I could hardly breathe.

I still didn't turn round to look but after a minute (of *course* I was counting) he went.

That's a relief then Chuck! MyMum is the best. It was as if she could still talk to me. I heard her say *Just go the other way then.*

I did super-duper fast walking and looking over my shoulder, like a spy. He wasn't following me. I could see him getting smaller and smaller. I kept watching because it was very interesting. Usually when you are walking you see things getting bigger and bigger.

But then I had a naccident. I bumped right into the blind man! He knocked me down so I was on my back!

—I'm sorry.

He was saying it to me! It was the funniest thing I had heard.

—Hahahahahahaha!

—I recognize that voice! Hallo.

—Hahahahahaha! I can't stop. (I really couldn't.)

—Are you all right? (That was two people both at the same time. A lady was asking him and he was asking me. That only made it worse.)

—Haaahaaahaaahaaa!

—We're fine thank you. (Him.)

—Come on, dear! Up you get! You're right in his way. (The lady.)

—He's fine. We're both fine. Thank you. (Him.)

—Make him stop! HAHAHAHAHA! (I couldn't help it. It was Alec. He was licking me.)

—He thinks you're hurt because you're on the ground. He's probably trying to make you better.

—Make him stop!

—He'll stop if you get up.

—All right. I'm getting up. (I stopped laughing too.)

—Good boy, Alec. Can I pat him?

—Well let's take him over to the chairs.

—He's supposed to take you. Hahaha.

—Don't start again!

—All right.

We sat in the deckchairs even though it wasn't sunny. I was out of breath. It was like the time I fell down laughing in the playground when the boy hit the dinner lady right after she told him What a good boy! You are really growing up.

Alec sat in-between us and let me pat him and the blind man let him let me.

I said He's a good dog.

The blind man said He's still learning.

I said What's he learning?

The blind man said How to be calm. How to be with people. Then we stopped talking. It was nice. I stopped patting Alec so we were all just doing sitting. All three of us. I liked it. The boat was rocking forward and back very very slowly. It was actually better than when you do rocking yourself. Sometimes one of the souls went by and said Hallo. Then the blind man said Hallo. And once I did. It made me start talking again.

—How did you know I was on the ground?

—I could hear you.

—Bats knows where things are.

—Exactly.

—You're very clever aren't you?

—I think you're probably quite smart too.

—And Alec is.

We were all quiet again. Just like before. Then he heard something. He said Those must be petrels. He spelled it for me. There were three birds like little black seagulls flying beside the boat. I wished he could see them. We didn't do talking for a long time but then I accidentally asked another question and that was the end of being quiet.

—What number are you?

—Pardon me?

—What number are you?

—You mean how old?

—No. On your door.

—Oh. sixteen forty-two. What number are you?

—Seventy-three thirty-three. (That's not really a lie because I don't have a door anyway.)

—Is it a nice room?

—It's a cabin. (Now it's a lie.)

—Of course. Is it nice?

—Yes, thank you. Is yours?

—Yes thank you. It's very comfortable.

—Can I see it?

—Oh I don't know about that.

—Well you definitely can't see mine hahaha.

—All right. Very funny.

—How do you find it when you want to go to bed?

—It's easy. A very nice steward showed me the way on the first day.

—You said *showed* me.

—Well that's what he did. It's on deck six.

—Does Alec know the way?

—He does now.

—How do you know when you get to your door?

—What do you mean? If I can't see?

—Yes.

—I count the doors

—One thousand six hundred and forty-two?

—Haha. No. Three. My cabin is the third one along from the lift.

—You go in the lift?

—You do ask a lot of questions.

—That's what MyDad says.

—You want to know how I know which button to press.

—Yes.

—It's easy. I asked someone on the first day to tell me how they were arranged. It's very simple. You just have to remember.

—I'm good at remembering.

—I bet you are.

—And you are and Alec is so that's three of us. Where's your mum?

—You mean my wife.

—No I don't. I don't expect you have one. I mean your mum.

—My mother's not alive any more.

—MyMum is not alive too.

—I thought you said you were with your parents.

—It was a fib. I'm with MyDad and MyAunty. (Another one! I can't believe I said that.) MyMum's dead. (At least that bit was true.)

—I'm sorry.

—It's not your fault. She was in her armchair.

—I'm sorry to hear it.

—It's better than being run over. My cat was run over and his eyes popped out.

—Shall we talk about something else?

—No. I like talking about MyMum. It makes it so she's still alive.

—All right then. Was she nice your mum?

—She was nice MyMum, but she makes people mad. Made. She was not a very obedient person. Miss Kenney probably hated her. And Father Morgan.

—Oh dear.

—Do you want to know what she did?

—Only if you want to tell me.

She had arguments all the time. With everybody. Once she had a nargument with Father Morgan outside the church and she called him greedy old bastard.

—Tell me about the nice things.

—She put her arm round Maureen's Mum and said you come back with me love. Don't listen to him. Then she gave her a cup of tea in the kitchen.

—She sounds like a good woman.

—That's what MyDad calls her when he's pretending to be mad. *Listen to me my good woman this is the last time you get away with murder.* Don't worry not real murder. MyMum hits things a lot. She used to. But only things. Not people. Do you want to know what else she did?

—Well all right. If it's not too private.

—Mashed potatoes. They're my favourite. And knitting but she wasn't very good at that. My sweater had a hole in the sleeve. She said that's for your thumb and she made a hole in the other one. I was wearing it the day we were in church when MyDad said we should go and there was a little baby doing toddling up the aisle—that's what they call the bit between the pews—and that's what they call the long seats and you have to try not to laugh because it sounds like bad smells. The baby was doing toddling all by itself while Father Morgan was doing talking and suddenly it fell down flat and started to cry and nobody got up to help it. Father Morgan just carried on talking but much louder and MyMum ran all the way down to pick it up and took it back to its Mum. Then she turned round and shouted at Father Morgan, You old windbag, you. Look at you still talking. And you lot. Sitting there like a bunch of pansies. What's wrong with you all? Come on Len. MyDad got up too. He was sort of ducking like he was in a low room and MyMum was still shouting. You won't get me back here in a month—no you won't get me back here in a *lifetime* of bloody Sundays.

Come on you two. So we went to the Feathers because they have a garden at the back for kids.

—I see.

—No you don't. Hahahaha. What? Are you cross?

—No. It's all right. It's just that that joke is very tired.

—You look tired. You don't have friends either do you?

—Yes I have friends. Just not on this boat.

—Do you want one on this boat?

—A friend?

—Yes. I can be your friend.

—I think you already are. But thank you very much. Now I really am tired and chilly too, so I think I'll go and have a little nap. And you'd better get back to your dad and your aunty. Bye-bye.

He did sort of groaning and he got up and said Walk Alec.

I said Bye-bye and Bye-bye Alec, but then I did a kind of spying.

I followed him quietly just a little bit behind. He didn't look blind at all. He just looked normal only with a dog. While he was waiting for the lift I went down the stairs as fast as I could. Holding on. I watched him come out downstairs. He walked along really close to the wall so he could feel when a door came. He stopped right at one six four two and turned round and scared me. He knew again!

He said, Now you have to find your way back again. Will you be all right?

I tried not to sound as if he had given me a fright. I said Yes thank you. I have a good memory. Remember? Hahaha. And then I couldn't help it I said But first I want to come in and see your cabin. Please.

—Oh, I don't think so.

—Yes I do.

—I mean I don't think that's possible. Bye-bye now.

—Just a look?

—Oh all right.

He opened the door a little bit. I could see a bed and a chair with some stuff on and lots of bottles on the dressing table like in the kitchen when MyMum did a birthday party for MyDad. I told MyDad there were thirty-nine and he said Are you trying to embarrass us? So I knew not to tell the blind man how many. (There were seven.)

He said Now off you go.

I looked at his face to see if it was a joke but I couldn't tell. Then he said Run along.

I said There's no running but I went anyway. He made me feel a bit mad. That's what friends always do. You're not supposed to say Now off you go to someone who is your friend. It's the same as saying Go away.

❧

At dinner time (that's what they call it) I stole a chicken leg. It was so confusing in the dining room that nobody noticed what I did. There was music playing and all the waiters were wearing big Mexican hats so probably they couldn't notice very well. I went up the stairs as fast as I could. A man said Woah there!—like you do for a horse—Where are you off to?

I said Oh no inside my head. I had to do some fast thinking. I said MyMum. She's waiting for me at the top.

I ran as fast as I could and the man called out No running sonny. She's not going anywhere.

I had never told such a big lie. MyMum would be ashamed of me.

When I got to the top I was nearly crying. But I don't do that. There was no one up there. It was too windy to stay and the sky was a bad colour like the evil potion the witch mixed up. My legs were all wobbly too so I went back inside.

I took my chicken's leg to the pictures because that is the only place you can eat stolen goods and no one sees you.

Stealing was worse than I thought. It is quite hard to do with no one finding out and when you have done it you don't feel very good. I don't know why bank robbers bother. It was darker than ever inside the pictures (a good thing) because it was always night-time on the film. I did not look at it after I saw a man with black eyebrows and black stuff running out of his pretend teeth. I felt a bit sick and I did not want to eat my supper (that's what I call it) but it was time. I made myself do it so I did not grow faint with hunger like Pinocchio. Pinocchio grew faint with hunger. It says that in Every Child's Big Book.

I started with the celery first (because I don't really like it) but it was too noisy so I put it in my pocket. And then when I took the cheese out of my pocket there was a really strong smell. You did not have to be a dog to smell it. I threw most it under the seat. Sometimes I think MyMum is watching me. I ate the chicken leg but not the skin. I threw that under the seat. It was lovely. Guess where I threw the bone.

Wrong haha! I put it in my pocket for Alec. So.

Bad Things 2
Good Things 1

When I had finished it was time to get ready for bed. There was not much to do because I didn't have any jarmies or a toothbrush but I had to be crafty. Like a nescaped convict. There were some people still outside even though it was windy. They were watching all the white squiggles on the sea. I had to go past them. They were sitting in deckchairs with their coats on and drinking beer and eating crisps. There was one lady and five men. They had travel rugs like the one in the back of the car for Gran. The lady had hers on like a cloak. They were play arguing. I think. When I was going by one of them said to another one No you've had enough and snatched the big bag of crisps. He said Here son. Want some crisps?

Nobody heard me say thank you when I took them because they were all doing roaring with laughter. They were salt and vinegar. My favourite.

A man said Want to play shipwreck with us? The lady said Ssh! Malcolm! She said You'd probably like a blanket too. You look cold. Here. Have Malcolm's and she grabbed the travel rug off Malcolm's lap and gave it to me and everybody roared with laughter all over again.

I wanted to get away quickly but I didn't want them to ask for their crisps back if I started walking so I stayed there to eat them. They asked me lots of questions and I made up lots of answers. I am a nexpert now at making things up. It gets easier and easier. I told them the blind man was my Uncle. I said he was MyMum's brother. And then I said the truth about MyMum. I don't want to say it again but you know what it was. They went a bit peculiar so I said goodbye to them anyway and carried on. They had stopped laughing. They let me keep the crisps. And the blanket.

I had to be quick. I went back round to my side and dived into my bedroom behind the mattresses. It was lucky because it was just when the boat tipped a bit and I slid in. I was a rabbit disappearing down a hole. The people round the corner were doing roaring and singing. They were not very good singers. I think they were having a party. At least I was not lonely. Actually I was. You know I said the Atlantic is a very lonely place? It's true.

I stayed awake a long time doing wishing. I wished I could be asleep. I wished I could be in the blind man's room. I wished I was Alec. I wished I had not done the lie when I said MyMum's waiting for me. It was worse than the one about my Aunty. It was terrible. But at least she will never know I put her in a lie so that is a good thing.

Then I thought about what the man said back to me and how it was true. MyMum was not going anywhere. So that was a bad thing. It was so bad it made me feel sick as if I really was down a hole. Where it was all dark and there was no one there. Except me. And MyMum was not going anywhere. That was true. And she was not waiting for me. And that was true too.

It was cold even with the travel rug. It was a good job the mattresses were thick. They made a barricade. One of my favourite things. You can make one with the cushions off the settee. It used to make MyMum mad. She used to say What do you want to spend all your time for barricaded behind the sofa cushions? It's a lovely day. And then I always knew what she would say next—Why don't we invite Martin over? You can play in the garden. Then I would say Can we take the cushions outside? And she would get all excited and say If you like. And I could give you a blanket. Then I would say No it's all right. I've changed my mind. She did shout at me quite a lot MyMum. It's all right if people shout at you if you know why they're mad. MyMum always wanted me to play with people. So did Miss Kenney. But when Miss Kenney said I had to MyMum got cross. She told MyDad I could do what I *mm-mm*-well wanted. And then she said it's none of Miss Kenney's business anyway. MyDad said the same thing MyMum said to me that other time. He said She's a *teacher!* MyMum said *Exactly!* She should be *teaching* him things! Not telling him what to do with his time for godsake. MyDad said Patti! (that's her name, I don't think I told you yet) and he did weird looking eyes at me where I was pretending to read on the floor. I didn't see them. I could feel them.

I wished MyMum and Dad were both with me. I wouldn't mind even if they were having a nargument. They didn't really mean it. They just couldn't control themselves.

The more I stayed awake the more lonely I was. It was all right when I was thinking of MyMum and MyDad. It was like they were in my head and it didn't matter even if MyMum was mad. I even liked it. But when MyDad said Patti! it went all quiet in my head and I felt like they were gone.

Only I was the one who had gone.

Every time I thought about MyMum I got sadder than I was before. I missed her. And I missed MyDad but I was going to see him again. He would be all alone (like me). It was very confusing. MyMum was still in my head but it was Saturday now and MyDad would have made them bury her before she started to smell bad. No one would be allowed to stay in their armchair when they're dead.

Can a dead person be in two places? I don't know what you can do when you're dead. Besides nothing. When I asked MyMum if it hurt being a skeleton like the one in the chemist's where she gets her medicine she said dead people don't see or hear or feel or anything. She didn't say they didn't know anything. But they probably don't. They probably forget everything. Like their name and their family and the whole world. But then MyDad told me that dead people live on. He told me that when my Granddad died. I said What do you mean? My mum said He means inside our minds. In our hearts. I said Yuk get out Granddad and started brushing my chest and MyMum threw the dishcloth in the sink and went out. It probably wasn't a very good joke. I said it because I thought she was lying. But here is the thing. She might have been right because she was inside my head when I was waiting to go to sleep and it seemed as if she was alive. So if she was in my head she must know all my lies. The ones about her anyway. So I said Sorry. In my head.

It was much too noisy to go to sleep. The wind was doing ghost noises and the boat was clanging and I could hear the seawater smacking and swooshing. It was like being in the pictures except you were in the film instead of in a seat. I couldn't stop thinking about when I had to go to school and leave MyMum in the chair. It was too terrible to think about with the wind and the lies and everything.

I probably should have told the milkman.

I wish MyMum had been at school with me when I tried to tell them she was dead. She would have made them believe me.

Gran

I said, Len, I don't give two hoots who you slept with in Ipbloodyswich. It could be the Queen of Sheba for all I care. Makes no difference now to your Patti. Nor me. I couldn't care less. You need to pull yourself together, you do. For Patti's sake, Len. For Frankie's. So don't keep harping on it. Sorry? I should say! But now's not the time. Just put it all behind you, for God's sake. It's not you you should be thinking of. It's Frankie. They said you're in the clear, so what are you waiting for? Jack would have been going door to door by now. He'd have the whole street upside down, looking.

Thing is, Len, I said, she died Wednesday. It's the coroner's word. He said no possibility it could have been after. It was Wednesday. And Frankie went to school that day. He was on the register. So maybe she took ill after he come home? And then what? He got scared? Went round for some help? Somebody took him in, didn't they. Where though? Where would he go? It don't make no sense. They would have called the ambulance. And anyway he went to school Thursday. You think anyone would just keep a kid and then send him off to school next day?

No. None of it made any sense. I said he's run off. Not far mind you. He always says his legs hurt. He's lost, that's what he is. Or hiding. He has to be. You'd do that wouldn't you, if you saw your Mum in a state? He's scared. No one's going to find him unless they look. And no use staying here no longer. I'm going back to the house. They've had a copper there all this time but that won't be no help, not if he was trying to get home. I told Julie to go to my house. Always a chance he could go there. He'd remember the way all right. No, your best bet, Len, I said, is get out there with the lads. They said they won't stop till they find him.

And there's poor Patti, still. Like she's waiting until you pull yourself together. The coroner's going to have his report signed by the end of the day and what are you doing about it? Do you think you can let her just lie there? And no one to send her on her way? Have you been in touch with McMorton's? What are you waiting for? A band of angels? You've got a lot to think about you have. I'll help, you know I will, but I can't make your decisions for you. You're the next of kin, not me. You know I'll help if you want it. I did it for Dad. And for Jack. It's not as if I don't know what's needed. You've only got to ask, Len. Tell me what it is you want for her and I'll see to it. I'll come round to yours so I can use the phone. It'll give you more time to look.

Len looked at me all strange like I was speaking another language. Then he said Frankie's all that matters now.

And his face. Well maybe for the first time in my life I thought I saw the man in him. Just starting.

Chapter 6

SUNDAY AM
(that's the morning)

I did not go to sleep forever. No, that's another lie. I know I
went to sleep because I woke up haha.

Actually I woke up lots of times in the middle of the night
because everything was woozy. The boat was sort of falling
over. It was tipping over one way and then waiting—eleven
seconds, I counted—and then tipping back the other way. (I
was terrified if you want to know the truth.) I wished I had a
life jacket. I think we must have been in a storm. But we
escaped. A storm is when boats sink. I made a plan to ask the
blind man if he had a nextra life jacket. Just in case.

The last time I woke up I had been having a nother dream.
I dreamed I was walking up our road like when I walk home
from school and right at the top of the hill there was this great
big ship in the middle of the road! It was taller than the roofs
of all the houses. Even taller than the church behind my school.
And it was coming down the middle of the road. With *no*

water—only mud so it could do sliding. I don't know why it didn't fall over because you know what the bottom of a ship looks like don't you? It's pointy like a V. It kept coming towards me and I was afraid I was going to get run over and squashed in the mud. By a ship! My heart was beating so fast I woke up. I was so happy! For a minute.

Sometimes it feels really good when things are not true. I don't think that happens in real life. I think in real life true things stay true forever. It is better to not think about that.

I have had a horrible thought. You know that thing when I said I did not go to sleep forever? It can mean a nother thing. And when it means that then the thing I said is true. I did not go to sleep forever.

I decided to make a number 4 on my plan.

4. Persuade MyDad not to go home again.

I did not want to go home to my house where MyMum used to be. I did not want her to be missing. It was all right when she was still there even when she was dead. I haven't told you about that yet. Have I? I will tell you when I've finished telling about getting up.

It was like dark daytime because there were black clouds everywhere. It was still windy and everything was soaking wet even though it wasn't raining. The water in the swimming pool was sloshing and some was coming out. I could not walk to the door where you go inside—it was too slopey—so I went round the other way. I could see red sky a long way away like someone had lighted the clouds on fire underneath. The sea was a nasty colour. It was the same as the clouds. Nearly black like our road.

Inside it was nice and warm but still tippy. I cleaned my teeth. Guess what with. The celery! Like Robinson Crusoe! It was all squeaky and bits came off but then my teeth were nice and clean and they wouldn't go bad like MyMum always says. Said. I wished she could see what I was doing. I checked in the mirror to make sure my hair wasn't sticking up and then I went to the dining room to get my breakfast. It wasn't even open!

I could feel the panic coming. I always get that when I don't know what to do next. I went to find a quiet place and stay there until I felt better. I did not even want to have breakfast anymore.

There was nobody at all in the pictures because there wasn't a film yet. It was lovely. One of my favourite things is when there's nobody. Like at my birthday party. MyMum didn't like it. MyDad observed that too. He said Don't fret pet to cheer her up. It didn't work. She said What about all this food? Look at it! I said Yummy. She said You don't even like jelly you. I said you can have mine and she started to cry. I couldn't see her face because she was going off to the kitchen but I could hear her breathing like a person doing crying.

I had made fifteen invitations because MyDad said. MyMum said it was too many but MyDad said I think it's probably a good idea. *You know.* (*You know* is what they say to each other when it's a secret that I don't know. But I think I knew this one.) MyMum said I don't even know most of these and I said That's because you don't go to school. I made sixteen invitations. I had seven boys and eight girls but it was equal because there was me too. I did one for me so I wouldn't feel left out. I couldn't get them all finished before bedtime so I did some the next day then I took them to school in the morning. I did not tell anyone what I had in my satchel. I went into the outside toilets and I put one in and pulled the chain. When I put the next one in it didn't work. I had to wait for the tank to fill up again. Then I had to wait all over again before I did the next one. So I did two together. I did that three more times. But then two came back up. So I had to do those again. I went back to one. I did three more and the duty teacher started knocking on the door saying Who's that in there playing with the chain? I said I am not playing. She said come out now and let me see to it. I still had five left (you will know that if you have been paying attention) so I put them away and did up my satchel. Then I came out and washed my hands thirteen times because that's how many times I had pulled the chain. (Eleven. Plus two for touching the door.)

I was a bit worried all through Nature Table and Arithmetic because somebody might say Don't take your satchel out to play but they didn't so I did the rest at playtime. I felt better then.

When I went home MyMum said Want to help me make fairy cakes for Saturday? I said No thank you.

When Saturday came it was a really good party. We waited a long time to get started. MyMum kept looking up the road to see if anyone had gone to the wrong house. And then MyDad went over to the table and said Right then. There won't be time for everything if we don't start soon. I said We have to do the games first and MyMum said I'm having a drink. That's when she opened the bottle of Bubbly. MyDad said That was for New Year's Eve. Do you know how much that cost? And MyMum said We're having a party remember?

We did all the games. They tried to let me win everything but I could tell when they were cheating so I made them start again if they were. Nobody quarrelled like at a real party and nobody cried. Except maybe MyMum when I told her it was the best party but it was hard to tell because she had been laughing a lot. I waited until after the cake to tell her about the invitations.

🐋

So anyway that was Friday and I already told you what I did for the rest of the day. So shall I tell you now what happened when I went to school? After I saw the milkman? I saw some other people on the way too but I didn't know them. There were some kids away in front of me and a Mum. The rule about not talking to strangers is a bit complicated because who counts? The people I don't know are definitely strangers even if I see them nearly every day like the man on the wobbly bike but the Mum one is a bit confusing because she is the Mum of the boy with the big clumpy shoe in Mrs Barret's class so I kind of know her.

When I saw the bricks of the school wall I got the panic feeling so I slowed down. It didn't help. The slower I went the more I got the feeling so I speeded up again and when I turned the corner I was right. As soon as I saw the gates it came and fell all over me like a huge big noisy downpour and I was inside it. It was terrible. I couldn't hardly see or even breathe and it was making me feel sick. And then I did some without even deciding to do it. It just came up. Actually down because there was some on my shoe. I had a handkerchief in my pocket but I didn't want to use it because then I couldn't put it back in my pocket and I couldn't throw it away because you mustn't litter and I would have to hold it and that would be disgusting.

I tried to kick it off but some of it stayed. I crossed over then because that is where the house is where they never mow the lawn and there are big clumps of grass. I felt silly trying to get it off because I had to bend my leg like the boy with the big shoe. But it came off. *That's a relief then Chuck.* I crossed back again and kept on doing going to school and nothing else happened. I could still feel the panic like someone was holding me round the throat like the girl at school who said I had to play with her.

When I got there everyone had started a massive game in the playground. They were holding onto each other like a train. Everyone had their hands on someone else's waist at the back and they were running around collecting people shouting Join on! Join on! If you didn't join on when they went by the one at the front turned round and they came back to run you over. They were being a bit rough and some people were falling down and then the bell rang and everyone went inside. That was a nother relief.

I saw Miss Kenney coming towards the cloakroom and I ran out into the hall to go and tell her before anybody came. She saw me coming and said Go and take your jacket off Frankie so I ran back. She called out No running but I had to be quick so I disobeyed. I threw my jacket on the peg—and it stuck! That was a good thing. I started running back.

I said Miss Ke—and she said What did I say? No running. Now walk back and try all that again.

I said Bu—and she said WALK! Or do you want to practice walking all day.

That was a really stupid question so I didn't answer and she said Do you?

I could feel a lot of angriness. It was like rocks filling me up and all kind of knocking together. I sort of pressed them down with my mind and said No. She lifted up her eyebrows and put her head on one side like dogs do when they want something so I said Miss Kenney and she said That's a good boy. While I was walking back I heard some other kids who were already talking to her so now it was too late.

We all went into our class. It's 1B. Like a bee. (2B is still 2B and not 2Bs but I don't care I still see two bees in my head when I go past their door). Miss Kenney started talking even before she got to her desk. She said Now now now now now quietly everyone hands on top of your desk and no talking I said no talking thank you Ronald thank you Sylvie thank you Julie thank you Arlene thank you Michael thank you Elinud. And then she was quiet for a long time. I thought she was going to say Thank you Francis but she didn't even though I was the first one who did it. She said Good morning everyone and then we said Good morning Miss Kenney back and it sounded all sarky like it always does but she never says anything about it. She just takes the register. When she got to Belinda Woleynski she said Stand. Nobody talks when she says that because it's the Our Father and we have to do In the Name of the Father once before and once after and everyone's scared of the Holy Ghost. Then we sat down. I didn't know how I was going to tell her with everybody listening. I decided I would have to be very patient because it was time for sixpences. She unlocked her tall cupboard and took out the jar. She said Hands up who has their sixpence today?

Only five people put their hands up.

Miss Kenney said Hmmm. One…two…three..

I said Five.

She said Thank you Francis. (So that was fair now. Well sort of.)

Then she called them all up to the desk to put their sixpence in the jar and go and move their souls up the ladder. Kevin pricked himself with the pin and it made the leg of his Red Indian come off so he started to cry.

Miss Kenney said Never mind. We'll mend it later. Now she said. She was looking at her list and poking it with her pencil. That leaves—

I said Seventeen.

She stopped poking and looked at me with her mouth all twisty.

I said Seventeen who still haven't brought their sixpence.

Miss Kenney didn't say anything so I explained it for her. I said Because ten people have already brought their sixpence plus five today so still seventeen not. It's like leftovers.

Miss Kenney said Would you like to come up here and be the teacher Francis? She was doing mean eyes like she does but she was smiling at the same time. It was a bit confusing.

I said Yes please and I was just going because I thought I can do whispering when I get there but she said Sit down Frankie.

You have to do what you're told so I sat down again and said But I want to tell you something.

She did the big puffy breathing people do when they're mad. She said Yes?

I said Yes and I was getting up again to go and whisper it but she said Sit down then and tell me.

I said I have to whisper it but I was already whispering so she said Pardon?

I whispered I have to whisper it and everybody laughed. It was really loud.

She said Go outside Francis and stand in the cloakroom.

That made me feel a lot better because I didn't like being inside anyway and because then she would have to come outside to talk to me and I could tell her without anybody else hearing it. I waited a long time in the cloakroom. I counted everyone's coats from left to right and then I counted them backwards from right to left even though I knew it would be the same. I like counting backwards so I decided to count backwards from one thousand and when I got to five hundred and one Miss Kenney would come out. But she didn't. I got all the way to one so I started again. I was near the middle (four hundred and forty-five actually) when the door opened. But it wasn't Miss Kenney. It was Belinda Woleynski. She started talking to me and pretending to be someone important at the same time. She said Miss Kenney says Do you want to come back in to the classroom now?

I said No thank you.

Belinda said Pardon?

I said No thank you.

Belinda said All right then and went away. She looked over her shoulder three times before she shut the classroom door. It was only twelve seconds (I was still counting) when the door opened again. It was Miss Kenney this time. Yes! I thought but she looked really mad. Her chin was all wobbly.

I closed my eyes because I don't like seeing mad faces. It makes me do laughing sometimes and I can't stop. You know that.

She said You can close your eyes as much as you like Master Francis, but you can't close your ears. And she was right because I could still hear her. She was breathing like when you blow your nose. It made me want to laugh as well so I thought I'd better be quick.

I said MyMum's dead but my mouth was still trying to laugh.

She said What did you just say?

So I said it again even though I knew she heard me the first time. I said MyMum's dead.

She said What do you mean saying something like that?

I said She's not alive.

Miss Kenney said Well I haven't heard anything about it.

I said That's why I'm telling you.

She said So how come you are at school?

I said I walked here.

Miss Kenney stared at me really really hard.

She said Do you want to tell that to Mr Bladgeworth?

I said Yes please.

She said Go inside and sit at your desk.

So I did.

I thought she was going to get Mr Bladgeworth and make me tell him but she didn't. She came in behind me and said Right boys and girls put away your News (I had missed my favourite thing! If you copy the News really fast you can take out your reading book until everyone's finished) and line up.

I said aren't we going to do Arithmetic? Because that's what we always do after News.

Miss Kenney said You were outside so you missed the announcement. Who can tell Frankie where we're going? And everyone put their hand up.

Miss Kenney said Derek?

And Derek said Mrs Mahoney's.

Miss Kenney said Thank you Derek.

I said Please can I stay here? I have to think about MyMum and everybody burst out laughing.

Miss Kenney said I think you know the answer.

I said No I don't and that was when she shouted out loud. She shouted FRANCIS! LINE UP RIGHT NOW!

It made my knees wobble even though she shouted THANK YOU! right after. Nearly everyone was laughing. I was the one who wasn't.

Miss Mahoney's class is right on the other side of the playground. I did not know why we were going there. It made my head all muddled up and lots of bad ideas started getting in. Then a good idea squeezed in-between. I could tell Mrs Mahoney. She might know what to do. She has grey hair in a bun like my Gran.

I waited a long time when we got there while everyone pushed their desks back so we could sit on the floor. Mrs Mahoney had a big white sheet hanging over her blackboard. I didn't like it. I didn't know how I could tell Mrs Mahoney because there were so many people who would hear me. Then I sort of heard MyMum's voice in my head and she was saying *Take a big breath Frankie. Be really brave. I'll hold your hand.* So I put up my hand.

Miss Kenney said Put your hand down please Francis. Then she whispered something to Mrs Mahoney.

I saw Mrs Mahoney's eyes looking right on top of my eyes and her eyebrows were doing *Really?I'mdisappointedinyouFrankie.* So I pretended to look at my socks. She said All right children. Sit down quickly and lots of other stuff then she clapped her hands and some of the children started clapping their hands and then everybody was clapping until Mrs Mahoney put her hands in the air and we all stopped at the same time and it was dead silent. She whispered Thank you, boys and girls. And then she said Now we can start and she put the lights out. A bright light came on the sheet and then some letters but they were all upside down you could tell. I thought it was a test so I called out the answer—Road Safety—and everybody laughed. Mrs Mahoney said Thank you but Miss Kenney stepped over three people and came really really close to me. She did a kind of loud whisper that everyone could hear and what she said was If you say one more word you will have to leave.

I said All right. But she didn't notice that I said one more word or maybe it didn't count because it was two.

Mrs Mahoney turned the letters the right way up and then there was a man talking and a picture of a zebra crossing and then there was a film about some children who wanted to cross the road. It was completely boring and no one got run over. The bell for playtime rang before it was finished and Mrs Mahoney said we didn't have to see the last bit. Perhaps someone got run over then. I hope not because that's not fair if we missed it.

On the way to the line I went over to Mrs Mahoney and I said I have something to tell you. She said Not just now dear. I have to take this back to the stock room. Come and see me in the playground. I'm on duty. I decided to spend playtime by the big tree and do spying until she came out but I didn't see her once.

When the bell rang we all went in until dinner time. It was Tests. I love Tests because no one bothers you and it's no talking. Not even Miss Kenney. I did counting in my head while everyone was finishing. When the dinner bell rang Miss Kenney was purposely not looking at me. I could tell.

Dinner was sausage and chips. It's everybody's favourite only my sausage had something in it like a tooth and I didn't know that until I bit it and it broke up in my mouth. It was really disgusting there were so many bits I didn't want to spit them out on my plate so I put up my hand to go to the toilet. I waited with my hand up but nobody came to see what I wanted. Then my throat jiggled up to get it so I swallowed them all. And then I was sick all over my plate. Everyone at my table said Eeeuk! really loud and one girl started to cry. A dinner lady came right over.

She said Oh Lord. Then she said You to one of the boys and told him to go and get a big boy. The big boy took me to the toilets. I didn't know what to do because I didn't feel sick anymore. He said wash your face then. You stink. And then one of the teachers came in.

I said MyMum's dead and the teacher said There there. I'll take you to the infirmary. I expect you're upset.

The infirmary is where sick people go. It smells a bit funny but it is nice and quiet and they close the door. It was so quiet I fell asleep.

When I woke up the lady who collects the dinner money was telling me it was time to go home. She said Are you feeling better now? I said Yes thank you. She said Don't forget your jacket then.

It was the only one in the cloakroom. It had come unstuck and it was on the floor. All the kids had gone and Miss Kenney had too.

Miss Kenney

Terrible night I had. Terrible. Worse than Friday and that was bad enough. It must have been about two when I woke up. I didn't even know which way I was facing, it was so dark. I was lying on my left side so I had to be facing the window. Not that you could tell by looking. It was worse than the blackout. Pitch it was. And quiet as the grave. I couldn't make out why I was awake, I just was. Just suddenly stone cold wide awake as if I'd heard something. I listened for it to come again. Just lay there listening with my eyes open. Nothing. But you don't really want to hear anything in those circumstances, do you? A door handle turning? A foot on the stair? The only thing I could hear was my heart thudding as if it were outside me in the room, like another person's. The more I listened the louder it got. In the end I couldn't think about anything else. It seemed much too fast and that worried me. It speeded up even more then. That really scared me. How long can that kind of thing go on before you give yourself a heart attack? I tried counting the beats but what does that even mean? I mean how many are you supposed to have? And how fast? Are they supposed to be like seconds? I was just winding myself up, I knew, so I stopped. I thought about getting up and warming some milk and then I changed my mind. I could have put the light on I suppose, but to tell the truth I was afraid of seeing something. Or someone. Mrs Walters for instance. In my own bedroom.

I hate that time of the night. They call it the dead of night, don't they? When there isn't a sound anywhere. Not in the house. Not in the street. Not even an owl, though that was probably a good thing. It's a terrible feeling. You're the only person alive in the world. No one to help you if you *do* hear something. When you can't even see the clock face it's like being lost. It's like being in the middle of the moors without any signposts. That's what it is. You're lost.

I tried everything. I mean everything. Sheep, penguins, alphabetical lists of countries—America, Belgium, Canada. I've never been able to get past Ireland. *Is* there a J? Then people. All the people I know beginning with A, all the people with B, et cetera, et cetera. That was my biggest mistake. I couldn't get past F, could I. It was even worse then. No hope of getting back to sleep. I kept seeing his face again the morning he told me. Those big blue eyes he puts on. Mr Innocent. It was on Wednesday. I remember because it was the day we went to Mrs Mahoney's for the road safety. I went over and over it because that could get me into trouble, that could. There could be, you know, repercussions. And then I realized:

It was too soon. They only found her on Friday. So she was probably only poorly when he told me. He was just exaggerating to get attention. Or making it up. Like when he told me there's a bird that can fly backwards. He must have been because he wasn't even crying, was he? His mum had probably been cross with him and so he was in trouble and that's what he was wishing. That's the most likely. No one's going to tell me it happened on Wednesday. He never said anything at all to me at school on Thursday, did he? He would have talked about something that important and I would have remembered. You wouldn't forget a thing like that, would you? No, of course you wouldn't. When that policewoman came round Friday night it was the first I'd heard. Like anyone else. That's right. A complete shock it was. A terrible shock.

I went back to counting sheep once I'd sorted it out but it was no use. Every time one of them got to the fence it stopped because there was a new thought there. The same thought every time, really. A question. How long till *I'm* dead? It was as if they wouldn't jump over it until I'd made a guess. But it wasn't healthy to keep thinking "dead." I scared myself silly. I didn't get to sleep until the white started to show round the edge of the curtain.

Chapter 7

SUNDAY AM
(the same one)

When I went back to see if they had started breakfast it was hard to walk along because you had to sort of lean against the wall and when we tipped the other way you had to hold on. They have handrails like for stairs so that's helpful.

But breakfast wasn't very good anyway. They had no baked beans and there was no one doing cooking. They had scrambled eggs in one tray and a pile of bacon on another one. The scrambled eggs were all lumpy but I had some anyway because there was nothing else to put on the plate—unless you were a person who wanted hairs on their chest. After I had the eggs I saw the cornflakes on another table so I had some with lots of milk. Nobody cares if you do things in the wrong order. And nobody cares if you have too much milk and it spills.

I sat with Goldilocks and Goldilicks again but I didn't call them that. Goldilocks said Stinky. I think she meant me. She said it in a whisper but I still heard. Then she said We're going to sink you know. I didn't say anything back because just when she said it we did a big tip to one side. Everyone went Whooo! like you do for fireworks and started doing talking all at once and they all did Whooo! again when we went back the other way. There was a huge crash when a big pile of plates slid off the table near the door. It sounded like the whole world breaking up. I had scrambled cornflakes in my mouth and they wouldn't go down. I left the rest because no one cares about that either and I went outside to spit the ones in my mouth in the toilet. The door was really hard to open. I spat them in and then I washed my hands because of touching the door. I couldn't dry them because everything smelled bad and I didn't want to touch the roller towel so I couldn't get out again because my hands were slippery and the door was like it was locked. Then all of sudden we leaned the other way and it came open. *That's a relief then Chuck!* Except it banged me on the head.

I wanted to see how high up and down the rail was going but when I opened the door to outside a whole lot of rain (like a whole bucketful!) hit me in the face and I changed my mind. I walked around for a long time looking for the blind man so I could ask him for a life jacket. I even went past his room. There was a message hanging on the handle. It said Do Not Disturb. So I didn't. It was hard to go back the way I came. Everything was hard. This was the notice board.

It said—

SUNDAY

Please note revised activities and locations

| 9:00 a.m. | Fit as a Fiddle! | Activity Room | Adults | CANCELLED |

10:00 a.m. Mary Poppins! Cinema (continuous showing)

11:00 a.m. Passenger Boat Drill Refresher! * Optional Queen's Lounge followed by a short slide show

12: 00 *Please note the Sundeck Grill will not be in service. We apologize for any inconvenience. Regular service will be available in the main dining room*

2:00 p.m.	Bingo!	Queen's Lounge	Adults	CANCELLED
3:00 p.m.	Wits Pit!	Activity Room.	All ages	CANCELLED
4:00 p.m.	Look Like a Star!	Beauty Parlour	16 +	CANCELLED
6:00 pm	Cocktails			CANCELLED

* Please note: You will NOT need a life jacket for the Boat Drill Refresher. Your life jacket MUST remain in your cabin. Thank you.

Reading it made me feel a bit more travel sick than before. Sea sick! Of course. I had seen that in comics. People with their heads over the side of the boat.

—Hey!

I said Oh-oh in my head. It was Kay.

—Want to play Goofy Golf again?

—No thank you.

—Why not?

—It's Sunday.

—Why can't you play on Sunday?

—Because it's not on.

—What do you mean?

(If Kay was clever like me she could have done a joke like Of *course* Sunday's on! But she's not.)

—It's Bingo.

—How do you know?

—It says.

—Clever clogs.

I didn't know if she was being mean. Sometimes it's hard to tell what people really mean. (Haha.)

—I know.

—Want to play Bingo then?

—No thank you.

—Why not?

—It's not time.

—When it's time dimbo.

—No thank you.

—Why not?

—Because I hate it when you think you are going to win and then someone else does.

—Where's your mum and dad?

—What?

—You're always by yourself.

—So are you.

—Oh. Where's your cabin?

—I don't have one.

—Neither do I! (She had a big smile on her face as if she had won a prize or snakes and ladders or something.)

—That's a fib.

—Well you just did one.

—I didn't.

—Where do you sleep then?

—Behind the mattresses. (But I was so stupid! I told her my most important secret.)

—Oh.

—But you mustn't tell anyone.

—All right.

—Promise?

—Promise.

—I have to go (I was lying! Again!) and see my friend (and again!). Bye!

—Can I come?

—No.

I went downstairs instead and went along one of the corridors where all the cabins are. I walked past ones with the doors open. There was a lady in green—a different one—making the beds in one of them. She had a big trolley outside piled up with white towels. Yes! (That's what I thought to myself.) I can have a proper wash. So I pulled one off. All the rest fell down and another lady in a uniform came out of the room next door and said Look what you do! (I think she was foreign) so I gave it to her. She said Just ask if you want one! So I said Please can I have a towel? She said What? Oh take! Take! and gave it back so I said Thank you.

I did not really know what to do with it. I put it round my neck like the people who do slow running. It came down to my knees. I looked as if I was going to have a bath. I was scared people were going to laugh at me. I was right! The next person I saw said Going for a swim? Haha. It'll be a bit rough!

I didn't say anything back but when I got to the other end I dropped the towel on the floor. I didn't really care about washing anymore anyway. I felt a bit sick. I went back up the stairs again. I went to the toilets and went in one and closed the door and waited.

I did not have to wait very long. It was horrible. I went all hot and sweaty and I could hear someone else being sick in the one beside me so the scrambled eggs came zooming up my neck. It wouldn't stop. It was disgusting. I waited until my knees stopped wobbling before I opened the door. A lady went in after me. She said You should be in the men's. I hope she saw my lump of egg on the seat before she sat down.

I had bits in my mouth and there was some in my nose too. Some of it tasted like the bad cheese. I had to do spitting in the sink. A lady said Here. Wash it away and she put the tap on. But while she was doing that her little girl was sick on the floor. It splashed on my leg.

Another lady in a uniform came in and said Uh-oh! Too late. Bags everyone! As many as you need!

She put a whole pile on top of the bin.

I took two. One was for the blind man. I went to see if he was up but the notice was still on his door. There was a sick bag on it too! There was a sick bag on all the doors! I kept the two bags for me.

I wished the blindman would get up. There were not many souls walking about. It was too difficult. I went to the pictures but I could not look at the film. It made everything go dizzy again. I closed my eyes and thought about Alec. I made another wish. MyMum says you can't rely on wishes but I made one anyway. I said I wish Alec could come and sleep with me tonight.

The Captain woke me up! He was making a nannounce-ment. I didn't even know I had been asleep but I must have been because I saw MyMum pushing a pram. I thought I would be in the pram but when I looked in it was a fish! (So I did see one. Finally.)

This is what the Captain said:

Ladies and Gentlemen this is a message from the Captain. All passengers are advised to avoid using the sport deck the sun deck the promenade deck and other outdoor areas that may be slippery even in the absence of rain owing to heavy spray. Those passengers wishing to observe the sea will find excellent viewing from the windows of the Queen's Lounge the Midships Bar and the Trinity Light Lounge. Please remember to use the handrails when walking about the ship or using the stairs.

So I went to the Queen's Lounge. I wished to observe the sea. I had done enough walking about the ship. I found a big arm chair facing the window. It curled round so you thought you were inside a snail shell. It was quite cozy but it was not easy doing observing because the water kept hitting the window. It was hard to see the sea (through the see water!) and very bleary like getting your hair washed and so there is not much to tell you. I will tell you the rest of what I did when I got home from school instead. I expect you want to know why MyMum died in her arm chair. Actually I can't tell you because I don't know haha. She just did. Die. I am one hundred percent certain. Perhaps it was a nelectric chair. No. I told you jokes can make you feel worse.

🦢

So. When I was outside the school I ran as fast as I could. I could not wait to get home because I thought Perhaps MyMum is not dead after all. It gave me butterflies. I thought she's probably awake now. I was so excited I fell down once by the bumpy wall but it didn't matter. I ran up the alley at the back and went through our gate and I didn't even mind that Denby was barking. I was going to call out Mum and then I didn't want to so I just said it when I was in the kitchen. She didn't answer.

I said I'll make a cup of tea and she didn't say I'll do it like she always does because she doesn't want me to pour the kettle so I knew she was still dead. So now it was the same as the morning. I didn't know who to telephone. No one not even a nambulance would take a dead lady to hospital because what for. You can't make dead people better. MyMum even told me that. I thought I could ask for the police when the operator said Nine nine nine. Which service do you require? But that seemed a bit dangerous. The police might think you've done something wrong or your Mum has. And anyway the police would be useless. They put people in jail in the police station and then they take them to court and then they put them in Westhill but they don't bury people.

Then I had a good idea. The priest! The priest buries people! But as soon as I said that I heard MyMum's voice only not in the room. She said *Over my dead body!* And she was laughing. I wished it was true. That she was laughing I mean.

I looked in the living room. She hadn't moved. Not even a little bit. She looked lonely so I said I'll telephone Gran. Then I remembered she doesn't have a telephone. And then I thought that Gran might come over—because that's what she does sometimes—and if she did she would know what to do. So I decided to wait. While I was waiting I made a cup of tea. I was careful. I pretended the hot water was a nanimal that could bite me. I got two cups out of the cupboard and then I put one back. Silly me! I put the milk in and then the tea. I was going to put sugar in but MyMum said it rots your teeth. I thought about it for about seventy-three seconds and then I thought If I turn round three times with my eyes closed and I can see the sugar bowl when I open them I'll put it in. Lucky me!

Then I got the other cup out again and put it ready for Gran and I carried my tea into the living room. Poor Mum. I put my cup on the stool and went to talk to her but I didn't know what to say. I sat down on the floor next to her leg instead. It was very quiet. Like everyone outside was dead too. It was a bit funny without anyone talking. MyMum says I'm either not talking or talking too much. I got up and put the wireless on. A man was saying

The rose is a rose and was always a rose but everyone knows that the apple's a rose and the pear is so I stopped listening but I let him keep on talking because somebody had to. Then I remembered biscuits.

I ate two in the kitchen and put two on a plate to take into the living room. I had to eat them both. Of course.

I waited a long time for Gran. While I was waiting I watched the telly. After Blue Peter it was the news and then it was four men having a quiz.

When it was nearly dark I knew Gran wasn't coming. I thought I should go next door to tell someone about MyMum. I put on both my pairs of long trousers and two jackets and a pair of gloves from the winter box under the stairs. Do you want to know why? Because that's where Denby lives. Denby is half a Doberman. He has pointy ears and jumps up. MyMum said He's all right, Denby is. Just scary. (But she's not as short as me.) She said Just don't put your hand through the gate. And now I had to put my whole body through! It made me shake quite a lot when I was walking round. I didn't know if Denby was inside or outside. The curtains were all drawn. I went right up to the front door. Really quietly. I was just going to knock when I heard something jingle. And bark! I nearly peed myself. He did a horrible growl and a kind of snort. He was round the side of the house. I could see him through their side gate where it's broken. There's all bits of planks missing. He put his mouth through and was trying to bite some more off. I have never run so fast away but I made sure I slammed the front gate behind me. Just in case. When I got back inside I thought it was a good job there was nobody in. They might have driven MyMum away to the cemetery or something and I wouldn't have known if I had to go too or what and then when they buried her I wouldn't have known what to do without her. MyDad would have but he wasn't there. Remember?

I put all the lights on at once even upstairs and I closed all the curtains because that's what MyMum does so no nosey parkers can see in.

I said Never mind Mum I know what to do next. I have to make my supper. I turned the radio up loud (it was a lady now) to keep her company and I opened a can of tomato soup. It was hard to turn the can opener but I did it. Some spilled then the rest went in the saucepan and I put it on the cooker and turned it to High. I filled up the kettle and put it on again and then I put two slices of bread in the toaster. When I pressed the handle down all the lights went out. I got a terrible shock. Don't worry. I just made that up to make you laugh.

A shock is when you're sort of stunned. So it was true. Everything had stopped at once. It was all quiet too and I couldn't see. It was like being in a cave. I couldn't see for eleven seconds and then I could because there was some light leaking out of the hall. I didn't want to cry—the noise is too scary—but I nearly did. And my nose started to run. I started to do In breathing with no outs like sniffing and all sorts of bad ideas got into my head at once. I really wanted MyMum to help me but you know why she couldn't. Then I really wanted MyDad to come home but he was in Ipswich wasn't he.

I hate it when I don't have a plan for what to do next. You know that. I have to rock and even bang. Why? Because it's helpful—silly! I really needed MyMum to get up and tell me it was all right but—well—you know what. I just did breathing really really loud with my eyes closed so all the bad ideas didn't have anywhere to stop. Like when newspapers do blowing all over the pavement. When I started to feel dizzy I opened my eyes. I could see the edge of the saucepan shining a bit. Then

I had a good idea. I opened the fridge. Well that was no good. It was all dark in there too! I put my hands out like a sleepwalker and went into the living room. Oops. It was not a very good name now.

I was glad MyMum was there because I didn't want to stay in a room by myself in the dark. I expect MyMum was glad I went in. Her hands were cold. Her face was too. I did sleepwalking over to the sofa and got the travelling rug. I had to drag it with one hand so I could do sleepwalking back with the other one. Then I climbed up on MyMum and covered us both up.

I could not remember what time it was so I just did a nestimate of how many seconds it would stay dark if it was nine o'clock. I did it in my head but I will write it out for you. Nine o'clock to twelve o'clock equals three. That's for hours. Twelve o'clock to six o'clock equals six. Three plus six equals nine. Sixty times nine—that's for minutes—equals five hundred and forty. Sixty times five hundred and forty equals thirty-two thousand four hundred. That's the seconds. (It's easier than you think. You just put the noughts on after.) So I started from thirty-two thousand four hundred and counted backwards in alligators and it worked. It was light when I woke up.

MyMum's mouth had come open and there was not a nice smell (actually it was really terrible but don't say anything). There was another smell too like cat's pee. I was worried in case it was me like when I was little but I wasn't wet. And we don't have a cat. So then I was embarrassed for MyMum but I don't expect she meant to do it. I thought when I get to school this time I will tell the first teacher I see and I if I don't see anyone I will just go in my classroom and tell Miss Kenney straight away even if she tells me not to and I won't stop until she does something.

I got down and went to the toilet and washed my hands a whole lot of times then I went in the kitchen and got a bowl and some Weetabix and some milk and made a nisland like before. MyMum says No sugar but she couldn't see me so I got some anyway. I didn't even like it. Then I did all the things you're supposed to do before you go to school except getting dressed because I was already. I took Jackie's cover off and gave him some food. He kept saying Pretty boy! I put it back again so it he wouldn't disturb MyMum. I couldn't think of any other things to do. When I looked at the time it was only seven o'clock. I did the washing up. Then I did drying. And the putting away. I sat down and waited. I am good at waiting. It's peaceful. There was a robin outside the window. It came back nine times.

When it was half past eight it was time to go so I went to say goodbye to MyMum. She looked funny, as if she wasn't feeling well. She wasn't! I said I am going to give you a kiss. I did that but I didn't like it. I never like kisses. They are too close to my head where all my mind is. I like it to be private there. I did it because I thought it might be important for MyMum to have a kiss especially if she had to wait a long time for somebody to come. I expect she couldn't wait to be buried. It's where you're supposed to be when you're dead.

Chapter 8
STILL SUNDAY

It was getting rockier and rockier and I didn't feel good. When my chair slided and hit the table beside me I got out fast. I really needed to have a cabin. While I was walking about the ship—remembering to use the handrails—I had a very brainy idea. I would go to the blind man's cabin and this time I would make up a really big lie and get it ready to say to him when he opened the door. This is what I made up.

—Hallo.

—Oh hallo. (The blind man.)

—MyDad wants to know if you have a life jacket for a kid and can we borrow it?

—Of course! Come in. (The blind man.)

(But if he was selfish he might say Why? What's wrong with yours? But then I could say It has a hole in it.)

Then when I got inside I would ask him if I could stay inside his cabin for a little while and if he said Why? I could say MyDad and MyAunty are having a private moment and their door is locked. (That is what MyMumandDad did on Sunday afternoon sometimes. Once MyMum said to me they were going to do Church and MyDad heard her and said Come on Frankie. I'll take you to the park.)

I went all the way along to number sixteen forty-two. The notice was still on the door but I knocked anyway. I heard the blind man say something and I pulled the handle down but the door wouldn't open. Something was stopping it. I could sort of see through the gap. It looked like his shoe. Then I could see Alec's nose. I got scared because the shoe was sideways, lying down. Not standing. Then the blind man said something again. I couldn't hear it properly. It was two things. It was Jush weave me first and then it sounded like I knee to die.

I closed the door.

Now I had no cabin and no life jacket either. I decided to go to bed early instead because at least the mattresses would be like a life jacket and anyway the lifeboats were out there.

I went up the stairs holding on—of course. The door was really hard to get open. It even hit me on the head like the other one! But it was no good. All the mattresses were put away. Everything was soaking wet and it was raining cats and dogs. And horses and pigs haha! It was much too loud. All right I thought. I will go to the red hand room. At least it will be dry and quiet and I will be right near the lifeboats when we start to do sinking. Women and children first so lucky me! BUT. I only took one step and I fell over. I slided all across the deck. Like a quoyt! But sideways. It is a good job I am lucky because one of the big metal box things in the middle stopped me. If it hadn't been there I would have slided straight to the edge and I probably would have slipped right over underneath the wire and then I would certainly have fallen all the way down. Twelve decks! When we tipped the other way I was even luckier because I slided all the way back to the wall. There is an iron bar all along the wall so I grabbed it tight. I decided not to let go until I got to the door with the red hand. Then I could not believe it because a real wave came up all the way from the sea like it wanted to get on the boat and it did! I saw it run off and it was all bubbles exactly like the beach.

Holding on was very tricky. My hands kept slipping. I hooked my arm through and used my elbow and held on with the other hand. I had to walk pigeon steps so I was getting soaked but it was better than sliding away. I was just nearly there when I could hear a man doing yelling.

HEY YOU! he yelled (that's just like in a book isn't it?) HEY YOU! HOLD ON! DON'T LET GO! (He didn't really have to tell me that. I am not completely stupid.)

I yelled back to him I AM HOLDING ON! (Now we were both yelling!)

He yelled DON'T LET GO! But he had already told me that. Then he came up behind me and grabbed my arm.

He yelled WHAT ARE YOU DOING OUT HERE?

I yelled I'M HOLDING ON!

He yelled LET GO!

I said You're squeezing my arm.

He yelled LET GO! Again. He yelled YOU CAN'T BE OUT HERE. WHERE ARE YOUR BLOODY PARENTS?

I said They're in their cabin. (!!)

He said Here! Get inside! and pushed me.

I thought Am I being kidnapped? because he still had hold of my arm.

He said What's your cabin number? Do you know it?

I said Sixteen forty-two.

He said Come on. He was walking really fast so I had to run but he didn't care. Then he started running too and we ran down the stairs. Now I was really scared because what would he do when he saw the blind man instead of MyMumandDad.

He said What number? So I told him again even though I didn't want to go in anymore.

OK he said. He was banging on the door and then he opened it. I could see the blind man's legs. They were on the bed now! And guess where Alec was? Underneath!

The sailor said Get in there! Go on! Keep this lad inside sir. Sir?

The blind man wasn't answering him but the sailor didn't care. He didn't care about anything. Not even me. He just went.

The blind man wasn't moving. Even when the door closed he didn't move.

I said Are you all right?

He didn't answer. I thought This is my second dead person. Good. I can do hiding and be safe with Alec.

Alec had his front and back legs stretched out sort of holding onto the floor under the bed. When I got down close I could hear him doing very tiny squeaking like a tiny tiny dog. I said Come Alec but he didn't come out. He looked really funny. Sort of frowning. His front legs were stretched out in front and his back legs were stuck out behind and his ears were all squished. Then I said Stay and he came out but he didn't even look at me.

He just sat down with his back to me right up close to the blind man. His legs still looked funny like he was sitting on something too wide and he was still doing the tiny squeaking. I think he was crying. Probably because the blind man was dead. I said Ssh. Come back under here. I'll stay here with you and I squeezed under the bed. We did a big tip and a bottle fell down and hit Alec on the head. He came back under straight away. Silly boy! It was a bit crowded. There was a little suitcase under there as well and a bottle. There were other bottles rolling about on the floor too. The blind man wasn't very tidy. Then we did a second really big tip and that's when the lights went out and it went a bit quiet and that's when I started to do shaking. Everything was black. I didn't like it with no lights. I kept my eyes closed. It was just what happened in my house. I thought it must have something to do with dead people. Or maybe I am blind too now I thought. Or dead. No I am not dead. I am doing breathing. I can hear me. I can even hear my heart running. And my head hurts. Dead people don't feel anything not even when you pinch them. I didn't want to try it on MyMum. I was too scared. It would be terrible to be dead and somebody was hurting you and you couldn't pinch back. Then Alec began making a disgusting noise and I could smell something bad. Not just the pub smell. I knew he had been sick. I didn't know dogs could be sick.

It was the worst day of my life.

I wished I was at home. I wished MyMum had never died. I wished MyDad was with me. Three wishes. But only stupid Alec and a nother dead person.

The whole boat was rocking up and down. And sideways too. It was making me do shaking. I wished the lights would come back on.

Four.

I'll tell you a story if you calm down. That was MyMum!
That's what she always said. But it was no good there was only
the stupid suitcase and stupid Alec. And all he could do was
tiny crying.

I put my arm over him and he licked my thumb. He really
stinked. I wished I could do rocking (five!) but there was no
room. I could hear clanging and crashing and a kind of giant
quiet noise. I tried to feel if we were sinking in case I had to
get out but I couldn't tell. I couldn't get out anyway because it
was too dark. I curled up tight with my eyes closed. It was just
like I said it would be — I was saying Help me help me help
me and there was no one there.

All the people in the world I knew were not there. MyMum.
MyDad. Gran. Grandad (he's a nother dead person. His head
was nearly all bald and he let Jackie walk on it when he came
over). Miss Kenney but I was glad she wasn't. Aunty Julie.
Philippa at school (she showed me her webbed toe). My little
sister. I haven't told you about her. She was MyMum's dead
baby. I know more dead people than anyone I know. She didn't
have a name so she might not count. She was one of the things
that made MyMum unhappy but she couldn't help it because
she was only just born. That's why she didn't have a name. My
Uncle Jack but he would be no use because guess what? Yes
dead! I was all alone.

Think of something nice Frankie. (That was MyMum.) *Think
of something nice.*

I thought about Cry Baby Bunting. I knew all the words
because MyMum sang it to me a lot.

Cry baby bunting
Daddy's gone a hunting
To fetch a baby rabbit skin
To wrap the baby bunting in
Cry baby bunting
Daddy's gone a hunting
To fetch a baby rabbit skin
To wrap the baby bunting in
Cry baby bunting

I sang it over and over in my head. I thought about when she put her arms right round me to stop a panic. She put them right round me in a circle and told me to cry instead. We were rocking. Like the boat. You can laugh if you want. MyMum always wanted me to cry. She said it was helpful. She did it once when I fell off my trike and my head was bleeding and I didn't like the blood. I wanted to cry but I wanted her to carry on singing too.

Cry baby bunting
Daddy's gone a hunting
To fetch a baby rabbit skin
To wrap poor baby bunting in

I thought if I sang it enough in my head there wouldn't be room for any scary things.

Cry baby bunting
Daddy's gone a hunting
To fetch a baby rabbit skin
To wrap poor baby bunting in.

My nose started running. And my eyes. And Alec started licking me. I had to turn my face the other way. Then he started licking the back of my neck. I think dog lick is probably good for you. It made me feel calmer and my heart stopped-running so fast. It was a good job it worked because it was a whole long time until the lights came on. They came on by themselves when the big quiet noise stopped all of a sudden. *That's a relief then.* You could hear the engines grumbling. (That was a nother relief.) But it was still the worst day of my life. I have never been so scared with all the rockiness.

We tipped a long way sort of sideways so Alec and me got pressed up against the wall under the pillow end. I needed to find somewhere else. I didn't want to go on the blind man's bed. He's not the same as MyMum. I couldn't wait till we tipped back the other way. When we did it felt a lot better. I even got used to it. After a while a speaker came on and said

Ladies and Gentlemen. This is the Chief Officer speaking on behalf of the Captain. He has asked me to apologize for the recent interruption of power and consiquent disruption of services. Standby power has now been established and full power is expected to be restored in all public areas within the hour. All passengers however are advised to remain in the safety and comfort of their cabins until more settled conditions prevale.

I bet you think I am making that up. I'm not. I'm remembering. I told you I can do that. It's another thing Miss Kenney makes me do at school remembering what people say because once I told her *Here is the news* and then I told her all of it. She looked at me like I look at Denby when he is watching me through the fence. She said You're making that up and I said No I'm not. She said You know it's a sin to lie? I said Pardon? because she knows I know. She said Never mind.

At playtime she said Just stay inside today Francis will you? There is something I want you to do.

She went to the record player and put Peter And The Wolf on. Then she took it off again and said Can you tell me what the man said?

I said *Shall I tell you a story? Once upon a time—well this is a musical story and like all stories it has caracters and each caracter is represented by a different instrument of the orkestra. So that you can recognize the caracters every time they appear I'm going to ask the various instruments to show them to you. First the bird. He is represented by the flute…*

She said Well. I expect you've heard it before. Lots and lots of times.

I said You play it when we have to wait for Miss Gibbins class.

She said Hmm and you could see she was thinking what to do next. Then she said Come with me and she took me to the Staff Room. She walked in front. I was doing Heel!

I had never seen inside the Staff Room before. It was full of smoke. It had tables and chairs and two settees and even cushions and a kettle and two teapots and curtains. But perhaps you already know what a Staff Room looks like so I won't tell you every single thing only the wireless. It was the same as the one at home.

Some of the teachers were sitting in the chairs eating and some of them were smoking and one of them was doing them both at the same time.

Miss Kenney said Excuse me everybody. There is something I need to check. Everybody stared at us. The man teacher said Don't bring any headlice in here thank you Miss Kenney and everybody laughed. Then he said We have plenty of our own thank you and everybody laughed a second time.

Miss Kenney said Trust you Mr Herbert and someone else shouted out Speak for yourself and everybody laughed really loud.

Miss Kenney said We won't be very long will we Francis?

I said I don't know.

She said It's just a test and she took me over to the wireless and said Listen hard and switched it on.

It was a man saying—*remains low west of the British Isles with a south to south west air stream covering most areas. A troff of low pressure over central England is expected to move slowly east to the north sea during tomorrow. In north eastern coastal waters of England from the Scottish border to Widbee winds will be south to south west mainly modrate or fresh but strong at times. Light rain at first will give way to bright periods but further showers are expected later.*

Miss Kenney was writing stuff down on a piece of paper the whole time and then she switched it off and said I can't keep up any more. Come on.

She said We'll leave you in peace now. Ta very much everyone.

Some teachers said Bye-bye and somebody said Be good and the man teacher said And if you can't be good be careful.

When we got back in the classroom Miss Kenney asked me to stand by her desk and she got her piece of paper and she said What did you hear?

I said The man doing the weather forecast.

Miss Kenney said And—?

I said *Have you got cucumber? You always have cucumber. I can never find any this time of year.* And *You don't look in the right places.* And *I don't know about cucumber but somebody's been eating hard boiled eggs in here again and I wish they wouldn't.* And *Who's got a light?* And *my lighter's over by the—* but Miss Kenney didn't let me finish. She said THAT'S ENOUGH! It was very loud like when the whole class is being noisy. I knew I had done something wrong but I didn't know what so I said What?

Miss Kenney said Go outside. Just go out to play Francis. Go now. Just go. I said All right. (She didn't have to say it so many times but I knew not to tell her.)

So anyway I waited in the safety and comfort of the blind man's cabin. At least I could do thinking. And listening. I had to listen to know when it was morning. It was all electric light remember? Alec was sleeping so it was probably still night.

I was a bit sad about the blind man. He was one of my three friends. You know what they do with dead people on a boat don't you? Put them in a sack and throw them in the sea. You probably don't believe me but it's true. MyDad told me about it when Great Uncle George died. He was on my list of Don't Like because of his moustache. I said I'm glad Uncle George is dead and MyDad said Ssh! Don't say that to Mum.

I said Why not?

MyDad said He's YourMum's uncle and she loves him.

(I don't want keep saying *I said MyDad said* all the time so I'll just tell you what we said and not who said it. You can work it out.)

—Why is she going to let them put him in the ground then?

—You can't keep people when they're not alive anymore.

—Why not?

—It's a health risk.

—What does that mean?

—Isn't it time for Blue Peter?

—I want to know.

—Well.

(There was a whole lot of not talking next while MyDad did thinking.)

—Well. We're just the same as animals. When animals die their bodies stop working and then they start to decay.

—Like your black tooth.

—Sort of.

—Why?

—Why what?

—Why do they start to decay?

—They need to go back into Nature. They're no good as bodies anymore.

—So they're rubbish.

—In a way.

—So why don't people just let the dustmen take them away?

—Well that wouldn't be very nice. Not for people you love.

—Or for the dustmen.

—Mmm.

—Putting them in the ground isn't very nice.

—It's the right place. For a dead body. So it can go back into Nature. Now go and put the telly on.

—But what if you were on a boat and you died? You couldn't be put in the ground then. You would decay on the boat.

—No. You're right (I think he meant Yes) but there is something very special called A Burial At Sea. Your granddad had one of those.

—How can you be buried at sea if there's no dirt?

—The person's coffin is put in the water instead.

—The box?

—Yes.

—Doesn't it float?

—No.

—Why not?

—You know—you are a very clever lad Frankie. I think you can work out the answer yourself.

—They put stones in it.

—Yes.

—And it sinks.

—Yes (MyDad said that even though I wasn't asking).

—And it never comes up again? (This time I was.)

—No.

—No it never comes up again?

—Yes.

—What if the person doesn't have a coffin?

—They would put the person's body in a sack. Now will you do as you're told and go and put the telly on?

Actually I think MyDad was wrong. This boat is much heavier than a coffin with a person and some stones in it and we are not sinking. We would only sink if there was a hole in the bottom. I expect they make holes in the coffin before they do a burial at sea. I heard a very loud splash on the second night when I was sleeping behind the mattresses. Perhaps they were doing one then. Somebody could easily have died. There are lots of old people a board. Probably somebody a board dies everyday. I am glad I am not old.

It was very quiet. And not at all tippy. Alec had stopped licking. He was busy doing sleeping. I was wide awake. Perhaps I had been doing sleeping for a long time. I don't know how much because the lights made it all look the same all the time. I could see something horrible stuck on the side of my sock. Alec's pewk! Eeuw. I took my shoe off carefully and managed to get my sock off without touching the horrible bit. Then I put I my shoe back on. I whispered Breakfast Alec.

I got out to see if the blind man was still dead.

He was.

Are you going to wake up? (I did whispering.) I could see a bit of blood out of his nose.

I can't hear you. It was true. I couldn't hear him breathing. It was just like MyMum except the blood. It was making me scared. I really needed to get out fast.

I didn't want to be on the boat any longer. Everything was a big problem. I changed number one on my new plan. It was not Stay on the boat and go back anymore. It was Get off when we get to New York and find someone to help me ring MyDad. Not the police because they will ask how I paid for my ticket if I'm only a boy. Maybe a nice looking lady or a granny. It was the second time I had to change number one.

Len

One Tree Hill, Patti. Remember? You wouldn't forget.
That Sunday afternoon when you were expecting and we
ran down together. I was pulling you. When it happened
that night and you lost the baby, you blamed yourself—
and I let you. You weren't the same after it happened. I
wanted us to try again but you never did want that. When
you found out you were expecting the next time you
looked me right in the eye and said Want to go back to
One Tree Hill? I remember that. Staring each other
down. I said, Yes I do, only to call your bluff, really, but
we went. It was late summer. The bracken on either side
had already turned and the dry grass underfoot was
slippery. When we got to the top we sat down on one of
the smooth rocks. We sat for a long time without saying
anything. The view was beautiful that day. All the gold
colour and everything. Then you said Len, I'm going to
walk down, all right? And you looked me in the eye
again like before. I was that happy. I don't know. It felt
like a new chance at something. I said, Right, I'll go by

myself then. See you at the bottom. And I took off. I ran and ran. I could have been flying. I waited for you at the bottom, out of breath. When I saw you walking down you were more beautiful than the view.

If I could see you that way again.

Dear God if you could be here now. Walking up the hill towards us. Holding Frankie's hand.

I keep saying we'll find him. Everybody keeps saying it. But still nothing. They were out most of the day yesterday, right into the evening. And everyone was up first thing to meet again at the park at the bottom of Colbourne Road and start all over. So it's another whole day search-ing now and not a single clue. Not one. It's only clues we're looking for now, I know that. Not Frankie. They keep saying there's still a chance. They don't really believe it. Not really. Even Mum has doubts. You know Frankie, she said. If he were alive he'd have contacted someone by now. He's not daft.

It's taking its strain on her. You can see it in her face. She's aged ten years. She blames me. That's pretty obvious. I've always been the one to blame. Never mattered what for. I think she blamed me for Jack, too. But my own son? I'd do anything, anything to get him back. Blaming me for having a job that takes me away? Blaming me for Frankie taking off? Him getting taken? Oh God don't let it be that. Don't let it be that. The darkest sight you can ever imagine locked away in the back of your mind forever. And that's what's become of him, our Frankie? Please not Frankie. Forever and ever. Locked away in that darkness. Forever and ever, amen. And no turning back. Ever.

Hundreds out now looking for him. They've been back to all his favourite places. Got the museum and the library opened up again today, the school. Probably his least favourite, you know that, but they went through it again all the same.

Last night a load of them met in the pub. Bill called in after. He saw my lights still on. He came in and told me all about it. They had it all mapped out hour by hour. Written it all down for me. I told him I'd find them when I was finished at the station today, see what they had to say first, whether there was anything new. On the way down there this morning it was as real as real in my mind—the detective sergeant waiting for me to come in, all smiles. *Mr Walters! We have some good news for you!* I tell you when I walked through that door—the feeling. No one was waiting to tell me anything. They were dreading seeing me. I could tell. Every time someone shakes their head or whispers, No, you can't imagine what it does to you. The worst pain you've ever known being dragged out of your throat, your gut, and leaving behind nothing at all. All your hope running out of you as if it's your blood and you've severed an artery. It is your blood. It's why you live. You don't know how you're still alive. You want to be dead too. It's all you want, just curl up and die, but you can't give up. You don't. That's why some of us are doing the hill again. People are good. They'll do anything you ask. Well you would, wouldn't you? A six-year-old.

We've been here about two hours now. There's a line of us making our way from the top of the hill diagonally down the south-west slope. You can see the water from here. The sun's on it.

All those times we ran him down here holding his hands, his feet pedalling air between us. *Again!* he always said. Remember that? *Again!* As soon as we got to the bottom. *Again!* Four, five, six times we'd do it. End up lying down, the three of us. On the ground. Out of breath. Weak with laughing. The sky.

I know now we aren't looking for him alive anymore. Not really. No one says as much. It's all hot air. *We'll do our best. There's always a chance. Never give up hope. Never. The weather's good, that's one thing. He's a clever lad. He'll know how to take care of himself.* But we have sticks, that's the thing. We have sticks and we're beating the new bracken down. We're looking for him on the ground.

We'll do the wood next. Before it gets dark.

Chapter 9

MONDAY AM
(You know that's the morning. Right?)

I was worried about Alec. I had to leave him behind. If I took him with me he would be a great big Give Away. (That's what you call it when you're hiding and people can see the bump or a bit of your foot or something.) Everyone would stop and talk to me and then I would have to tell them about the blind man and then they would want to talk to MyMumandDad. So I left him. He didn't have any breakfast but I filled his water dish in the bathroom and carried it back. I spilled quite a lot but there was still some left for him. I put it a little way in front of where he was lying. He opened one eye but he didn't even look pleased. I don't know what they will do with him when they find him.

I went up the stairs and looked out the window. Outside was darker than inside. You didn't know if it was nearly morning or nearly night. I went out and had a look.

The sea was all flat again but going up and down and everything was still wet and slippery. There was a great big black cloud in the sky and it was flat too, like a ceiling only low down and with a big slit in it. And guess what colour the sky was in the slit? Not blue. It was gold. Like a wedding ring. A squished one. Filled in. And here's another thing—there was all steam coming down from the black ceiling. But I still didn't know which one it was—nearly morning or nearly night. Then I got a surprise. I'll give you one too. I saw snowflakes coming out of the steam really fast. Millions of them. They got bigger and bigger and they made a huge whirry squeaky noise faster and faster and louder and louder. BIRDS! They were birds! Millions and millions of them all flying the same way. When they went past you you couldn't see the sea or the sky or anything. It was like you were in the blizzard in The Great White North. A blizzard made out of birds. And then they were gone and you could sort of hear them like blowing away. I looked round to see if anyone else had seen it but I was all alone. I don't expect anyone would believe how many birds I saw if I told them. Sometimes it doesn't matter even if you tell the truth. People are like Miss Kenney sometimes. And sometimes they are just not interested anyway. You can tell.

I didn't want to meet the sailor all alone outside again. He certainly would not be pleased to see me so I went back in. And anyway I needed to.

A lady with cleaning things came out of the toilets and said Well good morning! You're an early bird! I wanted to tell her what I had seen outside but I changed my mind. I just said I know.

The toilets smelled a lot better than yesterday. I expect that's because the lady had cleaned them. The sinks were all sparkly.

I checked to see if I looked dirty. I had sticking up hair. I stuck it down with my fingers. I had a drink of water. Then I had a wash. I couldn't clean my teeth because the celery was too bendy so I threw it away. Then I stole a whole lot of (clean!) toilet paper to blow my nose. I felt much better. I was just going to leave when I saw my feet. Dimwit! I had one sock on and one sock off! I took the other one off so I didn't look like a nidiot. It smelled of foot but I put it in my pocket anyway and put my shoe back on without it. It didn't look so stupid. It looked nearly normal.

When I went out again there were more people who had got up. They were doing walking and chatting and smiling. No one took any notice of me so that was all right. I had to be careful about everything. It was why I hated being on the boat now. It was exhausting.

A whole lot of people were queuing up for breakfast and I can't do queuing. That's when people start talking to me. I carried on walking instead. Guess who I met? Clue—one of my three friends. Kay! She said Hallo and I said Hallo back.

Her Mum and her Dad said Hallo too and I said Hallo back to them.

Kay said Did you throw up yesterday? I did.

Her Mum said Seven times! We ran out of sick bags.

Kay said Mum!

I said So did I. But only once.

Her dad said Only once? Then you're quite the sailor. What's your name again?

Kay said Frankie. I told you.

Her Dad said Of course. Frankie's the one who likes to play crazy golf. Bye now Frankie.

Kay said Goofy Golf.

I said No I don't. But they had already gone.

I thought I hope we get to New York before they ask me the question I don't want anybody to ask. Only one more day.

There were still lots of people having breakfast when I went back the second time. I was even more hungry than before so I decided to do Excuse me. I said Excuse me—Excuse me—Excuse me—Excuse me—all the way to the baked beans and then I filled up my plate. One of the cooks put a negg on before I could say No thank you and then another one said Toast? So I said Yes please. I took it to the little kids table. There was a big boy there too looking after a little baby.

My breakfast was delicious. Except the egg. I left it. When I had nearly finished the big boy said Where are your parents? Are they half dead like mine? I was really scared all of a sudden. It's sort of true. Half dead. He said parents have no sea legs. Not like us. I'm glad he didn't make me answer the question. I was eating my toast when he left. He said Want something tasty on that? I said Yes please. He said Here you go hahaha and he gave me the baby's plate of spit up.

I tried to watch a film in the Cinema. It was loud and blurry like the others and it was cartoons again. I hate cartoons. Nobody can be flat. I closed my eyes. And my ears. I was just listening to the engines. Do you know you can listen through your feet or your bottom or whatever is touching something? It's true. Sharks listen through their skins because they're touching the water all over and so do snakes. They can hear you walking on the ground. Do you want to know what I was thinking about while I was listening to the engines? I'll give

you three clues. Not MyMum. Not MyDad. Not the blind man.
I'll give you an extra one—Under the bed.

Alec!!

I couldn't stop thinking about him. I was one hundred
percent sure the blind man meant I NEED to die. When someone says they need to do something it means they really *have*
to do it and you have to leave them alone, like—YourMum
needs to be by herself for a bit. Or—I need to be with Your-
Mum for five minutes. People are always saying it. Francis
needs time to be by himself. Francis needs to do counting. So
really I *had* to leave the blind man alone. But if I did no one
would feed Alec. It was a cunundrum. That's a puzzle. Like
the pipes under the kitchen sink.

I tried to work it out like a notice board in my head.

<u>If I do tell someone</u>   1. They will put the blind man in a
  sack and throw him in the sea.
  2. They might let me keep Alec.
  BUT
  3. They will find out I don't have a
  ticket and MyDad will go to jail.

<u>If I don't tell someone</u> 1. No one will know about the
  blind man.
  2. No one will feed Alec and he will
  Starve to Death like a refugee
  from Hungary.
  3. They will put them both in a sack
  when they find them and throw
  them in the sea.

Somebody needed to tell them. Me? Probably. No one else would do it. I was the only one who heard what the blind man said and the only one who knew he did it. It was really terrible. I did not want to tell anyone. They would only think I was making it up again.

Be brave Frankie. You know who that was. I always do what MyMum says. Especially when she's dead. It would be horrible for her if she could see me not doing what she said. I did want to tell someone really but I didn't want them to not believe me again. They would just do asking questions instead. They would say things like How do you know? And if I said I heard him they would say What were you doing in the blind man's cabin? Is he your dad? And if I said No they would say Where is your dad then? And then MyDad would be in big trouble because they would find out I didn't have a ticket and you know what they would do then don't you. Jail for you Mister!

I could just do hiding until we got to New York. But that wouldn't be brave. I did not want them to throw Alec in the sea too.

After I had been round the big deck three times I still hadn't told anybody. I didn't even know who to tell. I hadn't seen any sailors all the morning. Not one. I could tell it to another soul but everybody I met always did jokes with me. They would think I was joking back if I said The blind man is dead. And anyway what if I made things go wrong? Sometimes it's better to keep things all to yourself. Like a secret.

I nearly told a lady who was standing by herself looking at the sea—with nothing to see (but you know that one). She was there for a long time. I went to stand beside her. She didn't say Hallo or Hallo sonny or even Hullo-hullo or anything. She just kept looking.

I did a little cough so she would know I was there but she turned the other way and walked off. I expect she needed to be by herself.

Then I found a sailor. Finally! He was near the swimming pool. He had a hose turned on. It was all across the deck and he was shooting water over everything then putting the hose down—without even turning it off so he could do mopping. He kept doing that—hose mop hose mop hose mop. I was watching him. The water was all running away and going along the edge. He was a bit busy but I wanted to tell him anyway. Then when I started to go there he shouted out Not this way laddie! See the rope? So I couldn't go there. I didn't want to shout out what I had to say. I don't expect you would either.

I looked for other people who were by themselves because I don't like saying things when there are two or three or four or five people together. They always do jokes to each other. It's embarrassing. It's like you are invisible. Not many people are by themselves on this boat. They are always with someone else.

I saw the man with the podgy hands but I didn't go near him—of *course*.

I kept on looking anyway. I did see one man. He had his shorts on and plimsolls on. He was doing extremely fast walking. I remembered *Be brave!* and stood in the way and said Excuse me. It didn't work. He did a kind of L. He stepped sideways and said Watch out son! and carried on one side sort of all in one go.

I gave up and went inside. Straightaway I saw a man by himself outside the shops. He looked bored so I thought Good news for me! He also looked a bit like my Uncle Jack so I went right up to him and said Excuse me. The man in room sixteen forty-two is dead.

He put his eyebrows up and looked at me and said My my my! I hope it's no one we know.

I said It is. It's the blind man.

He said Oh the blind man. I know him. That *is* sad.

I said But his dog's alive.

He said Well, that's good news. I'm glad to hear that. Ah!

He said Ah! because his wife (or it might have been his Mum) came out of the shop and got hold of his arm.

She said They didn't have it in my size but they said they're cut really large and I could try it on so I said I'll just get my husband. What was the good news?

He said Oh it was good news bad news. The—

And then I didn't hear anymore because they were in the shop. Some grown-ups are useless. A lot of them actually.

I looked all morning. At twelve o'clock I went up to the top deck where you get the beefburgers. I wanted one but all of a sudden I didn't want to go in without the blind man because everyone was helpful when I was with him. I wasn't brave enough today. *Not brave enough to have your dinner?* I wished I hadn't heard that. I thought brave was only when you have to get a splinter out or rescue someone from a fire. I didn't think you had to be brave all the time. I thought you could just be who you are the rest of the time. Like shy for instance. Being shy is the same as being mean or being a bully. You can't help it. I like being shy. It means you can stay by yourself and no one bothers you. But actually that's not true. They do. They come up and say Don't be shy! But they never tell you why not. As if you're supposed to be brave all the time. Perhaps you are.

Anyway I was being brave about one thing today when I found someone to tell so I didn't have to be brave about my dinner. It was equal.

I thought Alec will be getting hungry too. Like me! I would have to find someone soon even though I was scared I might make things go wrong and someone would get into trouble. Guess who?! Or MyDad.

I thought about telling the lady in the playroom but she is just like Miss Kenney. I think she hates me. I waited to go into the yellow tent to do pretend sleeping before I tried again. I had to wait for ages. Two girls and a boy were playing kissing in there. It was horrible. The boy said Do you want to play? It's Postman's Knock. That is a disgusting game. You have to go outside and kiss the person who knocks on the door but they were playing you have to go *inside* and kiss them. I said No thank you. I wanted to tell the lady who doesn't like me but you mustn't tell on people. Anyway I think she knew because all of a sudden she went over and said All right. That's enough. Time for someone else to have a turn. Come on out now.

Another boy went in afterwards but he got bored and came out again so I went in. He should have taken Five Go to Pirates' Cove in with him.

It was nice and quiet inside the yellow tent (and sunny!) for pretend sleeping. While I was doing that I had a kind of day-dream. I was walking on the deck behind some people and I suddenly remembered that I had not tucked my third ear in. Yes I had three! It was terrible. No one else had an extra one. It was growing across the top of my head. There was a sort of slot there where I could tuck it in so no one would notice and point at me. I had to tuck it in so quickly I was out of breath when the daydream stopped. Straight away I had a nidea. It was—*You don't have to tell anyone anything. YOU CAN WRITE IT DOWN!!!* You can write it down at the table where the paper and the crayons are for drawing. YOU CAN WRITE A SUGGESTION!!! Then you can put it in the Suggestion Box.

I got out and went over to the table. I picked a red crayon because red for emergency and red for first aid (and red for blood. *Obv*iously!) I wrote—

My suggestion is

Then I was stuck because I didn't really have a suggestion. *The blind man is dead* is not a suggestion. Then I thought of one. I wrote—

A sailor needs to go to see

and then I got a navy blue crayon and drew fifty-six wavy lines over the words because it sounded like the song I don't like.

The lady came and looked over my shoulder and said That's nice dear. I told you she wasn't very clever.

I started again. I wrote—

Someone should go to the blind man's cabin to see if he is dead. If he is someone should feed his dog. His name is Alec.

I had to use seven pieces of paper because crayons make your printing big.

The lady came back the other way. She sort of pushed all the pieces about while she was reading. Then she said Leave some paper for the others now.

I said All right but I didn't look at her. She sounded a bit cross. I got a nother piece of paper and wrote

PS The number of the blind man's cabin is 1642

I put all the pieces in a neat pile and folded them all up together so I had a very fat square then I stuffed it in my pocket.

There were lots of people at the Purser's Office. They weren't lining up. They were in a clump and everybody was listening to the sailor in a uniform. The Purser! *Ding!* He was telling them a story.

I didn't know how to post my letter without anyone seeing it was me who put it in so I went away. I thought of lots of ideas but none of them were any good. I went outside to wait. I stood at the rail to do looking. It was all blue like the first day when I got a board. I stayed a long time. The pointy corner of the fat suggestion was poking my leg. Sometimes I changed my place (so no one would get suspicious) and started all over again. It was very soothing. Once I saw the quoits boy. He was holding hands with his Mum. That was not fair. I only looked at him once because it made me feel bad.

After a little while (that's something else they say in books) I went back to the Purser's Office. Everyone had gone. Except the Purser. Of course. But that was even worse because now he could easily see me if I put it in the box so I went past and went to the Library instead. There were hundreds of books in the Library all the same. They were all brown or dark blue or dark red or dark green. Not lots of bright colours like at school or in my bedroom. They were sort of matching in long lines. I got a small one and took it to a round table. I can't tell you the title because I didn't know how to say the words (I think they were foreign) but I can spell them for you because I have a good memory. (I'm not boasting. I'm just reminding you.) They went J-U-S-T-I-N-E space O-U space L-E-S space M-A-L-H-E-U-R-S space D-E space L-A space V-E-R-T-U. I got a big surprise when I saw the pictures. They made me feel funny like the pictures in Here Comes Noddy Again when the robbers steal all his clothes and leave him without any. You could see the people's naked bodies like you can see Noddy's. They were being so rude I would be in trouble if I told you. So I put it back.

The next one I got was Lord Arthur Savile's Crime. I could read some of the words but there were too many hard ones I didn't know how to say like L-e-v-é-e and p-e-e-r-e-s-s-e-s so perhaps it was a foreign one too. Somebody went by the back of my chair and said Goodness me! Can you read that? I said No and put it back on the shelf and went back to the Purser's Office.

The Purser was busy showing a lady a map. Their heads were really close together. I reached up to the box and pushed my suggestion through the slot. They both sort of looked up for a second but then they looked back at the map. They didn't care so that was a good thing.

Every time there is a good thing there is a bad thing right after. When I was leaving the Purser's Suggestion Box I passed the notice board and this is what I noticed—

4:30 p.m. The Titanic! (slides) Queen's Lounge All Ages

I know a lot about the Titanic. MyDad told me one of the most important things was that no one thought it would sink but it did. I started thinking about that. I had really bad thoughts. Like No one thinks this ship will sink either. But just because no one thinks it doesn't mean it won't happen. I decided it would be a good idea to go to The Titanic! because it might have useful information about how to get in the lifeboats if you are only three foot nine.

It was a long time to wait. I did walking about the ship. Outside the dining room someone had put a blue rope where the gigantic pot had fallen over and broken. Some men were clearing up the dirt. Everywhere I went people were clearing up except some boys in the café outside. They were throwing tomatoes about.

Right at 4:30 I went to the Queen's Lounge. There were lots of people already sitting down. My tummy was all mixed up because everything felt so important. I wanted to remember exactly how to get into the boats. No one else looked nervous. I was just going to sit in a nempty chair when the lady next to it put her hand on it and said This one's taken. Go down to the front dear with the other children. It wasn't what I wanted to do because I could see one of the tomato throwing boys but I didn't want anyone to see me having a nargument so I went.

A man came in and said *Good afternoon Ladies and Gentlemen boys and girls.* He had to say it twice because nobody stopped talking. Then he said *Today I have a special treat for you. A privilidged look at some rare photographs from the arkives documenting the construction of the opulant fittings that made the Titanic the greatest lady of them all. A look if you like at her wardrobe and her jewels.* I didn't know what he was talking about. When he said *Lights* someone turned them off. Then the tomato boy kneeled up and I couldn't see all of the pictures.

The first one had lifeboats because it was the whole ship you could tell. But after that they were nearly all pictures of stuff inside like stairs and curtains and lights and mirrors and all the tables and chairs with the man talking about how much everything cost—A lot! All right, I'll tell you. Total (that means everything added together like all the stuff I've already said *and* the pianos and carpets and pictures and doors and sinks EVERYTHING even taps) cost. Two hundred million pounds. After he said that I could hear MyMum's voice in my head. *So that was a waste of bloody money then Frankie. I bet they were mad.*

There were loads of pictures but they were all about stuff. I had just started thinking about my supper when another man went up and gave the first man a piece of paper. He read it and said *Ladies and Gentlemen* (he forgot the boys and girls bit) *we have a surprise for you* and everyone went really quiet. He said *We have been informed by the Marine Navigational Services of the Canadian Coast Guard that on our present course there is an excellent chance of sighting one of several sizeable icebergs currently drifting in a south easterly direction from the Arctic Circle.* Apparently they are *within* (he was reading again) *one hundred and fifty nautical miles of the southern banks of Newfin Land* which puts us in a very good position for a close look.

I felt sick.

Someone shouted Not too close I hope! and everybody laughed. Except me because I knew the sailor had said it on purpose. Anyway it wasn't funny to think about.

The sailor said Well Ladies and Gentlemen (he still didn't say boys and girls), that's about all we have for you and—he looked at the clock—it's just about dinner time (he meant supper) so I think we'll leave it there and wish all passengers in the first sitting bomb appatea. And—well—for the rest of you—the rest of us haha—the sun's almost over the yard arm so…Good health!

The man behind me did a loud whisper to his friend. He said That means he's going to go and get hammered.

Sometimes you don't know what people are talking about.

Everybody got up and started going out at the same time. Nobody lined up so that was good. I could sort of squeeze in between people and no one took any notice.

And then one lady did. She smiled at me and said I bet you can't wait to see a niceberg. You'd probably like it if we ran right into one! Hahahahaha (she was laughing at her own joke).

I said No I wouldn't.

She said Oh pardon *me* Mr Sobersides.

I didn't go to have dinner. I didn't have a nappetite. Not one. It was as if I was already full up because I had eaten too much. If I thought about eating something—even a piece of cheese— it made me feel sick like in the storm. It was sort of like being dizzy. Everywhere I went I heard people saying the word *iceberg* or else *Titanic*. They didn't seem scared at all only pretend scared. Not like me. Every time I heard one of the words I got more frightened until I was terrified like in my dream of the ship falling over. I wanted to know what the blind man would say but he wouldn't be able to say anything. He would be dead quiet— haha. (That was only miserable laughing. Like MyDad when he pretends to be that man on the radio.) Or if they found my note he might even be already buried at sea. Poor Alec. I wished the blind man wasn't dead. And then I wished MyMum hadn't died in her armchair so I didn't have to be on this boat at all. I didn't want to see a stupid iceberg ever.

I went up to the deck with the sunloungers. The mattresses were still on them so I didn't have a bedroom yet. I went back inside all the way to the big armchair where I did observing the sea. I pushed it a bit so it was facing the window straight. It made me feel better. No one could see me properly and I couldn't see anyone, except sometimes I could see their reflections sort of walking through the glass. Like ghosts. Only real. I stopped watching the sea and watched for people walking by. (They were behind me really.) I started making secret bargains like If I count to ninety-nine I will see the blind man and If I count to one thousand I will see MyMum. After I had done a whole lot of counting I could not wait to go to bed and close my eyes to make the time go faster. I don't like being terrified for a long time. It's tiring. Being asleep is all right because you can't see or hear anything scary (unless it's a boat in the middle of the road!) and when you wake up it's the next day. When the sea was pink I went back and checked again. Yes! My bedroom was ready!

There were still too many people walking about who might see me go to bed. No one was in a hurry to go anywhere. I had to do walking about the ship all over again.

All of a sudden there was a new message. It said

Ladies and Gentlemen, This is a nannouncement from the bridge. A school of porpoises has been sighted on the starboard side of the vessel travelling westward at approximutly the speed of the ship.

A lady near me said That's on the other side. Do you want to go and see? She held out her hand.

I did one of my lies. I said MyDad will take me. He's just coming. And she rushed off.

As soon as I could I dived behind the mattresses. No one saw. I was really squeezed in tight so I felt a lot better. It wasn't terrible anymore. It was very safe and I could be calm.

I didn't know how I would fall asleep. I was not at all tired. I waited until the sky started getting dark so I could do counting backwards. The sky took ever such a long time because it had to do all the colours first. I could see through a teeny tiny gap. You have to be extremely careful. Like a spy. My favourite thing! It did pink and mauve and orange and purple and everything— and then it did blue-black. (You can have that. Two colours at once.) It was dark (except the lights were on) so I started counting. You have to pick a number. I picked eight hundred and forty-seven. I started from there. Backwards (of course).

🐛

It didn't work. Instead of going to sleep I only thought about MyMum and I thought about what happened after I gave her the kiss. I'll tell you. It was THURSDAY AM. This is what I did. I got my jacket and put my best shoes on (just because) and went out the door. I didn't push the latch over then Gran could get in if she came and anyway it's a bit stiff and my thumb's not strong enough. Then I went out. It was a lovely sunny day but I didn't like being outside at all. I felt as if I was walking on a high mountain and I might fall down the side. I had to bite the insides of both my cheeks so I wouldn't. I expect I looked like a nidiot.

It was really early when I got to school. I don't like that. I stayed in the toilets for a long time so no one would to talk to me in the playground but then someone came and started doing farts and that made me leave. When I went outside I thought This is my lucky day (but you know it wasn't) because Miss Kenney was on playground duty and she saw me coming. But she purposely turned round and walked the other way. I ran to catch her up.

When I was close I called out Miss Kenney! Miss Kenney! And she turned round again. She folded her arms tight like a cross person in a comic and said Good morning Frankie. But she really meant You!

I said Good morning Miss Kenney. And then I said Miss Kenney?

She said What? (Only it was like WOT full stop.) And undid her arms and did them up the other way and said What is it this time? Your Dad?

I said No. He's in Ipswich.

She said Ah.

I said It's still MyMum. She's still dead.

Miss Kenney said Frankie that is still more unlikely than it was yesterday. Who is at your house?

I said MyMum.

She said There you are then.

I said But she's dead.

Miss Kenney undid her arms really quickly and looked at her watch then she lifted up the bell and rang it right by my ear. It was the loudest thing I've ever heard. She kept on ringing and not looking at me and looking all over the playground instead where all the kids were screaming and yelling and running to line up. Except me. I stayed beside her while she walked over to the steps but she didn't take any notice of me. She likes ignoring. Ignoring is probably her favourite thing. I thought she would talk to me when the lines started going in but she didn't. She said INFANTS! in a fat voice and when they started going in she said Get in line Frankie (in a normal voice). You should be in your line.

I knew what her plan was. Her plan was to pretend to be deaf when I started talking to her. But I know she's not.

I decided not to talk to her anymore anyway. At all.

Or anyone else.

Except Mrs Mahoney.

If someone said something to me I just looked at them. But I didn't look right in their eyeballs. I looked at the air in front of their eyeballs. If you do that you can pretend they're not there and then you can feel safe. If someone said something again I just used my head like no or yes or maybe (you do eyebrows for maybe). I thought it was going to be a bit difficult when we did Calendar and Mission and Spelling. And Arithmetic. (That comes after Mission.) But Miss Kenney didn't ask me a single thing. Not one. So that was all right. Douglas said Can I use your ruler so I just gave it to him and when Angela said I've sent three souls to Heaven since Monday I just looked at her. She looked happy. I wanted to say MyMum's in Heaven but I didn't in case she wasn't there yet because she always said she had no plans to go there and anyway I couldn't because I was the one doing not talking.

I just thought about it.

(I'm still thinking about it. I think MyMum was still there with me. On the boat. Do you think I am a mad person?)

I kept on just thinking about it in class. I had done all my spelling and all my sums so there was a lot of time for thinking.

When the bell rang for playtime I was the first one at the door. Everyone lined up behind me. Miss Kenney said Right. Outside quietly everyone. No running. Frankie you go back and put your ruler away.

So I was last.

When I got outside I saw Mrs Mahoney walking across the playground towards the big gates. She had her handbag on her arm. I ran over but I was too late because she was already outside in the road. I shouted out Mrs Mahoney! Mrs Mahoney! But she didn't hear me because there were two lorries and a bus coming. I ran outside even though you're not supposed to and shouted Mrs Mahoney! again and she turned round and then the first lorry was in the way and when it had gone she must have got on the bus. But the bus wasn't going anywhere because the bus driver was jumping out. He ran round the front of the bus and bended down and he must have run over a dog because I could see something like fur and someone else was bended down and I could hear some high up squealing and then tiny whimpers. I didn't want to see a run over thing so I didn't bend down. I just kept on running. That's when I decided what to do next. I did not want to go back to school. Ever. And I did not want to go home either. I thought MyDad is a grown-up. He will be all right.

Gordon Knight

Good God almighty. Mouth like an open drain. One has
to suppose it's one's own. Someone's riveted my head to
my neck. Hurts even to turn it. How am I going to do
this? One elbow. Wait for things to stabilize. Christ. I
have to stop doing this. Now the dog. All right, sit Alec.
You're going to have to be patient. I may be some time.

Gordon Knight is shocked to find he is still wearing his shoes.
Like all habitual drinkers, he indulges in a series of promises
to himself as he negotiates the flotsam of his room. He steps
on Alec's water dish. Damn. Never again. A good job he *does*
have his shoes on. He has no recollection of putting it near
the bed. None. This time he means it. Really means it. When
he has relieved himself and cleaned his teeth he finds a glass
and takes a long drink of water. It does not taste as good as he
had hoped.

   Alec next. He takes the dish to the bathroom, empties out
what's left and half fills it with fresh water, then he sets it down
in the corner, sending a pulse of blood, hard as a cricket ball,

through the back of his head. He puts his towel round his neck and washes his face, smoothes the water through his hair, and dries himself. For now the only kind thing is to take Alec—at the moment happily lapping—down to the dog park. Gordon combs his wet hair and smoothes it all over again just to make sure. He tucks in his shirt, puts a jacket on, and waits for Alec to finish before he attaches the handle and they set out along the corridor.

Hard to tell whether it's me or the boat. I've acquired a sailor's roll. Rhythmic, not unpleasant. Not unlike dancing. Just as well the lift isn't far, though.
Or maybe that was a mistake. Dropping six floors with a long glass of water inside me…Never mind let's get through this, Alec.
Don't know what I'd do without you. I had a mind earlier to leave you in the room—imagine! Take my leave, make a final exit. Lucky for you I can't resist the bottle. You'd be the ship's mascot by now. Perhaps you'd have enjoyed that. Your new friend would have. He's taken a shine to you.

Gordon and Alec, somewhat recovered, make their way back to the cabin. As soon as they leave the lift, Gordon can smell the disinfectant. He walks a little way and feels Alec's hesitation. A little further still and he stops. The cleaning cart is right outside his room. He doesn't want to know what there is to clean up. All he wants to do is take a shower with some of that carbolic soap and pretend the night didn't happen. Preferring not to come across anyone in his half-baked state, he turns and goes back to the dog park to wait.

Now his lack of action last night seems like a serious breach of faith, a betrayal of his friend—let's not be coy, his lover. He's made the promise to Harry more than once and never kept it. Like his promises to himself. Weak. He told himself it felt wrong to meet his end in England, so far from Harry, to be forever separated. But now that he's so close he can sense, if he's truly honest, that he's deceiving himself again. He doesn't have the chops.

Feeling weak, despising himself, does nothing to help him keep faith. Instead, it distances him still farther. He feels unworthy of the act he'd always believed to be noble, an act he would one day perform. And he is slipping so far from Harry in this state. He wants his memory back, his love back, unsoiled.

The cabin smells astringent and faintly toxic. Gordon Knight tends to Alec first. Fills his bowl with chow and—receiving a second cricket ball to the skull—bends down to place it on the floor. He returns to the bathroom for the shower he's been wanting. As he pulls the towel from the rail, something falls to the floor. He'll deal with it later. He's not bending down a third time.

He takes his shower, noting that, as good as it feels, every pain-sensitive nerve is now wide awake. Never mind. He finds some fresh clothes and generally restores himself to a credible replica of a man.

The task ahead of him feels right. Never mind that he doesn't have his portable typewriter with him. *It's* sitting square in the centre of his empty desk at home, a carefully folded note beneath it bearing the name and telephone number of his solicitor. But that's not the point. Not the point at all.

First, he makes a call to Room Service to order tea and some sandwiches to eat later. He doesn't want to be interrupted. He pulls up the chair to the dressing table and locates the blotter and the pen. When the steward arrives he has him set down the tray on the fold-out shelf beside the bed and asks him, before he leaves, to find two or three blank sheets of writing paper. He locks the door.

Ten minutes later, using the blunt tip of his key against the back of the bible, he has scored the paper deeply with the guidelines he will need. But he has not yet begun. It is not that he cannot form the letters. He has had many, many years of practice. It is that he cannot find the words.

He drinks his tea. Eventually he begins. Laying his left hand flat on the sheet, forefinger and thumb splayed, he forms each letter against the side of his knuckle, sliding his thumb steadily along the guideline as he writes.

Dearest Harry, my dear, dear Harry,

After all these years, how he wants him still. As if he hasn't wept enough. But it is all so shallow this second-best choice of a letter. It is an excuse, and a comical one. Dear Harry, I was going to join you but I decided on a letter instead. You won't mind, will you? Sorry if my letters fall over each other.

He gets up angrily, knocking into Alec as he pushes back his chair. He puts the tray outside and locks the door, then he returns to his bed. He lies facing the wall to comfort himself with memory and brutal touch.

When he wakes, he has no idea of the time.

His watch is on the dressing table. He opens it. It's almost eleven. The tea has dehydrated him even more. He goes to the bathroom to get himself another long drink of water. Poor Alec. *His* day is a write-off. And he must surely need the dog park again. His water dish is empty. Gordon refills it and sets it down. Remembering that something had fallen, he feels underneath the towel rail. There's something soft and faintly damp. He picks it up. For a second his fingers are at a loss. And then they read it. It's a sock but not his. Assuredly not his.

He takes it through to the bed and sits down, lays it flat in his palm. He registers its small size and his heart pounds. It's racing to keep pace with his brain processing the information lying in his hand and making its deductions. He tries to find an explanation for the presence of this item of clothing other than that the boy was in the room while he was comatose. It can't be that. It mustn't be. Good God. He remembers the storm now. The reason he had started drinking. How could he have forgotten it? And if he had forgotten that, what else was there? When did the boy come in? Did he let him in? His heart is racing now. He may be many things but not *that*.

He tells himself to calm down, take control. He can imagine other scenarios: that the boy gave it to him; that he picked it up himself because the boy had left it lying in the deckchair; that the boy had dropped it when he looked in (that day); that it fell from the chambermaid's pocket; that, like a retriever with a duckling, Alec had carried it in. He eliminates each in turn rapidly, too easily, and his heart thunders on. He steadies his breathing. Think. He holds the sock in two hands, stretches it a little—and catches a whiff of something horribly familiar.

Whatever washing the sock underwent was not enough to remove the stubborn, unmistakable taint of vomit. The boy was in his room while he, Gordon Knight, was in a drunken stupor. The question now is what is he to do about it? Indeed, there is more than one question. Whom to approach? What does he expect the outcome to be? What would he think, as a ship's officer, confronted with such a vague and unlikely report? More to the point, once they are advised, what will the parents think? Even as he is formulating the question, he feels the disjunction. It is like a magician's box. The top, the sides clack open one by one to reveal—nothing. There are no parents. The boy does not have a cabin on this ship. The boy—he knows it now with one hundred percent certainty—is all alone.

In light of this knowledge, the question of his own good name becomes irrelevant. The question now, the issue, is the child's safety. Go at once—it must surely be close to half past eleven, possibly even later—rouse everyone to action in the middle of the night? The boy is a strange one. *It was a fib...* *She was in her armchair...*He's suffered some mighty trauma. If he were provoked to run, to enter an inaccessible hiding place, put himself in danger? He has eluded detection so far. He's highly intelligent. Trust him to his own devices for an hour or so more?

He puts his jacket on and ties his shoes, decides he'll wear his anorak too. He has no idea what the weather's doing, except that it's no longer rough.

—Right, Alec. Work. He fastens the handle on his harness. Just before they go out, he goes back to the bed and picks up the sock and puts it in his jacket pocket.

Miss Kenney

I haven't slept for three nights now. I didn't know how on earth I was going to face school today. He was on the BBC Sunday afternoon. Well not him personally but an SOS on the wireless. "*And now for an urgent SOS. Will anyone with information concerning the whereabouts…*" They gave his name and address and everything like they do and they asked people to go to their local constabulary.

So that was it for the rest of the evening for me. They hadn't found him. I was awake half the night again going over it all. It got worse and worse. And it wasn't Mrs Walters I was worried about this time. I'd close my eyes and I'd see him face down somewhere. In a ditch. In the old canal tunnel. On the railway line. I started to feel a bit off. I must have been awake for about three hours. I felt rotten.

In the end I got up and made myself a warm Horlicks to settle my stomach. Terrible idea. I've always disliked the taste. But at least afterwards I fell asleep—for an hour. Fat lot of good. I didn't get away from him even then. When the alarm went off I was in the middle of a long argument with him about how long a bus would take to drive all the way round the world, if it could. He was sitting at my desk, in my chair. Mr Bladgeworth was listening and he had an inspector with him too. An HMI. I was so glad to wake up. Only then, of course, I remembered straight-away. I don't know how I managed to get myself ready for school, I was that worried. And not without good reason. When I got to the gates, they were all there. They all knew about it. I couldn't even get across the playground. *Miss! Miss! Tell us about Frankie!* I said, There's nothing to tell and the next person who asks me will stay in at playtime and write out their seven times table.

The staff room was another ordeal altogether. I knew they'd just been talking about me because there was a distinct silence when I went in and closed the door. You can tell can't you? Even if someone coughs it sounds put on. Mr Herbert said, Any news then, Miss Kenney? The whole room was quiet. No, I said, Not a thing.

I knew everyone was imagining the worst. But I couldn't help that. Except it made me feel so guilty. And what for? It was nothing to do with me, was it? But still.

I said, Poor little mite. I'm so worried about him.

Mr Herbert said, Let's just hope he didn't get in a car with someone. So then they were all talking at once.

I thought, Thank you very much Don.

When Mrs Wainwright said, Oops! Time to ring the bell, I felt so relieved. But it only lasted a couple of minutes. It all started up again inside the classroom.

Where's Frankie, Miss? Is he lost? Is he dead, Miss? Is he? Is he?

Yes, is he? I thought. I sincerely hope not. We shan't see the end of it, otherwise.

I told them their nonsense had really got to stop. No one had any news to tell, and in any case it was nothing to do with them. It was wrong to keep talking about it the way they were. Of course then Mr B. calls an assembly and we all troop in. The noise in there was like a nature film I saw on the BBC. Gannets or something on a cliff. All talking at once. The volume was tremendous even though it was all whispers. It stopped just like that when Mr Bladgeworth came in, though. He only has to stand there. I thought, That's real control, that is.

Boys and girls, he said, I have some good news. Well! There was uproar. *They found him! He's alive!* And all sorts of other nonsense. Someone even shouted, *He's dead!* Mr B. was red in the face. But he just he stood there. That's his tactic. He waits until you can hear a pin drop. Mrs Mahoney, he said, is still in the hospital following her accident but I'm happy to say she's making good progress and she is expected to go home by the end of the week. You could still hear a pin drop. Miss Coleridge's class is preparing a giant get-well card and it will be coming to your classroom some time during the day for you to write your names on it. There was still silence so he said, Let's all thank Miss Coleridge, and everyone started to clap. Except me. I didn't know where to turn. I rummaged in my handbag and found a hanky and then—I hate to say this—I did a couple of fake sneezes to sort of cover the fact that I was bawling my eyes out, I don't know why. I think my emotions were all mixed up. When the clapping had stopped, he carried on. And now, he said, we'll say an Our Father and a Hail Mary for our little friend Francis Walters. Somebody said—in quite a loud voice—So he *is* dead?—and they all turned round. Mr B. said, That person with no manners will come to see me after assembly.

Our Father, Who art in Heaven—

And we all joined in.

We didn't really know what we were praying for. That he'd be found? That they'd find him alive? That his soul would go to heaven if he wasn't? That he was already there?

It seemed like a long day. It'll be even longer tomorrow. We have to stay for a staff meeting after school. Mr Herbert told me Mr B. is thinking of giving me Junior Ones next year. Guess who'll be in my class if they find him?

I don't suppose I'll get much sleep tonight either. It's the not knowing, isn't it.

Chapter 10

MONDAY PM
(because it's night-time)

It did work. I went to sleep. When I woke up I had to hold my breath. I could hear sniffing. Something was sniffing me! You can hold your breath but you cannot hold the smell of you. I could hear that tiny tiny whimper like under the bus after the high up squealing. I thought What if it's a ghost that came just because I thought about it? A ghost of the run-over dog. I didn't want to see it. I kept my eyes closed. I know ghosts are not real but I was still worried. You can't hold your breath forever. It will make you die in two minutes. In one minute and fifty-nine seconds. One minute and fifty-eight seconds. One minute and fifty-seven seconds. One minute and fifty-six seconds. One minute and fifty-five. One minute and fifty-four. One minute and fifty-three. It went away.

I said Phew in my head. I could do breathing. I thought I heard footsteps but then it was quiet. I could hear the sea hissing and plopping. Like a nanimal. Like a night-time animal licking the sides of the boat.

I tried moving ever so carefully so I could squeeze over just a bit and look through a little tiny gap.

Everything was white and black. It must have been midnight. I could see the painted white lines like for tennis and all the white painted railings underneath the long wood one. Everything was really bright with the electric light shining on it and the sky was really dark black. I could see white out on the black sea too. Little white worms. They kept appearing and then vanishing. Magic worms.

But I couldn't see the scary thing that was sniffing me. I was probably looking out the wrong side of the mattress. There was no room to turn round. Or maybe there was nothing there and it really was a dead dog ghost. *Don't be silly Frankie. You know better than that.*

A dog! I thought. A dog is the only thing that does sniffing like that and Alec was the only dog on the boat. *And* he always did that tiny squeaking. So who was with him? Where was the blind man? Still in his room? In the sea? Not here. Please I said in my head Don't let him be here.

—Who's there, please? Somebody's there. Who is it, please?

He was! He was right there somewhere beside me. Talking to me! Not dead I thought. Please don't let him be dead because if he is—

I heard my Mum's voice then. It said *Frankie? There is no such thing as ghosts. There is no such thing as ghosts. There is no such thing as—*

I was more quiet than a mouse—a dead mouse haha— but Alec's squeaking just got noisier and noisier.

— *189* —

—Who's there, please?

I didn't answer and I didn't move and he couldn't see anyway so I was really safe. Really really safe. But it didn't make any difference. I was shaking like when the sailor got hold of me.

I heard him do some footsteps going away. And then he stopped.

Very *very* carefully I squeezed round—without making any noise—and looked out the other side.

I could see him! And I could see Alec. He was real and not a ghost nor was the blind man. Of *course* they were not. They were real and they were both over by the rail and they were both listening. I could see they were. We all were. Alec had turned his head to look at me and his ears were up. The blind man doesn't have ears that go up but I knew he was listening because he couldn't be doing looking like I do when I stand there. I could hear Alec doing that tiny tiny sound again.

And then all of a sudden they were coming back. Right this way! The blind man had his hand out. And then I couldn't see him anymore. He was right there just on the other side of the pile.

—It's all right Frankie. You can come out. I won't tell.

What? I thought. He knows I'm here? And how does he know it's me?

He let Alec push his nose right in.

—I have your sock he said. It's washed.

—Thank you.

—Won't you come out and put it on?

—No. You can push it through the hole where Alec is.

And he did it!

—It's not quite dry. I'm sorry.

I said I don't mind. I'll put it in my pocket.

—Night-night then.

—Where are you going?

—I'm just going over there to sit on the sunlounger.

—It's night-time!

—I can't sleep in my room.

—Because it smells bad?

—Well perhaps yes. But it's mostly because I'm worried about you out here all by yourself.

He bended down now. He was really very close.

—I'm all right thank you.

—I know you are. I'm just wondering about a few things.

—Like me! I do wondering all the time. I was wondering if they had buried you at sea—

—You can come out you know and talk about it.

—No, it's all right thank you. I'll stay here. I don't have to wonder anymore about if they have and will they throw Alec in too.

He did not say anything.

I waited. Then he did.

—I've been wondering for instance why you are all alone and how you got onto the boat.

(He knows I did lying!)

—How do you know I'm all alone?

—I suppose I'm quite clever too like you and Alec.

—You know I'm clever?

—You told me. And you'd have to be smart to get on without anybody noticing.

—It was easy but don't tell anyone. I just walked on with all the other people and everyone was talking and doing kissing and stuff—

—Frankie?

—What?

—I really need to sit down. If you want to tell me the rest you will have to come and sit beside me.

—Can we do that? Sit on the sunloungers when it's night-time?

—Yes. There are some other people doing it.

—Frankie?

—Ssh. I don't want the other people to know.

—It's all right. They're on the other side and they're asleep anyway.

—All right.

Alec went crazy when I got out. He widdled a bit. I love Alec.

—I think he's pleased to see you.

—Hahaha.

—What?

—You look funny with your sunglasses on at night.

—I expect you look funny without your socks.

I helped the blind man pull a mattress out and put it on a sunlounger and then we got another one so we could have one each. It was freezing. He let me hold onto Alec. He said it's very important not to let him go. We lay down on the sunloungers. But not Alec. Of course.

I told him a lot of things because I hadn't talked for a long time. I probably told him about twenty-seven. More things than I tell MyMumandDad. They always have not enough time for all the things. I even told him my plan to get off the boat in New York. I put him in my plan. I said I will get off with you and I can help you—like a dog—see where you're going and you can help me phone MyDad. I'll dial the number for you.

He said Thank you Frankie. I'm actually an expert at dialling. But I won't be getting off.

I said You won't? But that was stupid because he had already said he wouldn't.

Then I had a bright idea. I told him I would come and stay in his cabin then and we could go back together. Alec would like that.

I said When two people sleep in a bed and they're not married they sleep one at the top and one at the bottom. That's how they put sardines in a tin.

He said I don't think so.

I said Oh that's just because you've never seen them. I forgot you can't see.

He said No. I mean I don't think it will work for us.

I said Why not?

He said People will think it's questionable. We're not in the same family.

I said MyMum said it doesn't matter what people think. He just went Oh Frankie! Like this—Oh Frankie!

I said You sound like MyDad.

Then these are all the things we said next without the saids. (I told you they make me tired.)

—Are you missing him? (I'll start you off. That's the blind man.) He'll be missing you so badly.

—I don't know what you mean. (Me. Now you can do the rest yourself.)

—Yes you do. It's like being lonely.

—I'm always lonely. I like it.

—But your dad might not. It's nice being with people you love.

—Unless they're dead. Can I sit on your sunlounger?

—If you like. Just keep hold of Alec remember?

—I don't forget anything. That's why my head is so full up. Miss Kenney said my head is full of nonsense but it's not true.

—I'm sure it isn't.

—It's full of important things like the capitals of all the countries and The Rime of the Ancient Mariner.

—Oh yes?

—Yes. Do you want to hear it?

—No thank you. Not right now. Can you see if this is one of the crew coming?

—It is. How did you know?

—An inspired guess.

—Will he tell us to go to bed?

—I don't think so. Excuse me?

—Yes sir?

—Could we have some blankets please?

—Certainly sir. Oh Mr Knight sir. Just give me a couple of minutes.

—How long are we going to stay here?

—I think we'll stay until we make you a new plan.

—What's wrong with my old one?

—I don't think you've worked out the details. There could be all sorts of difficulties too that we need to think about. You don't have a ticket or a passport.

—I could hide all the way back. People see me all the time. They don't care.

—Here you are sir. (That was the sailor with the blankets. I expect you guessed if you were paying attention.)

—Thank you very much.

—Shall I—?

—No thank you. We can manage. Thank you very much.

—See what I mean?

—I do. Here. You have this one. There keep it double.

—Thank you.

—That's better isn't it?

—Yes.

—Cozy?

—Yes thank you. What do you mean details?

—All sorts of things.

—Like where's the phone in New York?

—That kind of thing yes.

—And I don't have any money?

—Yes.

—I will find a kind old granny to help me and she will ring MyDad and he will come and get me.

—Not bad but a plane ticket costs a lot of money and your father might not have enough and then you would be stuck.

—Oh.

—You know what Frankie? I think you need to let me help you. Will you do that? If I think of a good plan?

—I might.

—Then let me do some thinking.

—I love doing thinking.

—Well then do some right now and we'll both be quiet.

We were quiet for a very long time. My eyes were closing and then opening again. Even though I was very tired but they kept on opening. Doing sleeping outside is very pretty. If you do staring straight up into the sky it is enormous. It is very dark black-blue but if you keep looking and looking in the same place you can see more and more stars as if they are peeping out. Like chicks. Peep! They are all different sizes and some of them go on and off. You can even see some that are different colours. I used to think stars were all yellow but it's not true. They're not even all white. Only some of them. Sometimes you think you know everything and then you look and you find a new thing. Like I thought the Milky Way was in Cornwall. It is like a river in the sky. MyDad showed it to me when we went to Mullion's Cove to go camping but guess what? I could see it on the boat even though we were nearly in America. Isn't that amazing? It is like being inside a magic trick.

I looked for a long time. It was like being on a ride at the fair but with no frights. I could feel the boat underneath the sunlounger kind of tipping just a bit just a bit and just a bit more then ever so gently tipping just a bit just a bit and just bit more back the other way. Like on a really slow swing. There was a lot of time for counting.

When I was at seven thousand three hundred and forty-two the blind man interrupted me. He said Frankie? in a really tiny whisper.

I said What? all tiny back and he laughed.

He said I was just wondering if you were awake.

I said Yes.

He said Are you lying on your back?

I said Yes.

He said With your eyes open?

I said Except when I blink.

He said Tell me what you can see.

I said I can see the chimney if I tip my head back.

He said The funnel.

(I knew that. I just forgot for a minute.)

I said It's huge and I can see a white thing. It has sort of sticks underneath and it's curved round like a piece of tangerine sideways. But it's not juicy haha.

He said Where is it?

I said Just beside the funnel.

—That will probably be the radar. It sends pictures to the bridge so they can see if there's anything in the way.

—I know.

—I thought you might.

—Tell me what else you can see.

—I'm asleep now.

—Night-night, then.

—Now I'm awake.

—Oh Frankie. You really cheer me up.

—Usually I make people really mad. Do you want me to tell you what else I can see?

—Yes please.

It's all stars. Millions and millions of them. I've been counting but I haven't got to the end yet. I haven't even got out of the middle. It's like counting sand. That's what they look like. Sparkly sand on a black beach. I'm a radar. I'm sending you a picture.

—Thank you.

—Could you see when you were a little boy?

—A bit.

—So you know what stars look like?

—Yes but I like to hear about them.

—Well you know it's all black right? Well then it's like some-one threw glitter on it millions and millions of glitter bits and they all stuck so now it's like tiny tiny lights and some are sort of right on the ceiling and some are higher up sort of past the ceiling.

—I can see it.

—You can?

—In my mind's eye.

—You have another one?

—Everyone does.

—Really? (It was just like the dream I had about my third ear.)

—Close your eyes. What can you see?

—I can see all white with hundreds and millions of black dots and a black radar.

—Wait a little bit. Keep your eyes closed.

—I'm waiting.

—A little bit longer.

—All right.

—Now think about something wonderful.

—Like what?

—Something you really like.

—All right.

— Now keep your eyes closed. Can you see something?

—Yes.

—What is it?

—Baked beans. A can.

—And your eyes are still closed?

—Of course. They're in the kitchen anyway.

—Ssh.

—All right.

—Try it again. Think of something really wonderful. Something you like.

—All right.

—What can you see?

—My two mice.

Tell me about them.

—One was white and one was black and white and they lived in a wooden cage with a wire door.

—So you were seeing all that with your mind's eye.

—I was just remembering. When I opened the door they both rolled out. It was my fault. They had frozen up like iceballs because I had forgotten to bring their cage inside and it was winter. No one told me it was going to be winter.

—Oh dear. Try something else. Imagine something you've never seen before.

—MyDad dead. Lying down.

—That's something wonderful?

—Oh. No. Can I do it again?

—I think you'd better.

—All right. You. My mind's eye can see you. You're in a sack and they're throwing you over the side because you're dead but actually it's wonderful because then they give me Alec.

—I see.

—Hahaha. I love that joke. Now it's your turn. Do you want me to tell you what to see?

—No thank you. I'll pick.

—I can see a thin silver waterfall plunging down a green-gray cliff and inside the waterfall are hundreds of tiny blue fish.

—Were you remembering?

—I was imagining.

—Like you've never seen those things?

—No.

—Like you have then?

—No. I've never seen them.

—You mean Yes. You've never seen them.

—Frankie I thought you were sleepy.

—You mean Go to sleep.

—Yes. I do.

—All right.

I didn't go to sleep. I wanted to ask him another question but I thought it would make him mad. That would be scary. A blind man mad.

I stayed quiet. And still stayed quiet. And then I gave up.

—What's your name?

He didn't answer. I thought he must have gone to sleep.

—What's your name? I whispered so I didn't annoy him.

—Gordon Knight.

—Like night-time?

—No. With a K.

—Oh. So I can't say Night-night Mr Night?

—You just did. You know Frankie we're going to have to find some other company in the morning or you and I will be utterly indistinguishable.

—Like when you can't put out a fire?

—No, that's—Oh just please—please—for mercy's sake Frankie just please—please—please go to sleep.

I wanted to tell him he sounded exactly like MyDad. But I decided not to.

—Can I keep holding Alec?

—Yes you may. Just hold the loop right on the end of the lead. Then he can lie down.

—He's already lying down.

—I know. Night-night.

(I still think he can see.)

—Night night Mr Knight.

I did a lot of thinking about going camping with MyDad and cooking baked beans on the fire. I was cold. When I opened my eyes Gordon Knight was sitting up on the edge of his sun-lounger. He had his blanket wrapped round his shoulders like an old lady and he was smoking a cigarette. I don't think he knew I was awake.

I could see the sea past his shoulder. I could see it through the wires underneath the rail. There were no more white worms. It was just black with a huge white road on it. Mysterious. I closed my eyes again and turned over. And just opened them a bit to check. I couldn't see the white road anymore but I saw something else white in the distance. I thought it was a ship. And then I knew. It was the iceberg! It wasn't very big but if it was coming after us it would get huge. I could hardly breathe. I needed to do screaming.

—Frankie? Are you all right? Frankie?

The blind man put his hand on my shoulder. I had to do tiny tiny screaming so he wouldn't hear. I could hardly hear myself. Alec was doing it too.

He said Frankie you need to let go of Alec for a minute. He's getting strangled. Can you sit up please so we can get him untangled?

I couldn't keep the screaming tiny for much longer. I thought Alec would die too.

Gordon Knight kept saying Ssh, please Ssh. It's better for you if we just stay quiet.

—I can't.

—Please shush now.

—I'll shush if I can come over on your sunlounger. (I had already stopped but my voice was saying P-p-p for please.)

—Then come on. What are you doing?

—Nothing. (I said N-n-n-n-nothing too. I was treading on Alec.)

—Can you see?

—Hahaha. No. But I've got my eyes closed. Can you? Hahahaha.

Gordon Knight didn't laugh. He said Ouch!

—Sorry!

—Could you open your eyes, please?

I said I don't want to see it again until I'm beside you.

He said Here. Now put your feet under the blanket. This is ridiculous. There.

I said Thank you.

—Everything all right sir? (That's the sailor again.)

—Yes thank you. (That's Mr Knight)

—Shall I bring an extra blanket?

—Yes please. If you wouldn't mind.

—Not at all sir.

—Now what is it you don't want to see?

—The iceberg.

—Ah.

—Mr Knight?

—I'm thinking.

—What?

—I'm thinking you might never get the chance to see another iceberg. You might as well enjoy the sight while you can. Frankie?

—I'm enjoying the sight.

—With your eyes open?

—Of course. I'm doing enjoying.

He's tucking the blanket round me tight. It doesn't feel so dangerous now.

—Thank you. Do you want to know what it looks like?

—Let me guess. It looks very *very* quiet and serene.

—What's—?

—Peaceful. It's like a brilliant white chunk of icing on a flat plate.

—You *have* been faking. Hahaha.

—I beg your pardon?

—You *have* been doing fake blind haven't you?

—No.

I said Well you were right. It looks just like that.

I told him MyMum made me an iceberg last Christmas when it was snowing outside in the garden. She was mixing icing for the cake with egg whites and icing sugar and it was all shiny. She had some left over.

Gordon Knight said Brilliant white, I bet. The whitest thing you'd ever seen.

I said How do you know?

He said I had a Mum too. You can keep good things a long time in the mind's eye.

He said The garden looked perfect. Like a magic land. I've never forgotten it.

I didn't answer him. I pretended I was asleep.

I was thinking about my problems. Here they are.

1. If the iceberg started coming our way I would have to do loud screaming and everyone would get in the lifeboats except me and I would drown because I can only do twelve strokes. (So it was quite a big problem. About as big as a niceberg. Joke.)
2. I didn't know what Gordon Knight was going to do with me. I was nearly sure he was going to take me to the Captain in the morning. So I ought to run away—while he was not looking (haha). But if I ran away from him he would still tell the Captain and then everybody would be looking for me. They would be on the alert. Like for a nescaped convict.
3. I didn't know what to do. At all! I mean it. And that was worse than the iceberg.

If I turned my head just a tiny tiny bit I could see Gordon Knight. He was still sitting up. I knew he would hear me if I moved. And Alec would make the tiny noise again. I was stuck. But at least I was cozy.

I was nearly asleep when Gordon Knight started getting up. Ever so ever so quietly. He thought I *was* asleep. I could tell. I only kept a tiny little slit in my eyelids to look out through and I didn't move. (Actually it didn't matter even if I did open my eyes. But I didn't think it was a good idea.)

Then he started walking. By himself! Without Alec! My eyes were open now. They were wide open because I was someone having a big surprise. He was walking straight out very slowly from the end of the sunlounger towards the rail-doing one step then another step. He had his hands out doing criss-cross like the magician at the fete who did abracadabra over a hat on a table.

When he got to the rail he felt along it and then he just stayed there. Once he leaned over like someone who could see and was having a look to see how far down the boat went. I could have run away easily but I was holding onto Alec. After a little while he took something out of his pocket. It was white. I thought it was a handkerchief because he put it on his mouth. But it wasn't. It was paper because guess what. He tore it up! He tore it about seven times and then he just threw it away! Doing littering! It looked like white butterflies flying. Like the white birds but not so many.

When he got bored with standing there he took a great big handkerchief out of his pocket and blew his nose and wiped his eyes under his glasses. It made Alec wake up and sit up. He was watching him too and doing the funny noise. He wanted Gordon Knight to come back but he didn't. He just stayed standing there. Just standing and not doing anything. Except eyewiping.

Chapter 11   (SAME)

MyMum did standing still like that last year when she got a telegram about my Uncle Jack. He was my uncle because he was MyDad's brother. He was MyMum's favourite person. Except me. And maybe MyDad. When he came over they always did loud laughing. Once he got some baby spit from Aunty Julie's baby on his hand and put it behind his ears like a lady doing perfume. He used to make MyMum laugh so much sometimes it made her cry. It made them both cry. Real tears. That's when MyDad would say So are we having tea or shall I wait till Christmas? He didn't get their jokes. Neither did I. Once he said I'm going down the pub and they stopped like they were a wireless and someone had switched them off.

Uncle Jack was in the war. He got shot in the head but he was all right when everybody stopped fighting except he had a bullet in his brain. The doctors in the war were too busy to get it out so they decided to leave it there. Kevin at school said I was a liar when I told him. He said it was impossible but

Kevin wasn't in the war so how did he know? MyMum said Kevin knows Dick but don't repeat that. She said Anything's possible and your Uncle Jack's a medical bloody miracle. MyDad said Patti! like he always did when MyMum said B-L-O-O-D-Y.

Anyway one day she opened a telegram. It was from MyGran. It said

JACK IN GUY'S STOP COME AT ONCE STOP.

I know because I was in the kitchen where she opened it and it fell down. She just dropped it and didn't do anything. I was five so I could read it easily. I read it out loud but it didn't make any sense and MyMum didn't say anything about it not even Well done! or Good boy! She just did standing and staring. I went round the front of her and she wasn't blinking or anything. I got scared then because she was like King Midas's daughter in my book—except not gold—so I went down the garden and went in the shed. I'm not really allowed. After a little while I came out. I could see through the back door that she was still standing there so I went to the door and shouted MUM! like that. Really loud. She did a big jump (but her feet were still on the ground) and said Oh God! Then she said Oh God oh God oh God oh God oh God oh God. Help me Frankie I have to go. You have to come with me. You can't go to Gran's and she ran upstairs to the toilet and ran down again. She got our coats and her handbag and then she ran upstairs again to find some money to put in it. She was saying Come on and Oh God oh God oh God. She doesn't even believe in God so I don't know what she was talking about.

We ran all the way down to the bus stop on the Barnham road and there was one coming so that was lucky. And we got seats. MyMum couldn't find her purse. She kept saying Sorry I'm sorry. Sorry. The bus conductor said take your time love. No rush. Then she found it. The bus conductor said You look after these now and gave me the tickets. I said Thank you. It was the first thing I had said since I said Mum. I was too scared to talk. When he had gone MyMum said No! I haven't got my watch. But nobody heard except me because she was sort of saying it to the inside of her handbag. Then she patted my knee and said We can only do our best. Dear God. She sounded like she had been running a race.

The bus conductor said Central Station and we got off. I told MyMum it took four minutes and seventeen seconds and she said That's nice look for Waterloo. She was looking at the blackboard. I said Is that where we're going? And she said Just look for it for God's sake. I'm good at looking so I found it first. I said There it is and MyMum said Platform three RUN! like someone was coming after us. And then she said NO! we don't have our tickets! so we ran back the way we had just come and bought one and a half tickets. The man said Platform three but you'll have to wait for the next one only she didn't hear the last bit because she was already running. She turned back and grabbed my hand. She held it up high so my feet were sort of dangling on my legs. I nearly fell lots of times and then a big black man sort of scooped me up and ran along with me beside her. You could hear the engine of the train really loud. The man put me down because we had to stop to get our tickets punched before we could go through. My Mum said Thank you Thank you Thank you. The man said Slow down. It won't leave without you.

We went in the first door that was open. A man got up to shut it and said This carriage is First Class and MyMum said Rhymes with arse. I'd get a smack for that. Then we went walking along between the seats and opened a door at the end where you could go through to the next carriage. The next carriage was just the same so we had to walk again and go through to the next one. I stopped half way with one foot on one bit and one foot on the other and Mum said Frankie! but she meant hurry up. After a whole lot of walking we found a seat to sit in. MyMum let me have the one with the window so I was really happy.

MyMum wasn't. She put her hands over her face like pretending to hide from a baby and then she got a hanky out (so that's two things like Gordon Knight.) I said are you sad?

She said A bit.

I said I'll cheer you up. Do you want to hear a story?

She said Can I close my eyes?

I said All right. I told her the one about the three billy goats gruff but when I got to the third billy goat she put her hands over her eyes again so I stopped. She didn't say Carry on or And? or anything so I didn't. I don't think she was really listening.

After that we didn't say anything. Not one word. MyMum did staring and I did kicking the seat with my heels.

At Basingstoke a man got in and sat next to me and crossed his legs. He went out again nearly straightaway to find another seat.

MyMum smiled. She said Good boy. It was a bit late to say that but I smiled anyway.

We stopped loads of times after Basingstoke—actually eleven. MyMum said it was a slow train. We waited in the corridor for Waterloo (which is a really funny name but I didn't think MyMum was in the mood to hear a joke so I didn't bother). When you stand in the corridor it is quite interesting because you are going to Waterloo sideways. We got there really quickly even though our train was slow.

We went through another gate and when we were on the other side we stood still. Like we were Hansel and Gretel in the wood. MyMum turned back to ask the man collecting tickets which way to Guy's Hospital. I didn't even know we were going to a hospital. I stood really still like my feet were nailed down. I was trying to stop the screaming that was starting to come up my neck.

I can't tell you what happened next because everything was too loud and too many people were holding me and moving me about. And then I saw MyMum's face right up close looking at me. We were on the ground by a lamppost in the middle of the floor and she was holding me tight and she was the one doing rocking not me. She was sort of doing it for me. Then she said Please. Can we go now? We're not actually Going To Hospital. We're only going to visit Uncle Jack.

My throat hurt so I just did a nod. I saw some money on the ground by MyMum's handbag when I got up and I wanted it. MyMum said Leave it.

We were still inside the station so we went outside and MyMum asked the way to Guy's again. She asked a lady and a man this time. They told her. Actually they told her three times but I already remembered it the first time. Then the lady looked at me and said Your little legs are going to be tired.

I said No they're not.

And she said Hmmpf.

The hospital was even bigger than the one I have to go to find out why I am not normal but it had the same smell. I held my nose.

MyMum told me not to so I did hardly-breathing instead.

We asked people where to go and we did reading on the walls and a lot of walking. We went in the lift and came down again and then went up again. When we got out MyMum said hold on a bit I'm not quite ready and she did a lot of looking in her handbag. She wiped her nose on her sleeve so I gave her my hanky.

She said Would you like to go up again to the very top?

I said Yes please so she said All right. Let's do that. We went back in and went up all the way to seventeen and then down again to seven and MyMum said Right. I'm ready now.

There was a big desk and then a long corridor painted green and a shiny floor and four nurses with hats. One of them looked at us and said Visiting is over. Sorry. And another one came over and said I'm sorry. Children aren't allowed on this floor. MyMum said But I can't leave him all alone and the second one said I'm sorry again.

MyMum said I have to see Jack Walters. The first one said Visiting hours are—but the second one put her hand on her arm so she stopped before the end. The second one said Your little boy can stay with me.

That's when I ran because I saw MyGran. She had come out of a room when no one was looking and she was walking down towards the other end of the corridor blowing her nose.

MyMum shouted stop but I didn't. Only Gran did.

She said Oh Frankie. Go back to Mum.

I held onto her legs and pretended I didn't hear.

She said What's she doing bringing you here?

I said We've come to see Uncle Jack.

She said Go back.

The second nurse came and got hold of me and said Let go or your Gran will fall down so I did even though I knew it was a kind of trick.

The second nurse took me back the way I had come and went behind the desk and said We'll wait right here. You go ahead Mrs Um and MyMum went ahead. She didn't say anything to me. The second nurse said Your mum will come back and get you.

MyMum walked down the corridor and put her arms round MyGran and after they had done hugging for a long time she went in the room. I was terrified but I tried not to let anyone see. Then the nurse said She'll come out in two shakes and I didn't know what she was talking about. I had a picture of MyMum coming out of the room all wobbly like a bad old woman so I fell down and did loud laughing and kicking. When I had finished MyMum was looking down at me. She said We're going home now but it was like she was talking to the floor. MyGran was there too. She was buttoning up her coat. She said Get up. I think she was really mad. The first nurse gave MyMum some biscuits wrapped in a thing like a tea towel and said You can give him these. MyMum didn't even say Thank you. She didn't talk to me at all—not when MyGran said take him down in the lift and not when we were downstairs waiting. I said I didn't say Goodbye to Uncle Jack but she didn't take any notice. She still didn't say anything when MyGran came. MyGran said We'll get the bus to the station. It's quicker. I said What if my legs are tired? No one answered me. They were really grumpy.

Gran did all the talking. She kept saying There was no warning none at all. And It's the doctors it's the doctors they should have known they should have. She was sitting beside MyMum on the train and MyMum was holding her hand. I was glad she wasn't holding mine because she looked cross. MyGran started telling when Uncle Jack fell down so I put my fingers in my ears and did loud singing. I stopped when her mouth stopped moving and carried on when it started again.

After I had sung all the songs I know MyMum got up and took my fingers out of my ears. She whispered Gran wants you to stop. I whispered I want Gran to stop. Gran said It's all right Frankie. I've stopped. I'm all done in. Let's all try and have a little nap.

They tried but I didn't. I just watched everything going by backwards. And then it was dark and I could only see myself. I watched myself blinking and then I closed my eyes.

When we got home MyDad was there. He was shouting a bit saying I was worried sick. MyMum said Poor you but she didn't really mean it. Straightaway after she said Oh sorry sorry sorry I'm so sorry. She said Mum (that's what she calls MyGran) is staying here tonight and MyDad said What's happened? I ran upstairs before they could start telling. Especially the bit about me. I did all the things I'm supposed to do all in the right order and got into bed but nobody noticed.

The next day was school. MyMum wrote me a note to tell about going to Waterloo and she gave me some dinner money. When I went home at the end there was no one there. I sat on the step at the back and waited. Denby knew I was there because he barked all the time. It was a good job we have a brick wall between our houses. I waited a long time but I didn't mind (except for Denby) because when MyMum comes back from the shops she has sweets. Except she didn't this time. She made me some baked beans to make up for it and then we went to the park.

When we got back she let me have baked beans for dinner too. She didn't have any. She didn't have anything. I said Is Dad having baked beans? And she said your Dad and Gran went to Waterloo. I said to see Uncle Jack? She said Yes. They didn't come back until after I was asleep.

In the morning My Dad was at work. My Gran was still asleep in the spare room. MyMum looked like Christmas morning when we all stay in our pajamas.

I said Uncle Jack's dead isn't he? I said Did the hospital kill him? You said it nearly killed me.

She stared at me for a whole long time then she said He's getting buried on Friday.

I said can I come? I really want to see the hole.

She got up from the table and went to the sideboard and opened the door and slammed it shut again. She said I have to go out.

I said To Waterloo?

When Friday came I didn't see the hole. I had to go to school instead.

Afterwards MyMum was always doing sleeping or drinking sherry or going somewhere to be private. Sometimes she didn't get up at all and MyDad was worried. He said I am I'm worried sick about you Patti. I'm the one who's lost someone. They did lots of arguing in the bedroom. I don't know what they argued about but MyDad was always telling MyMum to drop it for God's sake. One day he said You'll drive yourself mad. He said You can't bring him back. I didn't know what he was talking about because I was already there.

One day I asked MyDad if MyMum had driven herself mad yet. He didn't answer me. He just said Frankie Frankie Frankie. Then he went and had a great big row with her in the bedroom. It was so loud I went in the shed again.

Now I've told you lots of things I didn't mean to. I was only going to tell you how Gordon Knight made me remember MyMum because he had his hands over his face like she did. But you know what? You know I said I remember everything? It's not true. I have only just remembered going to Waterloo so that means I had forgotten it. Right? And here's another thing. One day MyDad did lots of shouting and got her hand-bag and opened it and tipped everything (EVERYTHING!) into the toilet. MyMum was crying and kneeling down and even putting her hands in to get everything out. And MyDad said Patti look at yourself! But no one can look at themselves unless they have a mirror and MyMum was kneeling down so I said That's stupid! She can't.

They stopped shouting at each other when they heard me. I said Anyway she's mad now. MyMum wanted to wipe her eyes but her hands had been in the toilet so she couldn't. She didn't even want my hanky.

She got up said I'll just wash my hands. And she sounded completely normal. But I didn't tell her that.

Now I feel bad in case you think MyMum was like the man up the road who shouts ALL'S WELL THAT ENDS WELL! She wasn't. She was completely nearly normal the next day and the next day and the next day and all the other days. Sort of. She still did shouting sometimes when she got angry-mad like with Miss Kenney when she said I couldn't do division yet because it would make me confused or like with Father Morgan when he said for us to tell our Mums and Dads they have to give a shilling week to Mission because God doesn't let little black babies into heaven if they haven't been baptized. She still did swearing too like B-L-O-O-D-Y and B-U-G-G-E-R. But most of the time she was just like a real Mum. She made me nice things to eat and cups of tea and she gave me butter balls when I had a cough. I liked her better than anyone else's Mum except when she got sloppy and wanted to do cuddling too long. It's a waste of time when you could be reading. (MyDad wouldn't have minded. But he was always in Ipswich.)

You know what? He did have tears Gordon Knight did when he came back from the rail and his nose was red too. He had been there a whole long time and he came back very carefully. His sunlounger creaked when he got on it.

I said Why didn't you take Alec?

He said You're awake.

I said Yes. Why didn't you take Alec? Were you going to jump in the sea?

He said Oh my goodness. Then he said Why ever would I do a thing like that?

(Do you want to do the saids yourself? The next one is me.)

—I don't know. That's why I want you to tell me.

—It wasn't a real question Frankie. It was a manner of speaking.

—MyMum said (I said that) sometimes people are so unhappy they'd rather be dead.

—What made her say that?

—Me. I was reading the Manchester Guardian. Why are you laughing?

—I'm sorry. It just sounded funny. Go on.

—It wasn't funny. It was all about a lady who put stones in her pockets and then sewed them up and walked into the middle of a deep river to get drowned.

—That's a sad story.

—I told you it wasn't funny. Is that what you were thinking about when you were doing standing?

—What?

—Getting drowned?

—No. Absolutely not. I was thinking I'm glad the six-year-old boy I used to be is still alive.

—What do you mean?

—Inside me.

—Hahahahahaha. Like a mum expecting a baby.

—It's a manner of speaking.

—Like pretend?

—Sort of.

—Well MyMum is inside me.

—Is that right?

—Yes. Only she's not pretend. She's real. Because my head's real. You're not saying anything. Do you believe me?

—Of course.

—People are always not believing me.

—They'll learn. You're going to have a lot to teach people.

—I'm not going to be a teacher. I'm going to be someone who helps people nobody listens to. Who was your first dead person?

—Weren't we supposed to be thinking of things we really like?

—I like MyMum and she was my first dead person. Except for Uncle Jack but they wouldn't let me see him. And Grandad but he was inside his coffin with the lid on so he didn't count and Uncle George but I didn't want to see him and my sister but she wasn't a person yet.

—I see.

—Hahahaha. You're funny.

—Thank you.

—So who was it?

—You've been thinking a long time now. (It's me again. I was being very patient.) Are you going to tell me?

—It was a friend. He was very beautiful.

—Beautiful! Hahahaha. A man! And a dead one. Hahahaha. And you can't see anyway.

—Ssh. You don't have to see to know if somebody is beautiful.

—But he was a man.

—Anyone can be beautiful. *Any*thing can be if you love it enough.

—I want to hear about your dead person.

—He was very kind and very funny. He used to make me laugh every day.

—But I want you to tell me about him dead.

—Why?

—Because I keep thinking about MyMum.

—All I know Frankie is that his hands were very cold.

—Same!

—It was like touching the statue of a person.

—You couldn't see him though?

—No I couldn't see him. But I touched his face. It was almost as if it were someone else pretending to be him.

—Like a nimposter?

—Yes. Exactly. Like a nimposter. You know what? It's much much better if I remember him alive. It's as if I can still talk to him.

—And he can talk to you.

—Yes.

—If I'm very quiet I can hear him again. It's quite wonderful.

—All right. Let's really be quiet this time.

—Let's.

Len

Mum's getting things sorted. That's how she is. She was
at McMorton's all morning with Margie. McMorton's
pulled some strings for her, got in touch with the right
people so it can be done straight away. I said I don't want
anything to do with it. I don't care about who comes, any
of that. I just want to put her to rest. She made me go to
the registry office. I gave them the coroner's letter and
waited. It was like killing you myself. I could hear the
clerk in the back typing out the certificate, the small thud
of his stamp, then two more. Like nailing down the lid
on you.

My Patti.

I don't want anything to do with anybody anymore, Patti.
I'm all at sea.

The lads have been good. They haven't given up. They're
exhausted too. Some of them look as though they've been
through the mill. But everything hurts. Even the sight of
my mates. I know they go back to their families when
they're finished. Last night I let it go, I'm ashamed to say.

It was just me here by myself. I told Mum I didn't want her to stay. She'd been gone about an hour when it came over me all of a sudden. I was in the middle of looking for my black shoes when it hit. I just let go. Did you see me, Patti? From wherever you are. Did you? Did Frankie see? It was one of his tantrums. I screamed. I yelled, I blasphemed. I hit the walls. It didn't last long. I pulled myself together soon enough. It was easy. There was nothing left in me. Nothing. Who did this to us? Who made this happen?

Only Mum and me on our own now. It's like time running backwards.

They take away everything you care about. No one left I can say I love.

Jack would be laughing. Serves me right. I can't say I ever shed a tear for Jack. Not if I'm honest. Oh, yes, tears at his funeral last year, I give you that. But the tears were for both of us. For him and for me, the two boys without a care in the world. For him, my little brother *little*—the four-, five-, six-year-old Jack—and for me, the seven-, eight-, nine-year-old me snapped by seafront photographers. Margate. Trailing our spades all along the promenade just for the rasp of tin on pavement. I was crying for the boys in the photographs. Not for the boy who was younger, brighter, funnier, and who got away with blue murder while I took the blame. Not for the boy who came back a hero with a war wound while I was stuck in non-combat up in Lin-coln. Not for the boy who could make my own wife laugh till she cried. Yes, I wished him gone many times before. I'll not pretend. But it shook me when it happened. As if I'd dislodged that ugly bit of shrapnel myself and nudged it on its deadly way so that in the end he became the boy who made you cry so hard, Patti, you were never quite the same again.

Oh God, Patti, I could forgive all that if you only tell me what happened to Frankie. Tell me where he is. It's not right, you and Frankie leaving me. Frankie gone without a trace, as if he never existed. It's not possible. Help us Patti. Tell us where he is. I'm finished, I am. If you're both gone there's no point. No point in going on. Why would I? I might as well end it as soon as I can. I don't want to be here. I don't. I want to be with you, with both of you.

How am I going to go on? Go through one day, go through the next? For a whole life? I pitied Jack his fate. Never imagined mine would be a hundred times worse. If I could die before tomorrow. If I could.

Oh Patti. How we could have loved one another if we'd only seen what was down the road.

Chapter 12

TUESDAY AM

When I woke up I could only open one eye. The other one was stuck down. I thought I had caught being blind so I said Oh no and Alec heard me and came and licked the stuck one open. That was a relief. I wouldn't like it if a person licked my eye but doglick is all right. I told you it was good.

It was early. Everything was pink again and only a bit yellow.

Gordon Knight said Well good morning! I thought you'd never wake up.

I said That's what I thought when you—But he interrupted.

He said We'll have some breakfast shall we? I'm starving.

He looked all right so I know he was just saying what people say. I said So am I. We weren't telling lies. We were doing manner of speaking.

Alec was happy we were getting up. He was shivery.

I said Alec is cold.

It was freezing when we got out from under the blankets. I wanted to tell Gordon Knight to hurry up but that would have been a bit rude.

I said I don't want to be late.

Gordon Knight said I'm going as fast as I can.

I said Thank you to make sure he knew I was polite.

We went along the deck. Gordon Knight said It's very wet isn't it? He knows a lot of things without seeing. It was all wet like our blankets. And then we opened the big metal door and went inside. It was lovely.

On the way down the stairs we met a sailor.

He said Good morning sir. Early bird!

Mr Knight said Good morning. Then he said It's funny how they see me but you're invisible.

I said Wha—

He said *In* a manner of speaking.

I said I don't understand.

He said Neither do I. Never mind. What would you like to eat?

You know what I said. Then I said But first I need to go to the toilet.

He said Lead the way. I'll wait for you right outside. And then we'll take Alec to the dog park.

I said To go on the swings hahaha.

I was glad to have something funny to think about. Usually I am embarrassed when I do urinating (that's the right word by the way. It's more polite).

When I came out Mr Knight said we're going to the lift now. Come along.

I said You know the way?

He said I certainly do. I take Alec there three times a day.

We got in the lift and went right down to Deck Seven. That's the bottom of the boat. I know you think it's not because I told you there are twelve decks. But there are five decks without numbers on top of number one. I don't make mistakes.

We went in the dog park. It's not a park at all. It's just a room with long sand pit in the middle and it's really stinky. I said I'll wait outside and Mr Knight said Oh no you won't and put his hand on the door handle behind him. He sounded like a kidnapper.

I said Excuse me and he said We won't be long.

Grown-ups are all the same. Even if they are blind. They are always the boss. It makes me fed up.

I pulled a face at Mr Knight and it made me feel better. Then I stuck out my tongue and actually that made me feel worse.

Anyway he was right. We weren't very long because Alec did one straight away. Actually he did three. Good boy!

We went back and got in the lift again.

I said You pressed the wrong button. You pressed two. Breakfast is one.

Mr Knight blocked me off again. He stepped sideways so he was in front of the buttons again. It made me start to do worrying. He said we just have to make an important phone call. Then we'll have breakfast I promise.

I thought No! This is definitely suspicious behaviour. Everybody knows there are no phones on a boat.

I got out just before the doors closed. I thought about hiding somewhere but I was still on the bottom deck and that would be the first place to do sinking if the iceberg came and then I thought I would just go up the stairs and have breakfast anyway. No one would kidnap me in a room full of people.

I was out of breath when I got up to Deck One. I went straight in to the dining room. A lady said You're in a rush this morning my goodness me.

Gordon Knight said He always is. Little monkey. I was so shocked. I didn't know where he came from. An ambush! But he had a nice voice when he said monkey not a horrible one like in *mun*key! and Alec was really pleased to see me again so when Gordon Knight put out his hand and said Now we absolutely *do* have to make that phone call and you will *abso*lutely hold my hand all the way there I took it. He could fit my whole hand in his like MyDad.

I said Who will hold Alec?

He said Who would you like to?

I said Me.

He said Right then. One hand for Alec. One hand for me. And do as you're told.

(I told you they are all the same.)

He said he didn't want to go in the lift again so we walked down the stairs.

I said You're going to give me away, aren't you?

He said Hmmm. You've already given yourself away. To me. So it doesn't matter does it?

I wanted to know what they would do when they found out.

He said My best guess is they will be so pleased to see you they'll give you anything you want.

—A hundred million pounds?

—Is that really what you want?

—No.

—What then?

—Some breakfast.

—Is that all?

—No. I really want to see MyDad. But not MyMum. Don't tell them I want to see MyMum.

—All right.

—Promise?

—Promise.

I told him I was scared because I didn't know how to get home. I didn't like it when I didn't know things and if I didn't find out I might have to do screaming.

He said Well you're lucky. You're about to find out. So you won't have to.

And then he stopped.

At the Purser's Office! Not a phone box at all!

The sailor behind the desk said Good morning Mr Knight. How are we today sir?

Mr Knight said Good morning. *I'm* very well thank you. How are you?

—Very well, thank you, sir. What can I do for you, sir?

—I'd like to speak with the Purser.

—Certainly sir. I'll just go and tell him.

(The counter was taller than me so I couldn't see where he went.)

When he came back he said I'll take you right in. He lifted up a piece of the counter like a door lying down—a trap door!—and said Oh my goodness! Two of you! (He meant two of us not two of Mr Knight.) *And* the dog!

He said We'll let the lad wait outside shall we? I'll keep an eye on him.

Mr Knight said No no. *The lad* comes in with me.

—Certainly sir.

He let us go through and then he took us to another room inside. It had a glass door and it was full of smoke like a bus. He knocked on the door. I could see the Purser inside sitting at his desk smoking a cigarette. He said Come in.

The man behind the desk said Mr Knight sir and went away. We went inside. I could not breathe because the smoke was getting in my nose before the air. It started coming out of my eyes. I could feel it.

The Purser got up and said Come in come in and put out his hand. Oh here he said and took hold of Mr Knight's hand to shake it. Leftenant Fawcett. We've met before of course. How are you Mr Knight? Do take a seat. (He didn't wait for an answer.) Mr Knight and...?

—Frankie.

—Frankie. How do you do Frankie.

I said How do you do. I'd never said that before. Can I take a seat too?

—Hahaha. Be my guest. (He meant sit down because he was pointing at the other chair.)

—Thank you.

I sat down. My feet stuck out in front. I felt a bit silly and I wished I hadn't asked but at least Gordon Knight couldn't see me. (He could only hear me coughing.) He said Sit Alec and Alec sat. Then he said Lie down and he did.

The Purser said So. What can I do for you Mr Knight?

—It's really a question of what you can do for Frankie. You haven't met Frankie before have you?

—No. I don't believe I've had the pleasure. What's your room number Frankie?

—I don't have a room.

—Perhaps you've forgotten it. Do you know it Mr Knight?

—He doesn't have a room.

—I mean his parents' room.

—Frankie's travelling by himself.

—What's the boy's surname Mr Knight?

—What's your surname Frankie?

—Walters.

The Purser moved his ashtray to make room for a big book. He flipped over lots of pages and used his pen like Miss Kenney to help him do looking.

—You won't find him in the list.

There was like a big hole then in the air. Leftenant Fawcett looked at Mr Knight and then he looked at me.

His face was going bright red like Lucy Mayberry's when she wet herself in the gym so I started to laugh. He stood up and said Excuse me and got a big handkerchief out of his pocket and turned away to blow his nose. I think he was pretending. He didn't want anyone (well—me) to look at his face. It was still red when he put his handkerchief away and sat down again.

—So you don't have a room?

—No. But I'd like one.

—Could I ask you Mr Knight—if you'll pardon my presumption—the nature of the relationship you hold to the boy?

—None.

—So you're his guardian.

—No.

—Young Francis boarded the ship with you though.

—No. Frankie boarded alone. Perhaps Leftenant Fawcett we should let him tell you how.

But Leftenant Fawcett didn't want to hear. He said I'm sorry to be dense Mr Knight but do I assume—since you said he does not have a room—that the boy has been sleeping…in your room?

—No. He hasn't.

—Except for Sunday. I slept there on Sunday only you didn't know. You were like a dead person. Hahaha.

Leftenant Fawcett put his eyebrows right up nearly in his hair like people do.

Gordon Knight said I'm afraid he might be telling the truth.

Leftenant Fawcett's eyebrows didn't come down.

Then he stood up and they did. He said Mr Knight I think it would be a good idea if we have this conversation in the presence of a third party. Perhaps Frankie can tell his story then from the very beginning.

I hate parties—you know that. I thought about all the people who would stand round in a big circle and I would be in the middle.

I said No but it was a bit quiet and maybe nobody heard me because Gordon Knight said That's a very good idea and Leftenant Fawcett said I'll just ask Warrant Officer Davies to step in.

—I don't want anyone else to come in. (I whispered that.)

Gordon Knight reached out sideways and said Hold my hand. You'll be all right.

I put my hand onto his and he took it but then I felt like someone in Infants and I didn't like it so I took it away again. I whispered I am all right thank you very much.

When Leftenant Fawcett came back with Warrant Officer Davies I said I don't want to go to a party and I don't want you to take me to a police station either when we get to New York.

They both laughed but I wasn't joking. I told them I wasn't and they laughed again and that's when I decided I didn't want to tell them anything else. They did not seem like people who would listen to me.

I started to do hard rocking. Warrant Officer Davies said Woah there Billy boy. You'll put that chair right through—and then I didn't hear anymore because that's the whole point of rocking. You can see people's mouths moving if you open your eyes but your ears are protected. I did rocking for quite a long time and I only opened my eyes once. Everybody's mouths were moving at the same time.

Now I was in trouble. I think I probably hit someone. Someone tried to make me stop rocking so I did hitting and kicking too. I hoped MyMum hadn't seen. She said I was too old to do that and if I wanted to hit something I should hit the floor. The carpet could do with a beating.

Leftenant Fawcett and Warrant Officer Davies had gone and so had Gordon Knight. There was a lady instead. She was enormous. If I sat on her lap it would have been like a narm-chair. She was wearing a striped dress and a stiff white apron with a watch pinned on her bosom (that's the polite word for her chest) so I thought she was probably a nurse. Too bad for her then because I wasn't sick.

I was still rocking but slower. I was doing looking through my eyelashes so she wouldn't guess I was watching. She was reading Woman's Own.

—So. (She said that but she didn't even look at me. She was still reading.) Do you think you can stop completely before I get to twenty-nine? One two three four…

She did counting!

—…five six seven eight…

So I stopped.

—Well well well! Are you feeling better?

—Yes thank you.

—Good. Are you ready for breakfast?

—Yes please.

—Right. Good boy. Let's be having you. (What MyMum always said!)

—What about Mr Knight?

—Who's that?

—The blind man.

—He's with the others.

—Where?

—I think they're with the Captain.

—Mr Knight hasn't had his breakfast either.

—He'll get some.

—Don't you want me to hold your hand?

—Why?

—In case I run away.

—What? Before breakfast?

—All right I'll hold it after.

—Good boy.

I liked it when she said that. I felt like Alec.

—Where are we going now?

—To have breakfast. While they make some phone calls.

That sounded suspicious again. And we were going down instead of up.

—It's the wrong way.

—We're going to my office. The breakfast is coming to us.

I was very confused. That is not a good thing for me.

—You have an office?

—I share it.

We went all the way to Deck Seven (twelve right?) and turned the opposite way from the dog park.

—Here we are.

There was a sign on the door that said Surgery. That's where surgeons cut people. I knew that.

I said I'll wait outside. I don't want to see the Surgeon.

She said You won't see him. You'll stay with me. Nurse Adeyemi. The Surgeon's gone to cut up his breakfast haha.

—Haha. (That was actually better than the jokes people usually do for me. But I was still unhappy.)

I said I still don't want to go in.

—You won't be in the Surgery darlin. You'll be in the waiting room. With me.

I could see that because the operating table was in another room inside the first one like the Purser's Office. The door was open and I could see there was a big light and a high-up bed and a stand with scissors and little bottles and stuff. I couldn't see a knife. Where we were was only a little table with magazines on—National Geographic—my favourite!—and some chairs.

—Sit yourself down there now and tell me what you want to eat.

She went and picked up the handle of a telephone. It was stuck on the wall next to the door where we came in. So it was true. Telephones on boats! She picked it up and said Yes Matron here. Send a breakfast down to Surgery please. What do you want darlin?

You know what I said then don't you? You're right.

She said Anything else? A negg? Some bacon?

—No thank you.

—No. No egg no bacon. Just the beans.

—And some toast. Please.

—And some toast please. Thank you. Good then. Five minutes. You're a love. (She put the handle back on the telephone without saying bye-bye.)

—There. And then after you've had your breakfast we'll go back and find the others.

—What are they doing?

—Collecting some information I expect. Like me. Let's get you measured.

She went in the Surgery. I didn't.

—What for?

—So they can get in touch with your family.

—I don't have a family.

—You don't have a mum and dad? She looked really surprised.

—MyMum's dead.

She was clinking some weights but she was still talking to me.

—Dear love. But a dad?

—Yes.

—Come in here and hop up.

I love measuring machines so I did.

—A brother or a sister?

—Only a dead one.

—Three foot nine and a half.

(I had grown!)

—A nuncle? A naunty?

—Yes. But one died.

—Three stone three.

(Perfect!)

—A gran or a grandad?

—A Gran.

—There you are then. You've got a family.

—But not all in my house.

—Don't have to be. Who's in your house right now?

—MyDad.

—He'll be so happy when he has you home again. Ah. Come in! It's your breakfast. (Not by itself. A sailor was carrying it!) Right there thank you.

The baked beans had an upside-down silver dish on top.

I told you I was lucky.

I was right in the middle of them when someone went knock-knock and came in. I carried on eating quickly in case it was the sailor coming to take them away again. It wasn't. It was the Captain because the nurse said Morning Captain.

He did Good morning Matron and Well well well well well. I've heard quite the story. Who is this young man then?

I turned round and said Frankie. You met me before remember? By the map. You said That wouldn't do at all would it son? And I said I wouldn't mind.

You know when I said the Purser went all red? Well the captain went all whitey-yellow. He did a big swallow and I saw his Adam's apple go up and down like in a lift.

He said It looks as if you're enjoying your breakfast. Don't let me stop you.

I said All right.

Nurse Adeyemi said You've met before sir? You know the lad?

The Captain said No. He's probably confused.

I wanted to say No I'm not but you mustn't talk with your mouth full.

—Well he thinks he's spoken to you.

—Must have been another officer. Anyway we're in radio contact with the marine service right now so we'll be talking to the consulut as soon as the office opens. I just want to have a good look at the lad so I can provide a fair description. He'll be a missing person in England.

—His dad'll be worried sick.

—Quite so. Not to mention his mum.

—His mum is D-E-A-D Captain.

—His mum is dad?

I said D-*E*-A-D. She said MyMum is *dead*.

The Captain did moving his mouth before the sound came out. I've seen people do that before.

—Oh how very awkward. I'm so sorry. Ah well look just send him along will you please matron? When he's ready?

He didn't even wait for an answer. He just went.

Nurse Adeyemi said There. You've even got the Captain running round after you.

I said Telling fibs. Big ones.

She said Tut-tut-tut.

I didn't know if she meant me or him.

Then she said You can go in that little room there to use the toilet. And don't forget to wash your hands after.

I didn't bother to answer.

I won't tell the next bit.

When I came out I said Where's Mr Knight?

She said Probably with the Captain. That's where we're going now. Captain's Quarters. And you're holding my hand remember?

I said I don't mind.

She was right. Gordon Knight and Alec were in the Captain's Quarters. My friends! I decided I would talk to them but not to the fibbing Captain. The Purser was there too with his lists. They were sitting in armchairs by a little low table except the Captain. He was sitting at his desk.

The Captain said Come along inside you two. Sit down, sit down. Now. We'll try to get everything straightened out and then we can make arrangements for your parents to be contacted.

Mr Knight said His father Captain.

The Captain said Right. Oh right.

I said I don't want to sit here. My feet stick out. I want to sit on the floor beside Alec? Please.

The Captain said Probably better if you come and stand here. Now. First of all tell us your full name.

I didn't say anything.

Gordon Knight said Tell him Frankie.

I said Francis Walters.

The Captain said Do you mind if I call you Frankie? Or Frank?

I didn't say anything.

Gordon Knight said I don't expect he would mind if you call him Frankie.

I said I would. It's only for people who are fond of me.

Leftenant Fawcett laughed out loud so I said Not for anyone else.

The Captain said Right then. Well—Francis—can you tell us where you live?

I didn't say anything.

Mr Knight said Francis they want to get in touch with YourDad.

I said You can call me Frankie.

He did a little sigh just for himself and said Thank you. Now tell them your address.

I said I'll write it down or they'll get it wrong. People always get it wrong.

The Purser said All right. Here. And he held out his notepad and his pen.

I said I'd like to sit at the desk, please. Gordon Knight put his hand over his mouth and wiped his face down like he had a bit of jam on it.

The Captain got up and I sat in his chair. The Purser pushed it in tight for me. I said That's too tight so he pulled it out again. I wasn't looking at him but I can tell when people are mad just by the way they breathe so I didn't ask for a cushion. He tore a piece of paper out of his notebook and gave me his pen.

I wrote—

7 Worcester Terrace Southampton Hampshire England The World

I said You say Wooster not War-cess-ter. I said it to the air. Just in case they didn't know. And so I didn't make anybody mad.

The Purser said And how old are you?

I wrote down *six.* because I wasn't speaking, remember?

—I don't suppose you know how tall you are.

I wrote it down for them. And how much I weighed.

—Eyes?

I wrote Yes but he bended down and looked at me and said Blue. He was writing stuff too in his own book. I crossed mine out and wrote blue on top.

—And do you know YourDad's name?

I wrote down Len Walters.

The Purser said And do you have a telephone?

I shook my head. I think I just wanted to be mean.

—Right. (That was the Purser.) Well I'll get this off to the coast guard. I think that's the quickest way to reach the consulut and they can take it from there and meanwhile we'll get in touch with Southampton via shipping.

—Thank you Fawcett. (That was the Captain). I don't think there's much more we can do at this stage.

—Except make sure he doesn't, you know, D-I-S-A-P-P-

—E-A-R (I was really mad I said that. I wasn't going to talk to them.)

Gordon Knight said I'll keep an eye on him.

I wanted to laugh but I didn't. It was all quiet. Nobody said anything for thirteen seconds. I counted (I used orangutans). And then the Captain said That's all right thank you Mr Knight. Matron can look after him now. You'll have plenty to do today I'm sure.

I said But he's my friend. And everybody went quiet again.

I don't know what's wrong with people all the time.

Mr Knight said Don't worry. I'll come and see you and did a great big smile.

Leftenant Fawcett said Right then. We'll go and wait for that call.

Chapter 13
TUESDAY (Still)

We went all the way back down to Deck Seven.

Nurse Adeyemi said What are we going to do with you now? It looks like a busy morning.

There were five souls waiting to see the surgeon. I could see through the window in the door. I said I can wait in the room next door.

She said That's the overflow. It's probably not a bad idea. If it's empty. I'll find someone who can stay with you.

I said Mr Knight said he would keep an eye on me.

She said Fat lot of good that'd be.

That was a bit rude.

I said He kept an eye on me all night.

She said Yes. We know all about that.

She said Come in here a minute and I'll find someone.

Everyone sat up straight as if they were in Miss Kenney's class.

Nurse Adeyemi said Good morning. I'll be with you in just a minute.

She picked up the handle of the telephone and said Yes. It's Matron. Have you got a spare body over there?

I didn't really like hearing that. I picked up a National Geographic (without looking at anyone) so I could have something to stare at without looking scared. And guess what? It was an orangutan. Just like my counting.

Nurse Adeyemi was still talking into the telephone. She said I need a hand...No...Yes...One of the girls from hospitality?...All I need is someone with a good head on their shoulders. I'm not looking for the Admiral of the Fleet. Yes. You can get that from Leftenant Fawcett...No. I know...But this is not a regular situation we're dealing with...Thank you.

She put the telephone back on the wall and said I'll be right back to all the people and took me next door. I tried not to think about the things I had heard her say.

Next door there was a little short bed and two armchairs. I got into one and held up the National Geographic. I said Look! An orangutan! I did thirteen of those this morning.

She said Good boy (I don't think she was paying attention). We can go and get some books from the playroom if you like.

I said No thank you. Shall I read you a bit?

She said Well you can try.

I said Wait a minute.

She sat down.

I couldn't find the orangutans. If they're on the front they're inside too. Then I did. I said Here they are. Listen. It says *The Sumatran* (I don't know what that is) *Orangutan is the largest tree-* what?—oh I get it—*living mammal in the world. A male orangutan can reach five feet*—that's sixty inches. That's fifteen inches more than me—*and weigh as much as three hundred pounds.* Is that heavy?

—Heavy just depends. I'm nine stone six.

—That's one hundred and twenty-six pounds plus six. You're tiny compared.

—Thank you.

—*...but it may take thirty years for him/a male to attain mature stature.* I don't know what that means but the next bit says *Newborns weigh only three and a half pounds and do not leave their mothers for at least five years.* But unless their mothers die right. Like get killed by a hunter. Or fall off the tree. Look! This is an orphan.

—He's a dear little fellow.

—What do you call half an orphan?

—I don't know. What do you call half an orphan?

—No. I'm not doing a joke. I'm asking you.

—I don't think I have an answer for you darlin.

—Can we ask Mr Knight?

—I have to stay here but when they send us someone you can go for a little walk.

—If I hold hands.

—Yes. If you hold hands.

—Or a long one.

—Or a long one. But not more than half an hour.

When someone came it was the lady from the shops with the bright red nails.

She said My my my. It's you. What have you been up to?

Nurse Adeyemi said He just needs someone to keep an eye on him while I'm on duty.

—The lady said Where are his parents?

—I said parent. He's in England.

She put her eyebrows up but they were sort of crooked. Then she said

—What's wrong with the playroom?

Nurse Adeyemi said It's better if he's not left. It's quite important.

The lady said Vee I Pee is it? Well that's not why I signed on. Doesn't the Purser know how to deal with it?

Nurse Adeyemi said Look if you don't want to do it just say so.

The lady said What's your name?

I said Francis.

Nurse Adeyemi said Just take him for a little saunter and you can take him for a bite to eat and then most likely I'll be done. By about two anyway.

The lady said Come along then Frankie.

I said Francis.

She said Pardon me for living.

When we were walking I said Can we go outside?

She said I suppose so. But we'll have to go to the shop first so I can get a scarf.

We went in the one where she works and got a red and blue scarf off a ring and said All right Sandra? Sandra said All right even though she didn't pay for it. When we got outside she put it on her head and said There. That'll save my perm.

Outside I looked everywhere for Mr Knight. Then I said Can we go down to Deck Seven? She said Whatever you like. You seem to be the boss around here.

She didn't do much smiling so I didn't either.

We went down in the lift.

I said I want to see the dog park.

She said That's disgusting. But we didn't have to go there anyway because Gordon Knight was just coming along the corridor with Alec.

I said Mr Knight. Guess who it is.

He said Frankie I know exactly who it is.

—Can I say Hallo to Alec?

—Yes you may. Playtime Alec.

Alec is always happy. He loves me. I think he loves me more than he loves Mr Knight. Poor Mr Knight.

—And who is your friend Frankie?

—You.

—No. The friend you're with.

—She's not—

He interrupted me and said How do you do?

—How do you do sir. Frankie has been keen to find you.

—Francis (that was me).

—And you are…?

—Miss Thatcher. The Land Ahoy Shop sir.

—Ah.

—Nurse Adeyemi has asked me to keep an eye.

—I see.

I didn't even want to laugh. I just wanted Miss Thatcher to go away.

—Well I'm just going up to find some lunch. Would you like to join me?

—I have to get a sandwich for Frankie.

—Francis.

—I'm sure he'd enjoy a beefburger right Francis?

—Frankie.

—Frankie.

—Yes.

—You could come as my guest no doubt. People rarely refuse me a request.

—Well…

—Settled then. Now the lift's gone. We'll have to call it again

So that's what I had. A beefburger. Miss Thatcher said they're not called Wimpys. That's just what common people call them. I didn't want to do chatting so Mr Knight and Miss Thatcher did it instead and I listened.

Miss Thatcher did the most. She said Haha at the end of everything like I suppose you're used to the high-life haha. And It must cost a lot of money being you know blind haha. And But I expect the government pays you quite a bit. They seem to have money to burn haha. And Of course I won't stay in shops forever haha. I expect I'll be offered a new position soon. People usually don't take long to see my potential haha.

I got bored so when I had finished I got down and talked to Alec.

Gordon Knight said You'd better sit up again. Miss Thatcher is supposed to be keeping an eye on you.

Miss Thatcher said My goodness that was a big sigh for a little boy. Do you have any children Mr Knight?

Gordon Knight said I'm not married. You could say I'm a confirmed bachelor.

Miss Thatcher said Oh goodness. It's almost two. We'd better get back.

I said Where are we going?

She said Back to the Surgery.

I said will you come too?

Mr Knight said I might come and see you yes. I'll certainly see you before tomorrow. I want to hear all about your phone call. Say hallo to Nurse Adeyemi.

Miss Thatcher said Time we were off.

When we got back Nurse Adeyemi was in the room next door reading about orangutans. She said Wonderful. I have you for the rest of the day. She had a little tray with a teapot and two cups and some biscuits. She offered some to Miss Thatcher but Miss Thatcher said No I won't thank you. I'm back on duty in half an hour. That was a relief.

I said Can I read to you again?

She said Darlin I'd love that.

I read fifteen pages and then there was a knock on the door.

Nurse Adeyemi jumped. Both of her feet sort bounced off the floor at the same time. I said Come in because she didn't know what had happened.

It was the Purser and another sailor.

The Purser said Well. We're making progress. I think we have contact.

Nurse Adeyemi said With…? And the Purser said Yes.

Nurse Adeyemi said On the line now?

The Purser said Fifteen minutes apparently. Is the tea hot?

Nurse Adeyemi said You're out of luck. It's cold and stewed. I can make some more.

The Purser said Splendid. Tell them we'll be along in fifteen Terry.

He was fiddling about in the biscuit tin. He kept turning them over. He was probably looking for a chocolate digestive.

Nurse Adeyemi thought so too because she said There aren't any.

He said Oh I was just looking for one for the lad.

I thought Pants on fire and sat down on the floor with the orangutans.

Nurse Adeyemi said Well give him one then.

He said Oh. Right.

I said No thank you.

Nurse Adeyemi got a kettle out of a cupboard and made some new tea and then she did chatting with the Purser while I was reading but I can't tell you what they said because I wasn't listening. I could tell you about what I was reading but you will probably only pretend to be interested. That's what people usually do when I talk to them about exotic members of the animal kingdom. Except MyDad. He is always interested in everything. If MyMum was still alive she would say *You and Frankie peas in a pod.*

When they had had their new tea the sailor called Terry came back and we went to the radio room.

The radio room had a whole lot of knobs and plugs and switches and dials and needles but I couldn't see even one telephone. There was a sailor with earmuffs on working all the controls. He said Sit down. We'll get your Dad up in no time.

I said He'll already be up. We did the minusses. He'll be at work.

He said Not to worry. It won't be too long now.

There were four chairs and a stool. Guess who got the stool. Leftenant Fawcett did standing with his bottom on the edge of the table. He started showing off and explaining everything to Nurse Adeyemi. She looked a bit tired. The radio officer said It's a busy afternoon. We'll have to have a bit more quiet in here if you don't mind. Nurse Adeyemi said Not at all sir.

Somebody knocked on the door and a foreign sailor put his head in said Do you want the Captain yet sir?

The radio officer said I'd say still about another fifteen minutes. I counted to see if he was right. He wasn't. When I'd done twenty sixties the Captain came in. It was really crowded. I counted four more minutes after that then the radio sailor said Ah here we are.

He twiddled some knobs and said There. That's better. Hallo? Southampton? This is WV6Ro. Warrant Officer Jamieson here. I'll put the Captain on.

The Captain said Captain Pondringum...*Mike* Alderton?... You're joking!...You got transferred? When was that?...Surprised no one told me. Do you miss Tilbury?...Haha. Who would—what? But we mustn't keep these good people waiting. You have Mr Walters there?...Good put him on...Hallo Mr Walters. How do you do? You've been briefed I take it?...Well let's hope it is sir. It's a pity we don't have radiovision. Haha. However I'm sure you'll be able to tell us as soon as you speak to him.

He took his earmuffs off and said come over here Frankie. Francis.

I went over and he put the earmuffs on my head. They came down to my neck.

He said Wait a minute and he adjusted them.

I said Ow.

He said You'll just have to hold them. Here.

He put my hands on the earmuffs and put them over my ears. I listened.

He said Can you hear anything?

I said I can hear someone sniffing.

He said Say hallo.

I hate it when people tell me what to say.

I said Here I am.

MyDad said Frankie. Oh Frankie.

I said Where are you?

He was a long time thinking. Then he said I'm at the Port Authority.

I said Is that like the Police?

He said Sort of.

I said Because of me?

He didn't say anything because he was blowing his nose.

I said Are they going to put you in jail?

He said No. Frankie. Oh Frankie.

I said What?

He said Are you all right?

I said Yes thank you. Have you buried Mum?

Captain Pondringum said That's enough now and pulled the earmuffs off my head and put them on his.

He said So. Mr Walters. Can I assume it's safe to say we have your son here? Mr Walters? Hallo? Hallo?

We may have lost the connection Jamieson.

The radio officer said Let me see. No we're fine. Here you go sir.

The Captain listened again then he said. It is. Speaking…Well we've only just found him, sir…No Mr Walters. He did not come to our attention before today…It is sir. Quite remarkable.

But the Gloriana is a very—*very*—large vessel as no doubt you're aware…

I said I want to talk to him again.

The Captain said. Indeed. Indeed Mr Walters. Mr Walters if you'd just excuse my interrupting you a moment I believe your son would like to talk to you again.

He took the earmuffs off and whispered Just to tell him goodbye then. He put the earmuffs back on my head but he didn't bother to put them in the right place so I had to listen through my neck.

I said Dad?

He said Yes Frankie.

I said You sound like an old man all crackly. But you didn't answer my question.

He said Which one?

I said Have you buried Mum?

He said Yes. She's sleeping now.

I said You mean buried. Then I said Stoppit because the Captain was trying to take the ear things away again.

I said Dad?

He said Are you sure you're all right?

I said Yes thank you. Then I said Dad?

He said Tell me.

I said I don't have any money.

He said You don't need any.

I said How will I get home without a ticket?

He said Frankie Be a good boy. Just do what people ask you to. It's all going to be taken care of.

But who will pay?

You don't have to worry one little bit about it.

But who?

The Foreign Office.

That was a surprise! I must have been a foreigner because I was not in England. Like Dad was a foreigner when he went to France.

I said Will you have to pay them back?

He said Oh Frankie. Oh Frankie. Oh Frankie.

I said What?

He said I'm so glad you're—And then I couldn't hear anymore because the captain had got the earmuffs off me.

He said I'm afraid we'll have to call it a day now Mr Walters. I'll let you say goodbye. The radio officer quickly took off his own and put them on my head.

MyDad said Bye-bye. Then he vanished. When I said Bye-bye he wasn't there. I think someone had pulled a plug out. I didn't want MyDad to disappear. I felt more lonely than when I'm all alone. A big panic was coming up inside me but it went down again all by itself like it was sinking in the sea and instead of doing screaming I did a new thing. I did crying. Real tears. It was like my eyes and my nose were melting all at the same time. I was completely wet! I wished I was still talking to him. I wanted him to carry on talking and be talking to me all the way to New York then I could close my eyes and pretend he was in the same room as me (but like MyDad not like a crackly old man). But here is the funny thing—all the tears were burning me. Burning water! Imagine! That proves there's no such thing as impossible.

Being on this boat I thought is like not having a Dad as well as no Mum. I am like a whole orphan. Like a baby orangutan.

Everyone was deciding where I should be and what I should do. And no one was asking me if I wanted to do it. I wanted to just go fast asleep until I could see MyDad again. I know he loves me even if he's a bit useless like MyMum says. Said.

Nurse Adeyemi said You look all in little man. Come along we'll let them sort everything out.

The Purser said Yes I'd better be getting back too. We're rushed off our feet. As usual. Last day and all that.

I spent the rest of the afternoon with Nurse Adeyemi. I didn't mind her. She left me alone. She said I have a lot of paperwork to do. You're going to have to amuse yourself. What do you think you'd like to do when you've done enough reading? Do you like drawing? Jigsaw puzzles? Do you want a nap?

I said I'll just read.

I didn't tell her I had some worrying to do before I did reading. Here's what I had to worry about:

1. Did they know I didn't have any money to get home?
2. Is it good or bad if they know?
3. Does take care of everything mean pay for it?
4. If it's taking six days to go New York will it take six days to go back?
5. When Gordon Knight gets off can Nurse Adeyemi be my friend instead-of?
6. Will they let me talk to MyDad again so I can tell him to wait for me and everything when I get off? It will be harder finding the way because they don't have a big arrow saying YOUR HOUSE like the one that said DOCKS.

That was more things than I've ever had to worry about at once. I hoped the panic that was stuck in the dent at the bottom of my neck wouldn't come up and spoil everything.

When I had finished I read three National Geographic magazines and then I said Can I have a jigsaw puzzle please?

Nurse Adeyemi said Yes. I'm ready for a little walk. We'll go and get one shall we?

I said Yes.

We went up to the playroom. The same lady was in there who's always in there.

She said Oh hallo Matron. Oh they've palmed him off on you now have they? You know I haven't seen his parents once this whole voyage. I don't know why some people bother having children—all the interest they take.

Nurse Adeyemi said I'd keep that observation to yourself if I were you Felicity. Where are your puzzles?

The lady said I don't know why I bother making conversation sometimes. It's not appreciated.

Nurse Adeyemi said You can say that again.

But the lady didn't. She just pointed to the shelf with puzzles.

I picked Conway Castle One Thousand Pieces and we took it back.

Nurse Adeyemi was using the table for her papers. She had to roll up the mat so I could make it on her lino.

We even had our supper in her room. She said it was better than getting mixed up with all the people because there was soon going to be a lot of nosey parkers.

Guess what I said for them to bring me? Nope. Haha. Chicken!

I didn't eat it though because it had a bone in it like a dead thing.

After supper we went to a special room to see the Captain again. It smelled like a pub. He said He wanted to let everyone know how things were progressing. He said We have been advised by the consulut in New York—listen carefully—*that the process of repatriation could be greatly simplified if the runaway were to remain on board otherwise the protockol would be costly and time consuming, requiring the services of both immigration and the judishary in the case of, as in this case, a minor. An exception could be made however for a runaway in tranzit provided the total time elapsed on US soil did not exceed twelve hours and provided the runaway was escorted by a citizen of his own country in possession of valid travel documents.* We're working on that one. So you see where we're going.

I said No.

Everybody laughed but no one bothered to explain where so I listened carefully.

The Captain said We're trying to make the operation as simple as possible. He said the Foreign Office in London have been in touch with the Home Office and they will take care of all his travel subject to reimburssment over a reasonable time period. They didn't spessify but one imagines they do know how to be reasonable.

That was when there was another knock on the door. Guess who it was. I'll give you a clue. Someone I like. A lot. Yes!! Alec! (But Mr Knight knocked. Of *course*.)

Everyone did Hallo and Gordon Knight said So. Are you making any progress?

Leftenant Fawcett said I believe we are. Indeed.

When everyone had done a whole lot more talking and a bit of arguing the Captain said Well it's bedtime for at least one of us around here.

Leftenant Fawcett said I should say.

I said I'll sleep in Mr Knight's room.

The Captain said That won't be possible I'm afraid.

I said Why not? We can do sardines. He's my best friend.

The Captain said I couldn't stay with him even if he *was* my best friend. He said I could sleep with Felicity Hicks from the Playroom. She's certified.

Leftenant Fawcett said he'd volunteer to go and ask her.

I said No not her. I hate her. But nobody heard. They were talking about the Surgery again.

I said Not the Surgery. Not at night-time.

The Captain kept repeating what he said about Felicity Hicks. Warrant Officer Davies was on his side too. Gordon Knight and Nurse Adeyemi were both talking as well but I couldn't hear what they were saying the others were so loud and no one was listening to me. No one at all. The Captain kept saying it was the best idea. Miss Hicks was properly trained in child minding. It was the best idea. It reminded me of when I tried to tell Miss Kenney. I gave up listening and did rocking instead and then I lay down and did kicking until I had to stop because I couldn't breathe. (I was lying on my face. It helps if you can't see people.) Somebody picked me up straightaway. Nobody ever picks me up. I hate it. It made me do loud screaming. It was Warrant Officer Davies. He said Crikey and put me down so he could hold his ear. Gordon Knight said What are you doing for heaven's sake? I screamed

I want to sleep with you I want to sleep with you about a hundred times. I had to scream because everybody had started talking again and nobody was listening. And then Leftenant Fawcett came back and said What's going on? Make him stop. Officer Davies said he's refusing to sleep with Miss Hicks. Or Nurse Adeyemi. Mr Knight said He's been through a lot. Leftenant Fawcett said It's probably because of where she's from. Mr Knight said Let me talk to him alone. And then Nurse Adeyemi said Rubbish. Get out the road the lot of you. She got hold of my hand and said We'll find our own place to sleep. Come along Mr Knight. And you (she was talking to me) you stop your nonsense or I'll pick you up.

I said I want to be picked up. She said Dear Lord give me strength.

I said I'm not very heavy.

She said Darlin you are no burden at all. Her bosom was lovely and soft.

Gran

Funny thing. I just want to tell Patti. Here we are just
come from her funeral and I just want to run over and
tell her the good news. Funny isn't it? You still can't
believe they won't be there. Even when they've been gone
for days. The dead I mean. Even when you've seen them.
Poor things.

Len is all in bits. It's the tension. It was only the tension
kept him together this morning. He looked like some of
the fellers come back from Dunkirk. Rigid he was
through the whole service. Hardly moved a muscle. And
her waiting for his goodbye under the flowers we chose.
I chose. It never came. I just hope he was saying it in his
head. Poor bugger. He did throw some earth in at the
grave, sort of snatched it up quick and did it fast. Like
throwing away dirt, rubbish. It was hard to watch. And
back at the house he was the same. Teeth jammed
together. He kept shaking his head if anyone offered
him anything. He didn't even move when the doorbell
rang later. We were in the sitting room. Just Julie and

her two and me and him. He didn't move so I said, I'll
go. It was the police again. I thought, No. He can't take
it. Not if you've found his body. I just said, What do you
want? Couldn't bring myself to say come in. They said,
We can't say, Mrs Walters. We need Mr Walters to come
down to the station again. Right away. I said, You know
there's a funeral here. They said, It's extremely important. And they didn't move an inch. So that was the start
of it. We left Julie to tidy up and there we were, the two
us in the back of the police car. We were only five
minutes at the station, just long enough for them to tell
Len they couldn't say with hundred percent certainty
but they thought they'd located him—alive!—and then
we were off again to the Port Authority, the two of us
shaking like leaves on a tree every time we went over a
bump and now here we are. I waited outside. I needed
the air. Len went in like a man who means business.
Giant steps. It seemed like he was in there forever. I
didn't know what to pray for. Kept thinking just don't let
it be a mistake. Don't. When he finally came out you'd
have thought he'd had the worst news ever, the look on
his face. He come up to me and I couldn't tell what his
expression was, his mouth looked like he was in pain.
He squeezed his eyes tight shut. He said, It's him.
Course I knew it had to be. There wouldn't be two
Frankie Walters, God help us. He gave me a hug so tight
I couldn't breathe. I said, Steady on, Len. But it was no
good. He wouldn't stop. At first it was like he wasn't
breathing either. Then he was crying. Great big heavy
baby sobs. I said, Come on, now, Len. He was crying so

hard. Snot all over my hair. I said, Let's go somewhere a bit more private, and we walked along and sat in the bus shelter. So here we are. The two of us sitting here in our black. Our shoes polished. We really need to get back to the house. I'll tell him in a minute.

Chapter 14

TUESDAY PM
(and Wednesday morning as well)

She carried me all along the corridor and down in the lift and then along again to a door called Private and said Fred!

When Fred came he said Good Lord.

She said We want some blankets Fred and some extra pillows up on the Sport deck please. We'll have nine blankets. No a dozen.

Fred said Tomorrow?

She said No right now please. We're going up there now.

But after we left she said After our ablutions. Right Frankie Chops?

I said Right. That's what MyDad calls it too.

She said What?

I said Urinating.

She said You are a case you.

She said Look we're all right now Mr Knight. You go along to your cabin sir. You know the way?

He said Yes yes. But I was looking forward to joining you.

She said You don't want your nice warm cabin?

He said I've heard New York at sunrise is not to be missed.

Nurse Adeyemi said And we'll be first to spot the Statue of Liberty. Oh. I'm sorry.

Mr Knight said Don't be. You go along and Alec and I will make our own way up.

So that's what we did. Nurse Adeyemi pushed three sunloungers together and made a fort. My favourite thing! She put blankets on top of the mattresses for cozy and said Good job we're flat calm. Get in the middle there you. We had special pillows that float and lots of blankets. Blankets underneath and blankets on top. Nurse Adeyemi got some other sunloungers over and made a kind of barricade and a sort of tent thing for over our heads. She said Mind how you go Mr Knight sir. Would you like me to tuck you in?

He said I'm not five.

The sailor who works with Leftenant Fawcett came to have a look. He said the Captain was not pleased. Leftenant Fawcett had said so. He said the Matron could find herself in hot water.

Nurse Adeyemi said That would be lovely right now.

Mr Knight said I sincerely hope not. Nurse Adeyemi has found an admirable solution to a very tricky problem. She should be commended.

I already told you blind people can do anything they want. Gordon Knight is good at making people do what he asks.

When he had gone Nurse Adeyemi said Look at the time. Eleven o'clock already. And we need to be up by four. Are you asleep yet Frankie?

I said No.

She said Well get cracking. Move your bottom.

I laughed so hard my tummy hurt. And then I think I must have laughed to sleep because I don't remember anything else until I woke up.

It was still dark but there was a purple line over on the edge of the sea.

Nurse Adeyemi and Mr Knight were whispering.

He whispered I promise.

Nurse Adeyemi whispered Thank you.

I said You don't have to whisper. I'm awake.

Nurse Adeyemi whispered GO BACK TO SLEEP but sort of loud.

It was exactly the same as when we went camping in the New Forest. It was nearly daytime and the rain had stopped and I heard MyMumandDad whispering and I said the same thing and MyDad said the same thing. GO BACK TO SLEEP and I did. When I woke up I remembered MyMum was at home. She didn't come with us. I asked MyDad who was whispering and he said No one. I said Yes someone. And he said You were probably dreaming. And I said or you were talking in your sleep and he said Most likely. I said With two voices.

I didn't go back to sleep on the sunlounger. I did thinking. I did thinking about MyDad all by himself. MyDad driving in the car with no one beside him and I'm not on the back seat. MyDad sitting at the kitchen table. MyDad making himself a cup of tea. MyDad saying Bye going out the door and nobody saying it back. I couldn't think about MyDad burying MyMum because that's too difficult. I don't know what it would look like.

All of a sudden Nurse Adeyemi interrupted. She said Come along now. Shift your bottom. She doesn't mind saying that word. It makes me laugh.

She said Don't start. Just don't. We have to hurry if you want to see the Lady of Liberty.

I said Statue.

She said Yes.

She said We need to do our ablutions first.

I said I just have to say Good morning to Alec.

Gordon Knight was already up. I climbed over the sunlounger and said it. Alec licked my mouth. That means the same thing.

Everything was a big hurry after that. After our ablutions lots of people had come onto the deck. Probably one thousand three hundred and sixteen haha. Everything was smokey pink except the sea and the sky. They were turquoyse. We saw the statue but it didn't last very long because we were moving by and then everyone moved over to the other side of the boat to see the buildings going past. I told everything to Mr Knight like—There's a skinny one and—That one's all windows and—There's a seagull just by us. Mr Knight said I'm really enjoying New York. And Nurse Adeyemi said It's a beautiful morning. I don't think I've ever seen such a beautiful morning coming in. Afterwards we went down to the Surgery. The Surgeon said Good morning Matron. There's a message for you to see the Captain. I'll keep an eye on the boy.

When she had gone I was bored. I said Can I get some National Geographics from next door, please? and the Surgeon said yes.

I read some of them while I was choosing so I was still there when Nurse Adeyemi came back. I could hear her shouting next door. She came in and said Lord give me strength. And he didn't even get you any breakfast.

All right she said. Now we hurry up and wait again.

I said What for?

She said You know what? I'm not exactly sure. But one thing I know. I'm not going anywhere until we get you sorted darlin.

We waited a long time in her room with the chairs. We had to go up and see the Captain three times. Once was for two people in uniforms. Once was for a policeman and a police lady and the last time was for a man I hadn't seen before. They all asked the same questions about MyMum and why I ran away and how I got on the boat and was I really all by myself and was I sure no one helped me.

The last man said Well not long now son. Are you ready for another journey?

I said Where to?

He said Where would you like to go?

I said Home.

He said What I was hoping to hear. You be a good kid now and the Matron will get you ready and you'll be home in no time. You'll see. Your Dad will be waiting for you. Run along now.

I said That's a manner of speaking. Right?

He said Haha. I guess it is. Bye now. Then he said Oh and Matron perhaps find him something clean to wear in the meantime. Or perhaps a bath. You know? He said You know? with his face all wrinkly like an old potato.

Nurse Adeyemi said Will there be time?

He said Yes. Plenty. The car won't be here until four. And the paperwork will be in the Purser's Office by two. We'll let Mr Knight know too.

I didn't understand why we needed a car. Everything had seemed all right until he said that.

I thought about it a lot while I was having my bath. (Yes a bath! On a boat! I know! Nurse Adeyemi said I could use hers and she would guard the door.)

When I had dried myself and got dressed I opened the door and said I'm not getting in a car.

She said Whatever do you mean? Don't you want to see YourDad?

I didn't answer because the last one was not a real question. She knew I did.

I said You can't get to England in a car. Someone is trying to trick me.

She said Come over here and she put her arm round me. She said Darlin you are still only six. You're going to have to let people help you get back. No matter how smart you are. There are lots of people working really hard right now to arrange everything to get you back to England. You even know one of them.

I said Leftenant Fawcett? I don't like him much.

She said No. Your friend Mr Knight. He's going to take care of you on the way back.

I said He's going back? He only just got here.

She said Well perhaps he's homesick too.

She said I think all the passengers are off now. Shall we go and find something to eat?

I thought Yes—a piece of cheese haha! But I didn't say it because she didn't know anything about the cheese and it would be too complicated (and a bit scary) to tell about the stealing part. So I just said Yes.

We went to a restaurant I had never seen before. Nurse Adeyemi said it was called the Mess. I said Couldn't they call it a better name than that?

She said Like what?

I said Like the Messo-Potamia?

She said Well they could try. But I doubt it'd catch on.

We got sausages and beans and tomatoes and then Nurse Adeyemi said Let's take it back to my room. We can eat in peace there. Too many nosey parkers in Messo-Potamia.

While we were eating she said You do know you're going home on a naeroplane right? That's why you need to go in a car. To get to the airport.

I said I don't want my second sausage. I'm not hungry anymore.

She said Aren't you excited?

I said No. Yes.

She said Well?

I said I'm too excited. I feel sick.

She said Lord you are a piece of work.

I didn't ask her what she meant. I was thinking about being in the air with nothing to hold you up.

She said Why don't you have a little nap while we wait. I'll wake you up when it's time.

At a quarter past three we went to the Captain's Quarters. Mr Knight was there with Alec. Mr Knight was having a glass of sherry and Alec was looking as if he needed someone to say Hallo and talk to him so I did.

The Captain said Thank you very much Matron. You can get on with your day now.

She said Sir?

He said That's all. You've been a great help.

She said I've packed him a sandwich and a bit of fruit sir. She was holding out a red-and-white cardboard box with Taylor's Flexible Dressing written on it. She said And there's a National Geographic in there for him too and a colouring book from the Playroom. I didn't like to take too many crayons though.

The Captain said That's very thoughtful and put it on the table.

He was holding the door open but Nurse Adeyemi didn't go out. She came over to where I was telling Alec about my bath. She bent down and whispered (even though you're not supposed to when there are other people). She whispered You look after Mr Knight. Promise?

I whispered All right.

She looked at me with eyebrows up so I whispered Promise.

Then she said Say Hallo to YourDad.

I said Well of *course*. Bye-bye.

🐋

Guess who sat beside me on the aeroplane. Here's a clue. Someone who belongs to me so their name begins with My. Haha it was not MyDad and not MyMum either. It couldn't be. Remember? I was trying to make you think that. It was *My* friend Mr Knight. He said he didn't really want to see New York anyway. And guess who was under my sticking-out feet. Alec of course!

I had a big wide seat belt on and that was one good thing at least. I had never been on a naeroplane before. Mr Knight kept saying Are you sure you're all right? I just said Yes thank you. It was only a tiny lie because it was secret. I held on to the armrest and Mr Knight covered up my hand.

I said Are we going to crash?

Mr Knight said No. My ticket says we're going to London.

That was the best joke I had ever heard. I thought I might laugh at it later.

Right then I had to be quiet because we were going to take off. Everybody was putting out their cigarettes. I decided to close my eyes and do counting until it was safe. Mr Knight said Don't you want to look? I said No thank you. I'm counting now. He said You might miss a treat.

I had only got up to three minutes when the roaring started. I was sort of pressed into the back of my seat with my eyes squeezed tight. There was so much noise I thought we were going to hit something.

Mr Knight said What can you see? Let me guess. All beautiful colours—purple and pink and turquoise and orange and navy blue and many bright lights twinkling all over like Christmas…

So I looked. I couldn't help it. I opened my eyes and it was true.

…And the runway is going super fast and then sort of dropping underneath us so you can see it even better with the trucks and the planes and the airport buildings and there's the river now and the whole sea. Are you glad you opened your eyes?

I said You *can* see. You've been pretending the whole the time.

Mr Knight said I'm afraid not. It's something my friend told me about and I've never forgotten it.

—Or your friend.

—Nor my friend.

I did not think we were going to go so high. I closed my eyes again so I couldn't see it. It was like the world was disappearing. It made me think I would disappear too.

I kept my feet on Alec's back and Mr Knight kept his hand over mine and I kept counting. When I got to four hundred and nineteen (I used Mr Walters. Like One Mr Walters. Two Mr Walters) a nannoucement came on and said *Ladies and gentlemen you may unfasten your seatbelts and resume smoking at this time*. So I opened my eyes again. I was right. There was no more world. Only clouds.

I said We're going slower.

Mr Knight said It's an illusion.

I said Like cutting the lady in half?

Mr Knight said Not quite. Would you like to undo your belt and put your tray down now? I expect they'll bring us something to drink.

I said I still don't have any money.

Mr Knight said Ssh.

I looked out the window again and it was all clouds and a funny coloured sky. I put my tray down and up again fifty-six times before the stewardess came to give us a drink. I had orange squash. So did Mr Knight except he put Scotch in his. That's whiskey. I know because I asked MyMum once. I asked her if it was her favourite thing and she said No Frankie. You are. And Dad. He's second. I said And Uncle Jack. She said Uncle Jack's special third. I said and then Scotch and she said Probably but don't tell. I don't know if it's all right to tell you now that she's you-know-what. I think she's probably more relaxed about everything.

When we were on the deck last night that's what Nurse Adeyemi said. She said It's funny how you're more relaxed about everything when you're outside. It's the air.

I was timing it. We had been on the plane for five hours and forty-six minutes. We had one blanket each and one pillow. Our seats went back like a dentist's chair. We had eaten two meals and two snacks. Mr Knight had smoked eleven cigarettes and drunk four whiskeys. He was asleep. So was Alec. I had had four little bottles of orange squash. I had read three magazines (I read them out loud so Mr Knight could listen) and Mr Knight had read half his special book. It's braille. That's dots for letters. He said he'd already read it once but that it was all he had. He said I could try to learn it if I wanted one day. It's interesting to touch words. He said I couldn't have any more juice for another hour because I'd be climbing over him to go to the W.C. That's what they call it on a plane. He let me have his special watch so I wouldn't have to ask him the time anymore. You have to open the front and be very careful and feel the time. If you make your fingers very very light you can feel the time passing. I needed to know so I could tell how many more minutes until I saw MyDad. There were four hours and twenty-one minutes left. Mr Knight told me it would be at nine o'clock in the morning which was four o'clock on his watch because London was five hours ahead. It was complicated but don't worry if you don't understand.

When it was dark I looked out of the window again. You could see the stars but only if you knelt up and put your blanket over your head and pressed it tight on the window so you couldn't see the inside of the plane.

The first time I did it the stewardess (that's like the waitress) came and said Is he all right sir? And Mr Knight—he was awake then—said I don't know. Are you all right Frankie? I said Yes thank you. I'm looking at the stars. He said Are there lots? I said Millions. Maybe trillions. If they were dots you could read them like braille. Mr Knight said Imagine! And then he ordered another drink.

When the stewardess came back she whispered something to him. He said Of course. Why don't we ask him?

She said to me Would you like to see some more stars ?

I said What do you mean?

She said Come with me.

Mr Knight said Yes. Go. Go.

The stewardess took me right up to the front and opened a door to the cockpit (that's what they call it) where the pilot sits.

He said Good evening. Come in come in. It was like the pictures but better. It was so big. He had a curved windscreen so he got a really good view and it was huge outside. Huge and dark and bright at the same time. Millions and millions of stars white and yellow and different colours like when we were on the deck but you didn't have to lie on your back to look at them. They were right there in front of you and you were flying right into them. At the bottom far away was a long line of bright orange curving round like the windscreen. I think it was the edge of the world. Except the world can't have an edge. It's a ball.

The pilot looked at me and saw what I was looking at. He said That's tomorrow.

When I went back I had another look at the stars. If I nearly closed my eyes but not quite I could see even more than before.

It wouldn't matter how hard you looked you would never see them all. And it would be no use counting. It doesn't matter how many there are anyway. There are probably just the right number. It was like a great big field where you could go to play. I thought MyMum could be out there instead of being buried. I said in my head she was. It made me feel better. She would like it anyway because she likes fresh air and she likes the sky. She could be out there and sort of watching this tiny little plane all by itself. And I'm in it! So she could say There you are! I was wondering where you'd gone! And I could say Don't worry. I won't go away again. You can do remembering forever if you want. Then she would probably say Never mind me. It's YourDad I'm worried about. And I would say. Don't be worried. I'll look after him.

The next time I opened Mr Knight's watch and felt the time it was two o'clock. So it was already seven o'clock in London. So it was two hours until I could get off and see MyDad.

It was all mixed up inside the plane. Some people were snoring (Gordon Knight!) and some people had their lights on reading and it was supposed to be still night-time but when I looked out the window it looked all pinky-orangey. If it was getting to be day why was it only two o'clock and if it was only two o'clock where did the stars go? They can't really go anywhere because the world is sort of in them. So where are they? It was the most complicated problem I had ever had to think about. I don't know how astronomers do it.

Chapter 15

I suppose you'd like to know if I got home all right and if MyDad came to meet me. Answer—Yes and yes.

I wasn't scared anymore on the plane. It was just sort of normal. Mr Knight wasn't. He said he had a headache. I said It's a good job I'm here to look after you when we get off and he said It is it is.

The stewardess brought us some breakfast. It was horrible egg and horrible sausage. I gave mine to Alec when Mr Knight wasn't looking (haha) but he still knew. He said If that dog is ill I shall know who to blame.

We had to tidy up and put our seats straight and everything so it was quite busy. There was a long queue for the W.C. Mr Knight said I had to go when he came back because it was still a long way to Southampton.

I said Is that where you live?

He said No. I live in Exeter.

I said That's where MyDad took me camping.

He said You'll have to come and visit. There's a lovely field right beside my house.

I said How do you know?

He said What do you mean how do I know?

—How do you know it's lovely?

—If you stand in the middle of it—with your eyes closed— you can hear larks and sparrows and finches and warblers. You can smell the wild flowers. You can smell hay if it's hot and the resin from big poplar in the corner when the wind rakes the leaves down. You can walk across it and you can go down and fish in the stream.

I said Can we camp in it?

He said I hope you will one day. What can you see now?

I said It's still clouds. Heaps and heaps and heaps. Oh and some going by the window. They're really fast. Oh and nothing. It's all white and foggy. No and a bit of ground. I can see the ground and fields and trees and buildings and roads and I can see everything. There's a river.

Can you see the airport?

I can see planes down on the ground. We're going so fast… oh. Is that it?

Yes. That's it. We've landed. You're home Frankie.

I said Only in a manner of speaking.

MyDad looked like someone who wants to cry when he saw me at the airport. He was behind a kind of barrier watching us all walking along and when he saw me he turned his back and walked the other way in a big circle and then he sort of ran low down and ducked right under the barrier and came and picked me up and turned me round and round and round in the middle of everyone so it was a real nuisance. He didn't say anything for a long time and then he said I'm sorry Mr Knight. Let me help you. And Mr Knight said I'm fine thank you. Let's just get out of the way.

So that's how I went to New York (but no one believes me) and then came home again.

THE END (Ta-da)

(I know Chapter 15 is a bit short but I didn't have any more things to tell you. Too bad for you. Haha.)

Frank Walters

A noying wasn't he? Haha. It's ages since I've looked at this stuff, ages. I can't believe what an objectionable little fart I was. I don't think, to be honest, I've ever read it over from the beginning. It's so long ago I can't quite remember. I know: I'm supposed to have an infallible, word-perfect memory. Make that *used* to have.

I wrote it not long after I got back. Dad wanted me to go to Aunty Julie's to take my mind off everything but I pulled one of my tantrums. I'm sure she was greatly relieved. I simply point-blank refused. You know the phrase "kicking and screaming"? Well, that was my forte. Poor Dad. He never did know how to handle it. Gran moved in for a while and persuaded him to let me just stay home. He asked what she thought she was going to do with me all day.

Gran said, "I'll think of something."

I remember joining in, then. I said, "You don't have to think of anything. I'm going to write a book." And I remember neither of them laughed at me. Gran asked me what it would be about. I said, "My trip. Of *course*."

To her great credit she took me to the shops the very next day. She bought an exercise book with a green cover and two pencils. I carried them home in a brown paper bag and started straightaway. I burned through thirty-three of those books. I called it, with a blinding lack of imagination, *My Trip*, a title that gave no clue to its unorthodox nature. It probably saved my sanity, writing that book. No doubt it also saved me from countless prying questions from all the visitors who turned up with a morbid—and ill-concealed—fascination for its impetus.

Gran wouldn't disturb me if I was writing. "I'm sorry. You can't see him," she'd say. "But he's doing really well. Considering."

By the time the book was finished, the long hot summer was over and my two heels were firmly dug in: I was not going back to school, ever. Dad resisted. He asked Gran exactly what she thought he was supposed to tell the authorities. She answered as she had before: "I'll think of something." I've no idea how she argued my case but I do remember being taken to the council offices a few times and being asked to perform my party tricks.

I did overhear a few arguments between Dad and Gran on the whole question of school. Gran wasn't as fiery as my mother but she was nowhere near as passive as Dad. She didn't mind looking after me at home and so she couldn't understand why Dad objected. "He never did like responsibility," she said to me once, years later. And I think she was right: he was afraid of assuming responsibility for my education, and failing. He didn't want to be held accountable. Gran took a simpler approach. She said just as long as she could get me to the library and back each day everything else would take care of itself. And she was pretty much right.

I owe a great deal to my Gran. These days I'd automatically be subject to counselling for PTSD. But, without any formal training, Gran knew what I needed. Peace and quiet she called it. What it gave me was space and time. Invaluable gifts. "Lucky me!"

My dad had a more difficult go of it. He kept his old job that took him away for almost a week at a time. When he came back for a few days, the house must have seemed dismal without Mum's energy. I wasn't any use to him. He used to wander around picking up items, putting them down again, adjusting a chair, a lamp, turning over a cushion. He was like a man waiting. I can see him now, finally settling in his own chair. He would sit forward a little, like a visitor. He'd reach for the paper and seem to be reading it, but he was really only looking at it, I could tell, like a patient in a doctor's waiting room. Gran would say, "Why don't you have a little drive out? Frankie would like it." Then he'd say, "Would you, Frankie?" And of course, being me, I'd say, "No, thank you," because there was always some reading to do or some complex mental task I had to pursue to its tyrannical conclusion. Often Gran would go back to her house. To water the plants, she said.

I walked in on them in the kitchen one day early on, when they were talking about Mum. I knew I'd stumbled on something important so I paused at the door. Gran was saying, "Never mind stopping. She wouldn't even have *started* without your "*help*." I remember that word and its tone. I was intrigued by the way adults could do that: say one thing and mean its opposite. "*Poor you*." Of course I didn't know the rules governing inverted commas or how to apply them. I just knew adults had access to a special tone of voice and it fascinated me. I used to try it out sometimes, but I never got it quite right. Gran's tone anyway succeeded in provoking my father.

I remember sensing his contained anger.

"That's it, is it? That's what you've been itching to say all this time? I'm to blame?"

My grandmother denied it. Of course. She said "It's just all those samples…"

I watched him turn into a bully I hadn't seen before.

"What? *What?* Why don't you say it? Lying around waiting to fall into her mouth?"

Gran was at the kitchen table and he was behind her, standing over her, bearing down, one hand resting on the table in front of her, talking far too loud right into her ear.

I ran off. I hated shouting.

That conversation is something I never gave much thought to afterwards. I imagine I suppressed it because of the volume and the anger. It's only come back to me now, in the last week, after reading and reliving that other drama I witnessed, the one when Mum was still alive, that sad and terrible drama that played out in the bathroom, my dad angry—so rare that—my mum on her knees by the toilet. Something else I suppressed. For fifty-five years. The dark matter of memory. Invisible. I could never have grasped the implications at the time or made the right inferences. I was five, for God's sake. I can't imagine what I thought they were doing. The moment I read it last week, it was as if a switch had been flipped on a dark soccer pitch. Floodlights! It was the era of Mother's Little Helper, after all.

I've been all over the internet since. *Obv*iously. Dad was a pharmaceutical rep. It seems outlandish to hope to God there was no connection. Without knowing what he was plying, it's hard to come to any conclusions. My mother was diabetic. Her heart had stopped. That's what the death certificate said. What stopped her heart, though, is a matter for conjecture. Too many pills, taken in a haze of grief after Uncle Jack—or a too-sudden withdrawal, under pressure from Dad. Without the name of the drug it's not possible to ever know for certain. Oh, Dad, oh, Dad. Poor Dad! Poor Mum!

And poor me? Not really. I was very matter of fact about it. There's a name for that now. Avoidant personality disorder. As if it's a thing. Like a viral infection. Or a congenital deformity. Or deficiency. Some people would argue it's exactly that… For me it's normal. I've lived my life that way. It's how I am. I experience people differently, that's all. I read an Irish writer recently. The entire book was built around a family gathering for a funeral. I was trying to get insights into family relationships. Still trying to figure out how it all works. Love. Empathy. Grief. But she didn't have any answers. She was still working on it, what drives us to "each love someone, even though they will die." She wrote that it seems like "such a massive waste of energy—*and we all do it.*" The italics are mine. She might have written "we almost all do it."

My own book raises all sorts of ghosts for me and they're not all about my mother. I'm just reading it again from the beginning—Ha! Certain things loom out at me, like figures stepping forward on a twilit stage.

The whispered conversation, for instance, that I heard on our camping trip. Who *did* I hear in the tent that night? And did I hear *anyone*? Was there another tent nearby? Was the sound distorted to seem as if it were coming from ours? I never spoke about it again after that first time I asked. Why would I?

And if Dad were alive now, now that I'm thinking about it again, would I have the courage to ask him? I don't consider it my business. *Was* he unfaithful? He certainly liked getting out of the house, but it was most often: "Just going down the Gardener's, love. Shan't be long." He came back reeking of beer, but so? Beer reeks. And he spent plenty of time there afterwards, that's certain, though not with women. He had a good bunch of mates in the Gardener's Arms. He explained to me once, when I was in my teens, how they had stepped up to help afterwards. How they'd had a whip round and a couple of raffles to help raise the money dad had to find for the Home Office. I know: it seems incredible the HO didn't fly me back. No. It was merely a loan. Gordon Knight of course paid his fare out of his own pocket. He was a man of some means.

He's another ghost, Gordon Knight. Stepping forward from the darkened stage into the spotlight. It's the moment I see him at the rail. Just standing there unseeing in the starlight. Alec was over by me. That's the real ghost in this memory. Alec who should have been with him. Alec who was intended perhaps to keep me safe, to ensure I was conspicuous, noticed there and gathered back to safety.

I know Gordon Knight had been crying when he came back and sat down—of that I'm certain. Fortunately he was wearing his dark glasses. An adult weeping is an alarming sight for a child of any age. A breakdown of order. And you know, if you've read this far, that I had a special relationship with order. Have. I haven't changed much over the years. Many, many people have had a go at trying to change me: other teachers—briefly; my dad, though his heart was never in it and he never had the time, anyway; psychs—a string of those; girlfriends, the two before Lisa anyway. But not friends. I've only ever counted three real friends—Alec (yes really), Gordon Knight, and Nurse Adeyemi—and they were friends because, as my mother did, they accepted me whole. They liked me just the way I was. No one after that. Perhaps *they're* the people I've loved. You might even call Nurse Adeyemi a passion. My six-year-old self had been convinced that Gordon Knight and Nurse Adeyemi had been plotting to marry. I wanted her to marry me.

A number of years ago, on one of my visits, I asked Gordon about that last night on the boat. He and I had taken a slow walk to the pub one lunchtime. We had been chatting about gay marriage, only just beginning to be a thing one *could* chat about. I ordered a couple of beers and carried them out to the table in the garden.

As I set them down I said, "Back on board…" A catch phrase we used often. "What about Nurse Adeyemi?"

He said, "What about her?"

I said, "I heard you making a promise."

I reconstructed the scene: the last night on the ship, the sunloungers under the stars, the three of us and Alec.

I said, "You were making a promise to each other."

He said, "I remember. Yes. She was making me promise to tell her how things went for you once you got home. She said I could write directly to the ship."

"And—?"

"It's rather sad. We lost touch. I had asked my neighbour to save any newspaper items she came across, so I had those, a couple from the local paper and one from the *Express*. Then after you came to visit with your father I typed a long letter to her. Got it sent off to the *Gloriana*—Haven't I told you all this?"

"Never."

"After a few months it came back to me with a note. The postman always let me know who my post was from—if he could identify it—in case it was anything pressing. I rushed over to my neighbour's at the end of the lane—I remember it—she was in the middle of hanging out her wash. She read it right there in the garden. *Miss Adeyemi is no longer in our employ.*"

I didn't know what to say. I settled for, "Bloody life, hmm?"

Gordon said, "Bloody people!"

I said, "Sometimes not, though."

And there we were, an elderly and a not-so-young man, contemplating our beer. Our bitters, *ob*viously.

Reminiscing, another question surfaced but I didn't ask it. And out of some kind of English reserve I never did. What puzzled me for a long time afterwards about Gordon Knight is not what he intended when he stood at the rail. That seemed clear enough later, even when the full ramifications of it were still beyond me. No, it was the reason for his tears when he came back. Regret? Shame? Relief?

Two weeks ago, just a week before he died, it all came into focus. I went down to see him as usual—yes, we kept in touch all those years. He was eighty-five, still in his own home, though he had help: someone to clean, someone who came in twice a week to do a bit of cooking, a gardener to trim and prune and keep the place looking nice. He was lucky, as I've said. He had a bit of money. But nevertheless he kept his independence. His bedroom was still upstairs in the house. He found ways of managing. He carried whatever he needed—book, biscuits, medication, a bottle of Scotch— up and down in a bucket. Made his builder's tea in a jam jar and drank it from the same jar too.

Anyway, I was there for a visit (so he had to bring out the teapot) and he told me something important.

He said, "Something I've always been meaning to tell you, Frank. Do you remember on the boat we had a long talk?"

I said, "We had a few long talks."

"And you wanted to know about my first dead person? I lied. I need you to know that. I know how important it was for you, growing up, to have people around you who would tell the truth. But I had to make it up. I knew what you needed to hear."

I couldn't believe what he was telling me. Over the years, he had become my lodestar for integrity: honesty and truth. He seemed different from every other adult then, and, to be honest, most I've encountered since.

I didn't know what to say.

He said, "I did it to help you, Frank. You had no one."

"So who *was* your 'first dead person'?"

"It was him, the man I loved. That part was true, except I never saw his body, never *visited* the body. Never touched him. 'Lost at sea.' Officially. He was completing his National Service. He'd deferred it while he was finishing his degree. I never liked his choice of the navy. Felt he was asking for trouble. You know, the times then were brutal for people like us. Cruel in every way. Harry's family were told there'd been an accident. Simple as that. He'd been lost at sea, in the mid-Atlantic. His body was never found. Whether it was an accident or something worse I didn't know. It was unbearable either way. Still is. I never saw him to say goodbye. The pain was so intense. So intense. I couldn't wait to join him."

I took hold of his hand.

"You came back from the rail for me that day, didn't you?"

"Not just for you, Frank. For my six-year-old self, too. It would have been such a betrayal otherwise. Such robbery. Anyway, as I said, I never did see my first dead person, but it seemed important for you to understand yours and not be afraid. So I lied. "*Oops!*"

His laugh was painfully hoarse as he mimicked my own six-year-old self.

"You do see, Frank, don't you, why I tinkered with the truth?"

I took hold of his hand and said, "I see. Haha."

He smiled.

"The stories we tell ourselves usually turn out to be wishful thinking, don't they. They're life jackets. For our survival. The story I told you that night on the *Gloriana* was for yours."

I said, "Thank you."

I made us both another cup of tea and made an egg sandwich for Gordon to eat later. I cut the crusts off like Mum used to do for me.

We drank the tea, ate a couple of biscuits, and then I took my leave.

I said, "See you next week." and Gordon said, "See you."

I sat in the car in his drive for a few moments and thought about what he'd told me with such conviction all those years ago. As I turned the key in the ignition I knew I was going to come home and look for my book. I hadn't turned to it once since I wrote it.

When people hear my own story now, they're aghast. They try to put themselves in my place and they find it unimaginable.

To sit with the body of your own mother. To spend the night with her. But it wasn't such an ordeal. It was just my mum. And she was gone. I got on with it. Looking at my mum that night I understood what people meant when they said to me, "Aren't you lonely? Wouldn't you like a friend?" I never really knew what they were talking about. But my mum looked like someone who might be lonely, who might like a friend. I was keeping her company. Plus I knew she liked me. I felt safe. The worst part wasn't being with her. By far the worst part was Miss Kenney next day. Imagine *that* if you can: delivering what every intelligent cell in your body is telling you is the most momentous news of your life—

I suppose running was my way of saying, "Sod them all." My way of saying, "There *is* nowhere here I really wish to be."

Looking back, I can see—I think—why people had difficulty believing me. If my story were true, they reasoned, why wasn't I in floods of tears, sobbing with fear and grief? They couldn't understand it. And what people still find disturbing is the thought that I was devoid of "real" emotion. They regard my six-year-old self as quietly horrific, some unnerving Stephen King creation.

I learned very quickly that the trick to fitting in is to fake affect. Just leapfrog the inconvenience of not really "getting" it and take your cue from others, reproduce the expected affect at will. It's a collusion with the systemic hypocrisy that keeps the social wheels turning. But it's bloody disastrous in relationships.

But it's all academic. In the short time I knew her, I loved my mother. I know what I know. I loved her in my own way, not the "normal" way, and she understood. Later, when I went back to school—yes, I eventually went back—my disrupted affect was taken as further evidence of what was usually referred to in shorthand as my "problem" and no doubt played a part in prompting the numerous investigations into the mysteries of my "disorder," my "abnormal" behaviour. Do you see how riddled with inverted commas my life was?

My way of loving—and living—wasn't problematic for me. I was fine with it, and to tell you the truth, I think my dad was too. But he didn't have the conviction to stand up to the teachers, the professionals who wanted to (here it is again) "normalize" me. And I didn't do myself any favours. After learning that bald statements like *I wrote a book*, or *I know what two million times seven hundred and forty two is—I've been to New York all by myself, MyMum is dead*—only incurred scorn, mistrust, and accusations, I clammed up even more.

Oh, I'm not looking for sympathy of any kind. (I wouldn't give it.) I'm only trying to explain why reserve looked like a good option for me. And still does.

And perhaps it explains my attachment to Gordon Knight. He accepted me right from the beginning, and then all through my formative years, exactly the way I was. And that was important because, to tell the truth, social behaviour has always been a great puzzle to me: how is a person supposed to know how to *be*? How do you determine the best spot to occupy in the trickily booby-trapped landscape of possibilities? Self-possession and independence get a gold star; cockiness and stubbornness a black mark. What's a six-year-old to make of that? Or a sixteen-year-old? A twenty-six- or fifty-six-year-old? Disarmingly shy or unpleasantly stand-offish? Wise or judgmental? Judiciously shrewd, or coldly calculating? Dignified and reserved, or frigid and withdrawn? Growing up has been no help at all to me. None at all.

Don't think my life was—is—unpleasant. Far from it. Beyond the barbarity of the mid-teens and the social complexities of university, I enjoyed my student days. Until I did my doctorate, I lived with my Gran. She needed looking after. It was a good arrangement. The rent was rock bottom and Gran liked having me around to do jobs for her and—this is important—do them efficiently without a whole package of faux concern or useless sentiment. Reading was my thing. And numbers. After she died, she left the house to me and suddenly I belonged to one of those families that quarrel over money. Dad was hurt, offended, even though I offered it to him and Julie. He wouldn't accept. I think you call it high dudgeon. Our relationship was never quite the same after that. He went out to see Julie in Australia and he never returned. I could have gone out there I suppose, at least for his funeral. The plain truth is it didn't interest me. My work is everything. I became interested in memory after taking care of Gran, went into neurological research, and found myself a niche at Cambridge. Just in time for the rotting brains of the boomers a step ahead of me. I devise the tests. I analyze the data. I leave it to my grad students to actually deal with the "subjects"—the polite name for my demented old farts. I don't have the patience, haha. I love my work.

I'm learning braille, too, twice a week. Gordon had volunteered his time to teach it to adults and that's what I'll be doing once I've mastered it. It's not as difficult as they say. Kay says it's all our relationship needs, another obsession. I'm pretty sure she means *doesn't* need. I haven't mentioned Kay, have I?

I'm not really asking. I know I haven't. She's an embarrassment. No, she makes *me* feel like an embarrassment. She found me on the internet—like a new appliance—though, to be fair, she wasn't looking for me. I blame Annichka the muttnik. It was in 2010, the fifty-year anniversary of the successful re-entry of Annichka, the first Russian space dog to return from orbit alive. Kay was googling for more information. She landed on the site of a space nerd who had posted photographs of the original front pages of the *Daily Mail*. That was where she came across the subheader: "More on *Gloriana* Boy." (Yes, I'm afraid I'd been "the *Gloriana* Boy" that summer. You can see why school wasn't such a hot idea when I came home...Probably one of the reasons Dad and I spent so many weekends in Gordon Knight's field that autumn.)

Kay anyway was persistent, dogged, when she turned up this archived material. It took her a while, I understand, but eventually she tracked me down in Cambridge and located me through my faculty. Her marriage had just fallen apart though she didn't tell me that right away.

We had a good time reminiscing on Skype. (Skype is good for someone like me. It's safe behind a screen.) I could remember a lot more about the trip and she enjoyed that, being able to reconstruct it all again, the Mexican dinner, the burgers, and the ridiculous Goofy Golf. We talked about Gordon Knight, too. I told her he was my best friend. She said, "He's still alive?" I said, "Yes, but Alec is long gone. His present dog is called Stephen. After Hawking. The one before that was Albert."

She came over to see me the following year and I took her to visit Gordon. We camped in his field. That's where—Oh but you don't want to hear all the intimate details. If you want that sort of thing I'm sure you can find it online. More easily than information on Annichka or the *Gloriana*. Anyway the camping was very special and we did our fair share of whispering in the tent. So much so that I began to wonder if what I heard when I was four was voices from the future.

We stayed for a few days, getting up in the morning to join Gordon for a breakfast of eggs and toast and coffee and going for long walks on the moors, stopping on the way back at the pub. Of *course*.

Gordon had no trouble remembering Kay. He said his memory for voices was pitch perfect and he could still hear her even through that accent.

She came over again last year, visiting a sister who lives in Twickenham. She asked if I wanted to go to a rugby match. I declined. Told her crowds were never my thing.

She said, "I guess you won't be taking me to U2 then, either."

I said, "I'd rather not, thank you," and she laughed.

I showed her what I do when I'm practicing my braille. I tie a scarf over my eyes so it forces me to make guesses and move on, instead of allowing myself to cheat. She was very interested in that. I showed her the first five words of the page I was tackling so that she could try it, but she wasn't really serious. She put the scarf on and then put her hands on my face instead and said, "Let me read your lips. Your jaw. Your throat." Actually I was quite interested in *that*. Maybe another time. I enjoy her company, I really do. Sometimes we laugh so hard it reminds me of Mum and Uncle Jack. Laughing's important, isn't it? I think sometimes that it's a kind of life jacket, too. But I *have* learned not to fall down.

We went down again to see Gordon before she went back. More long walks, more pub lunches; for us, that is. He was pretty much confined to his house by then, you could tell. Stephen had grown quite fat. Gordon on the other hand was wasting. He seemed tremendously tired.

He gave me a whole set of his books before we left. On the way back, Kay said it was tremendously sad. I said I didn't think so. It was life unfolding exactly as it should. She heaved a great sigh.

I've just finished reading through my book a second time. It's still releasing minor revelations, like little fireflies illuminating the pages (my writing's terrible by the way). I've only just realized it was likely Kay who gave my hiding place away. "*Promise you won't tell?*" Of course she did. *Of course.* Neither of them ever mentioned it to me. Maybe they thought it was too obvious. Or maybe they were being loyal to each other. I'll have to ask her. If she comes over again.

I must say it's all taken me right back to that summer I turned six. I started writing it at home up in my room, birds noisy in the apple tree outside my window. But shortly after that conversation with Gran, Dad took time off again and we went down to see Gordon for the first time. Gordon—Mr Knight then—had extended an invitation and Dad took him up on it. I took some notebooks with me and Dad took his fishing rod. He was a bit nervous on the drive down. Kept asking me how much Gordon Knight could see. If he needed help and so on. I said he looks after himself and he looks after Smart Alec too.

Mr Knight had heard the car and was waiting for us at his gate, with Alec, of course. He let him greet me—a free lesson in unconditional love. The house was as all houses looked then, in picture books at least: stone walls, roses round the door. He offered us his spare room, but Dad said no. We'd come to camp. So after we'd had some tea he showed us the field. Not very big, gently sloping down to a stream. He said there were plenty of fish in it. Sticklebacks. You could hear them break the surface constantly if you were quiet enough. I started to cry then. Dad was astonished. He said, "What's wrong?" I said, "I'm thinking of my fish." Neither of them said anything for a minute and then Dad said, "Well, it's a start."

The rest of our stay was, well…Have you any idea how wonderful it feels to lie in a yellow tent, a pungent, musty yellow tent—not cool, not warm, just right—smell the sun-warmed hay outside, hear a lark somewhere above an adjacent field, and pour your heart out onto the pages of an endless supply of notebooks, with no one to interrupt, and no one to say it isn't true?

PAULINE HOLDSTOCK is an internationally published novelist, short fiction writer and essayist, whose novel *Beyond Measure* was shortlisted for the both the Giller and the Commonwealth Writers' Prize. Her most recent novel, *The Hunter and the Wild Girl*, winner of the City of Victoria Butler Book Prize, was shortlisted for the BC Book Prizes' Ethel Wilson Award and listed by both the CBC and the *National Post* as one of the Best Books of 2015.